# THE
# ONYX
# SEED

*a novel by*
R.W. Harrison

*To Dad, I wish you could have read this.*
*To Mom, I hope you're surprised.*

# THE ONYX SEED

**Prologue**
**Cabanatuan POW Camp, Philippines**
**Tuesday, January 30, 1945**

PRIVATE FIRST CLASS Charlie Castle adjusted his pack and grabbed his friend and fellow private, Larry McConnell, by the arm. "Hey, do you have any more of those bennies the medic gave you? I'm dog tired."

"No, I popped my last one a couple hours ago. C'mon, it won't be much farther."

Castle frowned as they trudged through the grassy trail. He looked up to see Lieutenant Payne heading their way. "Ah, Christ, what does he want?" he whispered to McConnell.

The lieutenant stopped in front of his two men. "Can you idiots at least try and keep up? We're only a few miles from the target. You're going to have to double-time it to catch up." With that, he turned around and trotted up the path, shaking his head at the stragglers.

McConnell started to follow, but Castle pulled on his pack and held him back. "Charlie, let go. You heard Payne."

"Larry, Payne is a pain in my ass. We'll get there when we get there."

McConnell's shoulders slumped as he sighed. The two of them continued at their leisurely pace through the grass.

After a few minutes, Castle held up his hand and they both stopped. He turned to Larry. "Do you hear that?" Both men turned their heads, straining to make out a low moaning sound coming from the brush. They advanced a few steps and Castle pointed toward a palm tree several yards off the trail. Guns at the ready, they made their way slowly through the grass.

A few more feet and they could see the source of the noise. It was a man, a Filipino guerrilla, on his back. Scattered around him were his helmet, pack, and a rifle, in addition to a machete and several coconuts. His face was contorted in pain, heavy with sweat. They could see that his right hand was red and swollen. His breathing was labored as he looked with pleading eyes at the two Americans.

"Poor bastard," Castle said. "I bet he was stopping for a snack and a snake got him. Probably a cobra."

"Should we get the medic?" McConnell asked.

"The medic? Why bother? It's not like he's one of ours."

"Yeah, but he was probably helping the first group of scouts."

"Larry, I like you, but you're too soft. You gotta think practical. Fetching the medic would mean running—or double-timing it as Pain-In-My-Ass just told us—to the rest of the company. In this heat. And by the time the medic got back here, you know this little Buk-Buk would be long dead. So what's the sense in exerting ourselves?"

McConnell looked down at his boots and said nothing.

"What we *can* do," Castle said, "is help ourselves to his gear." Castle leaned down and began pulling supplies from the man's belt. He tossed the canteen to Larry and wrestled a pistol and its holster from the Filipino's belt and stuffed it in his own pocket. He then knelt down and rifled through the man's pockets.

Castle pulled a small photograph of a young Filipino woman, its white border torn and a crease across the face. "Sorry, my little brown buddy," he said with a sneer. "You won't be seeing her any time soon. Maybe I'll visit her in Manila." He kissed the picture and stuffed it in his shirt pocket.

The fighter tried to protest but his body was too weak. He was used to the racial slurs, but having the picture of his *mahal*—his love—treated with such disrespect was too much to bear. The guerrilla's dying eyes burned with hatred toward this American soldier.

Castle ignored the man's looks and dug into another shirt pocket. His fingers curled around a small, smooth object. He pulled out a small stone, even and featureless like a river rock, all black in color. It was about the size of a slightly flattened golf ball.

Charlie turned it over in his hands looking at it. "What's this, Buk-Buk? A good luck charm?" The Filipino mumbled something inaudible. "What'd you say? If it's for good luck, I don't think it's working." Castle laughed and rubbed his fingers over the small, black rock.

A few unintelligible words tumbled from the guerrilla's mouth and Castle leaned in closer. The Filipino took as a deep breath as he could and whispered a single word to Castle. "*Aswang*." His eyes blinked open and shut a couple times and then stayed shut.

Castle made no effort to understand the man. He simply stood up and flipped the stone to McConnell who caught it. He examined it briefly. "Doesn't look valuable to me, Larry. You can keep it." Larry carefully put it in his pants pocket.

The two men turned around to find Lieutenant Payne staring at them from the trail. "What the hell are you two doing?"

"Just taking a piss, Lieutenant," Castle said.

"Goddammit Castle!" Payne hissed. "Get over here now, both of you!" He glared at them while they plodded through the grass. When they reached the trail, he pushed them forward, forcing them to run. "I'm not going to miss this raid because of you two. Now move out!"

Several hours later, Castle and McConnell had joined the rest of the company and they began their cautious advance on the POW camp.

Overhead, a P-61 Black Widow began its decoy flight low over the camp at dusk, cutting one of its engines and restarting it, backfiring with a loud bang. The Japanese guards studied the plane as it made lazy, looping circles, all the while losing altitude. As the plane disappeared over some nearby hills, the soldiers waited for a ball of flame that never appeared.

The twenty or so minutes that the P-61 looped and swirled in the sky was all the time needed for the two hundred Rangers and Filipino guerrillas to crawl toward the gates of the camp unseen. At precisely 19:40, the guard towers and pillboxes came under heavy fire and were overrun. A sergeant raced to the front gate and shot off the padlock. The main force rushed in and engaged the Japanese soldiers. The raid to rescue five hundred American POW's and survivors of the Bataan Death March had begun.

Privates Castle and McConnell ran side by side to the tank shed. They heard a truck engine trying to turn over as Castle ducked his head inside the shed. He turned back to McConnell. "I count six Japs. Four trucks. We can take 'em. There's three on the left and three on the right. You take the ones on the right. Go!"

They darted into the garage while the sound of small arms fire peppered the air outside. McConnell aimed his submachine gun at the driver of the nearest truck. With a quick squeeze of the trigger, four rounds exploded from the barrel and shattered the windshield of the truck. Two of the bullets hit the Japanese soldier in the head, killing him instantly.

Without waiting, McConnell aimed a little higher toward the truck in the back where two soldiers were unloading a heavy machine gun. Startled by the gunfire, they dropped the machine gun and reached for their pistols. Reacting to the movement, McConnell squeezed the trigger and swung his gun in a quick left-right motion. A burst of rounds hit both guards before they could get a shot off.

McConnell had heard Castle firing his own submachine gun and looked left, ready to fire on anything that Castle had missed. He saw two soldiers on the floor of the shed, blood pooling around their heads. Castle always went for the head, and rarely missed.

Castle was advancing toward the back of the garage on the left wall, and motioned with the barrel of his gun that there was one more soldier in the back. McConnell nodded and headed down the right side, keeping his head low, occasionally bobbing up above the trucks to see if he could spot the remaining guard.

McConnell's ears were ringing from the gunfire and the acrid smell of gunpowder filled the small enclosure. Two trucks at the rear of the garage blocked their view, but he saw a hint of movement crouched at the back. McConnell stopped and pointed to the wall for Castle to see.

Suddenly there was a pistol shot and Castle screamed. McConnell looked and saw Castle hopping up and down. "Bastard shot under the truck at my legs!" He looked down. "Tore open my boot but I don't think he hit anything. Just a little blood but it hurts like a bitch!"

McConnell cautiously craned his neck to see over the back of the truck, positioning his feet behind the tire of the truck he was next to. He raised his weapon and nodded to Castle, mouthing, "I can see him."

Castle shook his head. "He's mine." He unhooked the canteen from his belt and threw it across the garage into the back corner where it crashed into some tools. Instantly the Japanese soldier spun around and fired into the canteen. At that moment Castle leaped forward and fired three rounds into the back of the soldier.

The guard fell against the back wall. He tried to raise his pistol but he was paralyzed, his spine shattered by Castle's bullets. All he could do was blink as blood soaked through his uniform.

McConnell turned away, ready to head out of the garage and finish securing the camp with the rest of the men. Gunfire still surrounded them and he heard the occasional *thump* of a bazooka being fired.

But Castle wasn't turning back. He was slowly walking toward the paralyzed Japanese soldier. "Hey McConnell! Come here!" McConnell turned toward the back wall and approached.

"Looks like our friend here is in a bad way," Castle said, grinning. He looked down at his own torn boot. Leather was stripped away along the side and a small amount of blood was now leaking out. "He tried to cripple me, you know. What do you think his punishment should be, Larry?"

"I think he'll be dead in a few minutes. Come on, let's go."

"Not yet. This pig needs an appropriate punishment for spilling my blood. And he's destroyed U.S. Army property. Look at my boot." Castle didn't wait for McConnell to look at his boot. Instead he pressed the sole of it against the Japanese soldier's face. He pressed harder and they both heard a groan coming from the soldier.

"What are you doing, Charlie? Come on, let's get out of here."

"Larry, we're partners, right? I back you up and you back me up, right? That's how we stayed alive on the godforsaken sixty mile march to bring us here. And that's why I told the MPs that you were with me instead of screwing that nurse back in Pearl Harbor." Castle pressed his boot harder into the soldier's head. "What if I had told them the truth? Where would you have been? You would have been locked up instead of having fun with me here."

McConnell frowned, but knew that Castle spoke the truth. Castle removed his boot from the soldier and stood back. "Your turn. Show him your boot. Show him that we back each other up. Show him that shooting me was just like shooting you. And he deserves to be punished."

"Aw, come on, Charlie—"

"I said do it! Stick your boot in his yellow slant-eyed face!"

McConnell hesitated and Castle shoved him. McConnell staggered back and fell against the back of a truck. "Hey! Knock it off. Let's just get out of here."

"If you don't stick your foot in his face, I'll have to change the statement I gave a couple months ago to that nice MP puke. Now do it!"

McConnell lifted his foot up slowly toward the frightened soldier. The soldier blinked several times and shook his head as McConnell's boot pressed lightly on his face.

"Harder, Larry. Harder!"

McConnell pressed harder and the soldier stopped moving his head, his cheek squashed against the wall of the shed.

"Kick him!"

"What?"

"Kick him. Kick him in the head. Do it!"

McConnell released the soldier and stood back. "I can't do that. What are you trying to do anyway, Charlie? You're insane!"

"Okay, I'll kick him first. But then you have to. Remember, you always back me up." With that, Castle reared back and kicked the Japanese soldier square in the face. Blood spurted from his nose and his head flung back, banging on the wall.

"Your turn," Castle said flatly.

"No. He's practically dead anyway."

Castle pulled his .45 pistol from its holster and aimed it at his buddy. McConnell's eyes widened and he backed up, bumping into the truck. "What the hell are you doing, Charlie?"

"Kick the slant. Kick him now, or I'll shoot you right here."

"You're crazy, man. No way."

Castle fired a round over Larry's shoulder. "Last chance." He leveled the gun at McConnell's head.

"All right, all right. Put the damned gun down." McConnell took a deep breath and leaned back on one foot. He swung his other foot into the Japanese soldier's face. More blood spurted from his nose and a tooth fell onto the floor.

"Again!" Castle yelled.

McConnell kicked him again, tearing the skin on the man's cheek.

"Again! Again!"

The more Castle yelled, the more McConnell kicked. He kicked harder and harder, not noticing that Castle had holstered his pistol. McConnell stepped back, breathing hard, and Castle began kicking the man again.

Life had long since ebbed from the Japanese soldier but McConnell and Castle kept taking turns kicking him in the head. His face was a mass of purple and red, swollen into disfigurement.

The gunfire had ended in the camp, but neither Castle nor McConnell noticed.

"Hey!" a voice called from the front of the shed. "What in the hell are you guys doing now?"

Castle and McConnell spun around to see their lieutenant with his hands on his hips. Looking around the garage, Payne frowned. "Nice work, boys, but I don't think you can kill that one any more than you already have." He waved them forward. "Now fall out. We've got a lot of POW's in pretty bad shape here."

**Chapter One**
**Kingsbridge, New York**
**April, 1946**

FROM THEIR SMALL KITCHEN Margaret McConnell watched her husband gather up his fishing pole and tackle box. He pulled on the ends of his favorite red flannel shirt. It was well worn, but he wouldn't let her buy him another one. She rubbed her stomach and wished that he were someone else. Wished that he were the same person she met before he shipped out to fight the "filthy Japs" as he called them.

Everything changed when he had returned. She thought Larry would be happy to be home, happy to resume his role as head of the household. And at first, he was. He got a job for a while at the cannery in town and was even excited when Margaret told him that they were expecting.

But then Charlie, his old army buddy, had moved into town. Soon after, Larry had lost his job and spent most of his time with Charlie and a local, Slim. She didn't mind Larry hanging around with Slim, but didn't like the influence Charlie seemed to have on her husband.

Now he couldn't find steady work and shouted at her

all the time. Sometimes he did more than shout. He would get angry with her over the smallest things and if he were drinking, his shouts would turn physical. If he wasn't yelling at her or worse, it was like she was invisible. All he wanted to do was drink and go fishing.

"When will you be back?" she asked as sweetly as she could.

"No idea. Me and Slim are going to see what's bitin' and then head over to The Grotto for a beer. Charlie can't make it. I still can't believe he got hired on with Sheriff Grady. So it's just me and Slim today against the fish." He ran his hand through his black hair and wiped it on his shirt. His tone was even, and Margaret wasn't sure how much she could push him.

"But aren't you going to finish the crib? You haven't touched it in so long. And you did such a great job on the dresser. The baby will be here in just a month." Margaret watched her husband slowly put his fishing gear down and braced for what was to come. She had gone too far and she knew it.

"Maggie," he said, lowering his voice to a near whisper, "the last thing I want to do is turn dowels on that stupid crib. I'll have it done by the time your precious kid pops out." Larry's voice rose and his face turned red.

"It's *our* baby, Larry," Margaret said. "And please, you know I don't like being called Maggie."

Larry's face tightened as he drew in his lips. "Dammit! I'll call you anything I want. Quit nagging me about the crib. I'm going to the lake with Slim. And then we're going to get stinkin' drunk. I don't know when I'll be home. Maybe I'll go home with the barmaid!" He was yelling now and took a step toward Margaret. She shrank back to the edge of the counter. Tears were welling in her eyes and she quickly wiped them away.

Her long, pale red hair swept downward as she looked to the floor. She had a smattering of faded freckles on her face, which was twisted in fear as Larry advanced.

He swung his hand up and Margaret sank to the floor cowering. She wrapped her arms around her round belly and waited, shaking, hoping he would catch himself.

Larry took another step toward her but slapped the counter in disgust. "Stupid woman!"

By the time he had grabbed his fishing pole and stormed out of the house, she was trembling on the floor of the kitchen wishing and wishing her life had turned out differently.

* * * *

The church was filling up with mourners. Margaret watched her mother dabbing her moist eyes with a lace-edged handkerchief. They sat in the front pew, but Margaret was turned around in the bench, watching as people filed in. She recognized a few people from the cannery Larry had stayed in touch with after he was fired, but so many of the women entering weren't familiar to her. She didn't realize that Larry had so many friends. She figured most were his drinking buddies. All to mourn the man who was so very charming to Margaret in the beginning but who came back from the Pacific and kept fighting, it seemed.

Margaret interrupted her mother's quiet tears as she turned to face forward. "Why are you crying, Mother?"

"I don't know. Funerals are always sad."

"It's not a funeral. It's a memorial service."

Her mother frowned. "You know what I mean. Plus I'm scared for you. You're going to have that baby in a few days and no way to support the two of you."

"Mother, please don't worry about me. I told you I'll

have Larry's military pension and he had that small life insurance policy. The coroner said he would be issuing the death certificate in the next week or two. And I'm thinking of renting out that attic bedroom. And, even though I've never touched it, I still have the money you gave me from Papa when he died. If things get tight, I can always get a job in Geneseo, at the college. I'm sure those professors need assistants or secretaries."

She paused, then spoke again in a low voice. "Truthfully I'm glad he's gone. I can't imagine raising a child with someone like Larry around. What if he got tired of hitting me and started," her voice caught, "hitting the baby?"

Margaret took a deep breath and looked squarely into her mother's eyes. "I hate him, Mother. I truly hope he's dead."

The pastor of the church, who didn't know Larry, began his opening prayer.

After the service, everyone moved to the parish hall for juice and cookies. Margaret's next-door neighbor, Frances, stood close to her at the punch bowl. "You okay?"

"Of course, Fran. I know I should be the typical widow in mourning. I am wearing black, you know. But, honestly, I feel like a huge weight has been lifted off my shoulders. And maybe I'll wear black more often—it really sets off my red hair!"

"Oh, I can't believe you Margaret! Your husband drowned in that lake a week ago, you're about to have a baby, and you're cracking jokes?" Fran took Margaret by the sleeve and headed toward the door. "Let's go outside where nobody can hear you. Plus, I need a smoke."

Once they were safely out of earshot and on the small lawn of the church, Fran lit her cigarette. She faced her friend and said quietly, "Now c'mon, I have a serious question for you...do you think there's any way Larry might still be alive?"

Margaret straightened the pleats of her black dress. "I know what Slim told me and I know what the Livingston County sheriff told me. Slim wasn't ready to go when Larry went to pick him up, so Larry went to the lake without him. He said Larry smelled like he had stopped off at the bar ahead of time and was mad that Slim wasn't ready. By the time Slim got to Sullivan's Landing, Larry was already a hundred yards or so out and had just cut the motor. Slim was waving his arms trying to get Larry's attention but either he didn't see him or was ignoring him. He saw Larry stand up in the boat and toss the anchor over." Her voice was calm as she turned slightly from the bright sun.

"And that's when the boat tipped?"

"Yes. The sheriff said that the anchor rope must have been caught on something. If Larry hadn't been drunk, he might have been able to keep his balance or, once he went into the water, held onto the boat or even tried swimming to shore. But Slim said he probably had quite a few beers before he arrived at his house, and the sheriff said he found some more empty beer cans in Larry's car and in the boat."

Fran looked at her friend and puffed on her cigarette. "So there's no chance he's alive? I mean, it's a pretty small lake and they spent three days dragging for his body."

Margaret looked around to make sure no one was listening. "Fran, this is going to sound crazy, but that afternoon, right around the time Slim said he went down to the lake, I got the funniest feeling. And the baby was really kicking. Larry had been gone for several hours and suddenly, I don't know, I just felt…at peace. I don't know how else to describe it. You know how much we fought and how loud he would get. You heard it. All that tension I've been feeling, especially since I got pregnant, just left me."

"I believe you," Fran said. "I think everything is going to work out. So, you still need a crib, don't you? It's too bad he never finished it. If it was anything like the dresser, it would have been beautiful."

"I'm getting a crib from the pastor's wife," Margaret said. "You know as much as we fought, especially after I got pregnant, I *do* love that dresser. He was excited at first when I told him we were going to have a baby, and that's when he started building the dresser. He worked day and night on that thing. He'd even work on it after breakfast before he left for the cannery. It's almost like he was getting rid of all the demons he came home with from the war by building something so exquisite."

A slight breeze blew a wisp of hair into her eyes and she brushed it back. "He was so pleased with how it turned out. But shortly after he was finished with it, he lost his job and things went downhill from there. He couldn't find work and he began drinking a lot more. His army friend coming to town didn't help things either." Margaret's eyes looked downward and she blinked a few times. "He became much more, well, vicious towards me."

"Well, look at the dresser and remember better times. Keep looking forward, new chapter and all that, right?"

"You're right. Thanks Fran."

Later that evening Margaret was alone in her house, sitting in the rocking chair in the nursery, drinking some lemonade. The baby was kicking again. She rubbed her tummy and smiled. It had been a long day but she felt like everything was behind her now. She struggled up from the chair and pulled open the top drawer of the dresser.

Her mother had presented her with a quilt she had made for her baby at the memorial service. Mother was so thoughtful, wanting to give her something positive to think about during such a troublesome day. But Margaret truly felt at ease now that Larry was gone.

The new widow didn't feel like a widow at all. She actually felt optimistic. She and her mother were very close and she was best friends with Fran who lived right next door. She loved her house and the town she lived in.

Kingsbridge was such a friendly town where neighbors looked out for one another, waved hello, and genuinely cared about each other. Just forty miles south of Rochester in western New York State, it was close enough to the big city that she could drive in for shopping once in a while, but far enough away to enjoy the rolling hills and farmland of the Genesee River Valley.

Her favorite stretch of road was Route 39 between Geneseo and Avon. Looking west over the valley to the farms and silos that dotted the landscape was such a peaceful, tranquil view. She smiled just thinking about it.

And she really did love this dresser, she mused, turning her thoughts to the joy that was to come in just a couple days. She traced the carved walnut handles with her finger. There were two small handkerchief drawers on the very top of the dresser and each one had a keyhole. Margaret touched the key for the lock that was on a chain around her neck, clutching it in her palm.

She imagined little keepsakes being stored in those two drawers, mementos of her baby's life as he grew up. She just knew it would be a boy. Lots to tell her son of her own life but she would leave a lot of it out. No need to tell him what a monster his father had been at the end.

Margaret gently rubbed the line of scrollwork on the very top of the dresser and as her fingers slid down its back, a sliver of wood thrust itself into her pinky finger. She winced and jerked her hand back, examining her hand. Right there, a small shaving of wood, just under the skin.

\* \* \* \*

Brenda Singer uncapped the bottle of beer for Slim and set it on the bar in front of him. The Grotto was pretty slow but it was only a Tuesday night. There were a few regulars scattered among the tables but Slim was the only person sitting at the long, highly polished bar. Brenda lit a cigarette and brushed her almost-white blond hair back from her face.

"Did you know that Larry always bought me my peroxide?" She exhaled a stream of smoke away from Slim. He looked at her without saying anything and tipped the bottle to his lips.

"What does that have to do with anything?"

"Well, dummy, who's going to pay for my hair treatments now?"

Slim slowly shook his head and took another sip of beer. There was just something not right about this woman, he thought. And why was his friend buying The Grotto's weekday barmaid stuff for her hair? He had heard the rumors that Larry and Brenda were having an affair, but didn't want to believe it. Slim couldn't figure what he saw in her anyway. She was attractive enough, but the years of smoking and drinking had taken their toll. And she had a mean streak that came out when she'd gotten to know Tom Collins a little too well. After her fourth or fifth, she would dispense with the lemon and sugar and sometimes even the soda water and stick with straight gin.

A few months ago at the bar, Larry and Slim were shooting pool while Brenda was tending bar. Larry said something to Brenda that Slim didn't quite catch and suddenly a full bottle of beer rocketed across the room and narrowly missed Larry's head. It exploded on the wall behind him, sending beer and shards of glass everywhere. Brenda stormed out of the bar and didn't come back until the next night. Someone evidently had called the bar's owner, Brenda's uncle, because he came over within a half hour and cleaned up the mess.

Slim never did find out from Larry what he had said to her that evening, and was in no hurry to ask Brenda, tonight or any other night.

"Let me ask you something, Slim." Brenda said, squeezing some lemon juice over a spoonful of powdered sugar into a tumbler. "Do you think Larry's really dead?"

Slim raised the beer to his mouth and looked at Brenda. He could swear her wrinkles had gotten deeper in just the last couple weeks. "Of course, he's dead. Just because they never found his body doesn't mean he's alive. This is the second time this week you've asked me, anyway. Why are you so interested?"

"He was my best customer!" she said too quickly. "Always left me at least two bits for each beer he drank! Now who's gonna tip me like that? You? Hah!"

Slim's annoyance came out in his voice. "Look, I was there! I saw him go in the water."

"Why didn't you try and save him then? Why didn't you swim out to him?"

"I can't swim. Never learned how. But I did run to the marina office and yelled to old man Norwood I was taking one of his boats out and to call the sheriff's office. By the time I got to Larry's boat, he had gone under."

19

Brenda had finished making her Tom Collins and had drunk half of it in one gulp. "Couldn't he have swam to the other shore?"

"'Couldn't he have *swum* to the other shore.'"

"What?"

"Never mind. He was practically in the middle of the lake, Brenda," Slim said. "He would have had to swim over a hundred yards—at least—to get to the nearest shore. Three or four hundred yards to get to the far shore."

"Maybe he swam to the north or south end?"

"Impossible. Baylor Lake is two miles long. There's no way he swam even a third of that distance. Under normal circumstances he couldn't do it. And he was well on his way to being completely bombed that afternoon." Slim brought his volume down as he noticed people in the bar glancing at him. "Look, I feel terrible about the whole thing. Had I been ready on time, we would have been on the boat together and maybe I could have saved him. And, more than anything, he was my friend. I know he wasn't perfect—far from it—but I miss him, you know?"

Brenda had calmed down as well. "I'm sorry, Slim. I know you and Larry hung around a lot. I guess I just miss him too and was hoping that, well…"

"You know why I'm so sure Larry's gone?" Slim said suddenly, pointing to the entryway with his beer bottle. "'Cause I owe him ninety cents from our last gin rummy game and he would have collected it by now." Slim chuckled ruefully.

"You're right about that. He kept a very careful ledger when it came to cards." Brenda smiled as she put down the empty Tom Collins glass and reached for another lemon.

\* \* \* \*

Sheriff James Grady put the phone back in its cradle on his desk and glanced up at his senior deputy who had just walked in the front door of the building. "Just talked with Albany. They'll be sending an investigator tomorrow."

"You still think there's something more to the McConnell drowning?" Deputy Malden asked.

"I don't know, Bill. Something just isn't sitting right with me. We dredged that lake for three days and nothing. No body, no trace. Even the dogs couldn't pick up anything along the shore that led to anything."

"That's 'cause he never made it to shore. He's at the bottom of the lake feeding the fish and the worms. There was nothing for the dogs to pick up."

Sheriff Grady chewed on a toothpick for a moment before responding. "You know, that's what I thought at first too. But," he continued, taking the toothpick out of his mouth and gesturing toward his deputy, "why didn't the dogs pick up his scent at Sullivan's Landing?"

Malden started to speak, but pursed his lips instead, unsure of how to respond.

"That's where his car was, and that's where Slim said he put in. So why didn't the dogs detect anything at the landing?" Grady said.

"What are you suggesting, Jim?"

Grady threw the toothpick down in frustration. "I'm not suggesting anything. Yet. Things just aren't measuring up. If that idiot Norwood hadn't been asleep in the marina office, he could have verified Slim's statement. All he remembers was waking up to Slim banging on his window."

"Are you doubting Slim's story?"

"Surprisingly, I'm not. He's not a bad guy, born and raised here, never been in any trouble. I think he believes what he saw. He's not making it up."

The town of Kingsbridge was too small for its own police department, so law enforcement fell to the Livingston County Sheriff, James Grady. He was assisted in this part of the county by Senior Deputy Bill Malden and his new deputy, Charlie Castle. Most of the crimes committed in the town were minor; a stolen bicycle or the occasional fight at The Grotto. Sheriff Grady and his deputies could easily cover the misdemeanors within the town and the larger county. For a drowning without a body and clues not adding up, Grady felt he should at least call the State Police and see if they could spare an investigator.

Sheriff Grady didn't feel like Kingsbridge suffered a great loss with the death of Larry McConnell anyway, but if there was a crime committed in his county, he wanted it solved. And he wasn't too proud to ask for outside help. He'd worked with some troopers before and always admired their professionalism and attention to detail. He'd heard good things about this investigator, Ted Perkins, who was on his way from Albany.

Perkins had actually started in the Crime Laboratory in Schenectady and just recently moved to the Bureau of Criminal Investigation where he was already making a name for himself. He may not have had the street sense that a cop working in the field for years had, but Perkins certainly had the smarts for the job.

Maybe with Perkins' help, they could figure out exactly what happened to Larry McConnell.

## Chapter Two
## Wednesday, June 9, 1948

"DAVEY, COME HERE right now," Margaret said, more amused than frustrated. He could be a handful sometimes, but he *was* almost halfway to three. Her son was still in the "terrible two's" her friends had warned her about but was fun and well behaved for the most part. "David Raymond McConnell, I'm only going to tell you one more time. Come over here now." By using his full name, they both knew she was getting more serious.

Davey ran over to his mother who knelt down and gave him a quick hug as she examined him for leftover food and stains on his shirt.

"We want to look good for our new tenant, right Davey?"

Davey returned an impish smile and let himself be kissed on the cheek. The doorbell rang and Davey ran toward the door. Margaret stood up and walked to the foyer. *That's strange. I can't see anyone through the glass.* As she approached the door, the bell rang again.

Margaret felt uneasy, her stomach quivering a bit, as she hesitated with her hand on the doorknob. The bell rang a third time and Margaret jumped back. The glass was rippled so she could never see through it clearly but she could always tell if the postman or milkman was standing there. This time there was no one. *Were they standing off to the side?* The steps were narrow so they would have to be standing in her perennials to be ringing the bell.

She finally grabbed the knob and twisted it with a jerk, flinging the door open. Nobody was there. No one on the steps, no one in the flowers, no kids running down the street after playing a joke on her.

Davey stood in the doorway next to his mother, pointed up and said, "Man?"

"No. No man," she said. "I'm not sure what that was, Davey."

Davey pointed again, this time thrusting his finger upward. "Man! Let man in Mommy!"

Margaret looked down at her son, puzzled. "Davey, there's nobody there." She looked around the quiet summer street and slowly closed the door.

She guided her son back toward the living room, her hand gently on the back of his curly blond head. She sat down slowly in the wingback chair. What had Davey seen? He'd never developed an imaginary friend, but she supposed this could have been his first appearance. She'd have to ask her friends when their children developed pretend playmates.

When there was a rapping at the door, Margaret almost leaped out of the chair, startling Davey who had begun stacking some blocks on the floor. Davey ran toward the door again, but she stopped him. "Stay here, Davey."

Somewhere between brave and cautious, Margaret marched toward the foyer. This time she could see a figure through the glass. She breathed easier as she reached toward the doorknob and opened the door.

"Mrs. McConnell? I'm George Carmichael—I wrote you about renting your attic bedroom?"

"Mr. Carmichael, I'm very pleased to meet you. Won't you come in?" Margaret stepped aside and the man entered the foyer, taking off his hat as he came in.

Davey ran toward the prospective tenant and shouted, "Man!" He held up his forefinger on each hand and squealed, "Two mans!"

Mr. Carmichael raised his eyebrows. "Two men? No, just me. Have you rented it out already?"

"Oh no," Margaret said, "There was, um, another gentleman here a few minutes ago. For something else."

"Ah, very good. Because I would very much like to see the room if it's still available. This is a perfect location for me." Margaret turned her head slightly, wondering why the sleepy town of Kingsbridge would be perfect for anyone so obviously sophisticated and...was that a British accent she heard? "You see, my company has sent me on a bit of a mission. Nothing so daring as the RAF missions in the war, of course."

He chuckled modestly and continued. "You may know that your cannery has been looking for a buyer recently. It's no secret, and they approached us last year to see if we would be interested in acquiring them. So that's what brings me across the pond, as they say. The company asked if I wanted to transfer from our London branch office to the States and I said yes. Fresh start and all. So they want me to check out the books, the facility and so forth to see if they would be a good fit for us. Plus I'd be closer to headquarters..."

Margaret realized she wasn't breathing and took in a quick gulp of air. She could listen to this Mr. Carmichael talk all day. The only time she'd heard a British accent was in the pictures. She hadn't really paid attention to exactly what he was saying, but it didn't matter. And he was so, well, handsome. He didn't look anything at all like Larry. Her late husband wasn't much taller than she was and had been growing quite a belly with all his drinking. Plus his eyes were small and too close together. What had she seen in him anyway?

Mr. Carmichael, however, was tall but not overly so. Maybe just shy of six feet, she figured. His sandy colored hair was neatly parted and he had kind eyes. But that voice. It wasn't just the accent. His voice was firm, authoritative, and as friendly as his face. Margaret made up her mind right away—he would make a perfect tenant.

"I am sorry, Mrs. McConnell. I've been going on ceaselessly about why I'm in your fair town and being positively boring, I'm quite sure."

"No need to apologize. I've not been a good hostess. Would you like some tea?"

"I'll drink tea in a pinch, but I actually prefer coffee."

Margaret raised her eyebrows in a delicate arch.

"I know, we English are supposed to make time every day for our afternoon tea, but I've never liked the stuff."

"That's good," Margaret laughed. "I don't have any tea anyway. I'd have to borrow some from next door. Why don't I get some coffee going? I can show you the room while it's percolating."

A few minutes later, Margaret was leading Mr. Carmichael up the stairs. Actually, Davey was leading the charge to the second floor, hurrying up the steps ahead of both of the adults.

"My room. Toys!" Davey exclaimed, pointing to his bedroom. "Potty room," he said as he ran to the door of the bathroom.

"Okay, Davey," Margaret said with a smile. "I'm sure

Mr. Carmichael isn't interested in your toys. And he knows what a bathroom looks like."

"Actually, he's quite charming, Mrs. McConnell. So full of energy."

"You have no idea! But don't worry, he's very well behaved and won't make too much noise, I promise."

Mr. Carmichael patted Davey on the head and smiled. "He actually reminds me of my boy when he was that age."

"Oh, will this be enough room for you? You didn't say anything in your letter about a son. Or a wife. I guess I just assumed…"

George Carmichael slowed as he walked down the hall toward the staircase that led to the attic. "Um, yes, both my wife and son perished in a doodlebug attack on London. Ian was just eight years old."

Margaret stopped and faced Mr. Carmichael fully. "Doodlebug? I don't—"

"Sorry, we also called them buzz bombs. They were the V-1 rockets the Germans launched. They had no precision, no aiming mechanism, but when they struck they did terrible damage. I was at Station Broadwell in Oxfordshire at the time. They would just launch them toward London and hope they hit something. Most of my block was destroyed and Ian and Maureen evidently never heard the terrible buzzing the bombs made when they fell and so…" His voice trailed off.

"I'm so sorry, Mr. Carmichael," Margaret said, placing a hand lightly on his arm. "I had no idea."

He smiled gently and stood a little straighter. "Thank you, Mrs. McConnell. You would have liked both of them and I'm sure little Davey here would have become fast friends with Ian." He smiled more broadly and said, "Now, if you'll have me, where shall I be staying? Oh, and please call me George."

After a quick tour of the attic bedroom, George brought his suitcases from the car and later joined Margaret at the kitchen table for a cup of coffee. Davey sat down on the floor next to them, sorting his collection of toy cars and trucks. He eagerly showed each of them to their new boarder who patiently examined the toys one at a time and asked questions about them. *He has such a way with Davey,* Margaret thought. He must have been a wonderful father to his own son. Davey seemed quite taken with him as well.

As Margaret was clearing the coffee cups, there was a knock at the kitchen door. "That'll be Fran, from next door. She usually comes over this time of day with her daughter." Davey ran to the door, eager to see his playmate. Margaret opened the door and greeted Frances and her five-year-old, Caroline. "Davey, take your cars to the living room. You and Caroline can play in there while we visit."

George stood and shook Fran's hand as Caroline and Davey ran from the room. Margaret made the introductions and the three of them sat at the table.

"We've just had coffee, Fran," Margaret said. "Do you want some?"

Frances hadn't taken her eyes off George since she walked in the house. "Fran?" Margaret repeated. "Coffee?"

She quickly looked at Margaret, her face red. "No, no coffee. Sorry." She turned back to George. "So you'll be staying in the upstairs bedroom here then?"

"Yes, I think the bedroom will be most suitable, and Mrs. McConnell and Davey are going to be wonderful hosts."

Margaret saw that her neighbor was again staring so

she cleared her throat a little. "Fran, is your husband still working the late shift at the cannery?"

Fran's eyes darted to Margaret and with a smirk on her lips, she spoke. "Yes, although he'll be back to working days soon. You know how much Dick hates getting home so late."

George began to ask Fran what her husband did at the canning factory, but the doorbell rang. This time Davey was playing with Caroline so he didn't run to the door, but Margaret got up and walked into the hall. Just as before, she could see no one at the door through the glass. "Not again," she said.

She opened the door and stood on the steps looking around. From behind, she heard the doorbell chime again. She jumped at the sound. Margaret whirled around half expecting to see one of the neighborhood kids hiding in her flowerbed, but saw nobody. This is the strangest thing, she thought.

She returned to the kitchen and explained what happened both this time and before George had arrived. He suggested that it was probably a short in the doorbell and he would be happy to take a look at it. Margaret directed him to the shed where Larry's old tools were stored. Fran was smiling when Margaret returned to the kitchen.

"Hubba hubba," Fran exclaimed. "Handy around the house and good looking too!"

"Oh stop it, Fran!"

\* \* \* \*

George was very complimentary towards Margaret's cooking that evening, his first in the home. "Wonderful pot roast, Mrs. McConnell. Thank you very much," he said, folding his napkin neatly and placing it on the table.

"Remember," she smiled, "you're to call me Margaret."

"Of course. I'll try to remember," he said. "Let me help you clear the dishes."

Davey interrupted as the two adults were getting up from the table. "Mister George! Mister George! He had too much trouble pronouncing "Carmichael" so their new tenant suggested Mister George instead. Davey seemed very pleased with that and had little difficulty in saying it. "Pay with me!" Margaret sighed and helped Davey down from his chair.

"*Play* with me," she said, emphasizing the missing *L*. Davey ignored her and ran to George.

"I don't mind playing with him, Margaret, if you can manage all right here."

"That would be wonderful. Thank you." She'd only known this man a few hours but already seemed very much at ease with him. At first, Margaret wasn't sure what to think about a man as a boarder. For the last two years she'd had a few women as tenants, but no men. Two of the women were widows, both in their 60s, and the third a college coed attending the nearby state university. But after the girl graduated she was left without a tenant and needed the income. She put flyers up at the college, the cannery, and placed an ad in the newspaper. The only response came after several weeks, from George Carmichael. She was happy with the prospect of collecting a rent check every week so didn't think too much of the fact this would be her first male boarder. Fran obviously approved and she hoped there wouldn't be too much gossip about it in town.

Margaret stood at the sink washing dishes and glanced in the living room. She couldn't believe how comfortable Davey felt with him. They were both sitting on the floor, her son rolling his cars on the braided rug. George was assembling little buildings out of blocks and Davey was careful to avoid them with his car.

George reached over and tussled Davey's brown hair. Margaret always kept her son's hair combed over to the side and now it was every which way and even standing up in places. She smiled as Davey giggled.

Then for a moment, Margaret thought about how polite George was and remembered that Larry was a charmer at first too. *But no, George seems genuine.* Looking back, she should have seen through Larry. She was young and naïve and unable to see past his initial allure. He wasn't particularly handsome but he was a talker and made her feel special, at least at first. She dwelled on the differences between the two men for a moment longer then finished drying the dishes and stacked them in the cupboard.

Removing her apron, Margaret headed into the living room and spied the sprawling city on the rug. "My! What do we have here, Davey?"

Davey jumped up and ran to his mother. "Lookie what Mr. George made! Our house," he said pointing to a few blocks stacked on one another, "Fire house! Libary!" Then, with a big grin, "Ice cream shop!"

Margaret knelt down and corrected Davey, "Library," emphasizing the *r*. "Can you say that?"

"Libary!" he repeated. Margaret and George laughed as they both stood up. Margaret crossed the room to sit in the rocking chair and offered a seat on the sofa for George.

"Davey, you can play for a few more minutes and then it's time for bed, okay?" Margaret said. Davey frowned but didn't protest. He promptly sat back down and steered his cars on the rug to the various "buildings."

George pulled a pipe from his jacket pocket and a pouch of tobacco. "Do you mind if I smoke, Mrs.—er,

Margaret?"

"No, of course not. My father and grandfather both smoked a pipe. I love the smell of it." She passed an ashtray over to him while he began loading the pipe. They chatted while he lit it, puffs of white smoke rising from the bowl. After a few draws on the pipe, the smoke lessened and George sat back in the well-worn sofa.

The conversation was light and enjoyable and before she knew it, Margaret realized that it was well past Davey's bedtime. Indeed, Davey had lain down on the rug and was fast asleep. "Oh dear," she said to George, "could I ask you to clear Davey's bed? He had his crayons and coloring books in his bed earlier today and I don't want him sleeping with them." She laughed. "I know he shouldn't be coloring in bed, but I do indulge him from time to time."

"I'd be happy to," George said. He walked quietly up the stairs with his pipe clenched between his teeth, smoke trailing behind him.

Margaret gathered up Davey's toys and placed them in a small wooden box in the corner of the living room, then picked up her son. George was just coming down the stairs and pronounced the bed clean and ready. "I put the crayons back in the tin and put them and the coloring books on the dresser. Hope that's okay. And I left the dresser lamp on."

Margaret nodded and smiled and made her way up the stairs while George settled back down on the couch. None of her other tenants had been so good with Davey, and they were all women. He must have really loved his wife and son, she thought as she reached the top of the stairs.

That's strange, why is it dark in Davey's room, she thought. Margaret was sure that George said he left the lamp on. She rounded the corner with her son in her arms and turned the overhead light on. Margaret's mouth hung open but no sound would come. She blinked and blinked again. She stared at Davey's bed, crayons and coloring books strewn all over it.

Margaret stood just inside her son's bedroom for a full minute, her eyes wide at the impossibility of it. George said he stacked everything on the dresser. He wouldn't have lied about it, but what other explanation could there be? And why would he lie about it in the first place?

Davey's mother slowly walked to the bed and, holding him tightly against her chest with one hand, began clearing the crayons and books with her free hand. Satisfied that the bed was truly clear this time, she laid him down softly and covered him with the blanket.

Margaret double checked the now-full tin of crayons on the dresser. She hadn't missed any and she began to breathe again. This just didn't make any sense, she thought, as she turned off the light and tiptoed out of Davey's room. Suddenly she had a horrible thought and she halted at the top step. *What if George being so pleasant and charming was just an act? What if he were as evil as Larry? What had she done? How could she be so foolish?*

She took a deep breath. *No, now you're being foolish. George is everything he seems. He's a good man.* Margaret took another deep breath and started down the steps to the living room.

George looked up at her with a smile. He took a puff from his pipe and put the newspaper he was reading aside. "Is everything okay?" he asked.

"Yes, yes, I think so," Margaret replied as she crossed to the rocking chair. She didn't sit down though. She stood in front of it and faced George. "This is going to sound stupid but, you did put Davey's crayons away, right?"

"Of course," George said. His brown eyes narrowed a bit in his confusion at the question. "Why do you ask?"

Margaret paused and drew a breath. "When I went into Davey's room, it was dark and when I turned the light on all his crayons and the coloring books were still in his bed."

George put his pipe down and shook his head. "That's not possible, Margaret. I put all the crayons in the tin, all twenty-four of them. He had three coloring books in the bed and I placed them on the dresser and the tin on top of them." He leaned forward. "Are you quite sure all the crayons were in the bed? Perhaps I missed one or two, but I'm quite sure there was no room left in the tin."

Margaret tightened her lips and her chin quivered slightly. She spoke slowly. "The empty tin and all the crayons were in the bed, along with the coloring books."

For the longest time Margaret and George sat silently in the living room, trying to work out what had happened, and how. In Margaret's mind, the only explanation was that George merely said he had cleared the bed, but really hadn't. But why would he say he did? To George, he must have simply missed a couple crayons and Margaret somehow exaggerated how full Davey's bed was.

Davey's screaming shattered the stillness of the evening.

## Chapter Three

SHERIFF JAMES GRADY pulled his cruiser to a stop outside the Wadsworth Diner, the only restaurant in the town of Kingsbridge. His senior deputy, Bill Malden, drove up just as the sheriff shut his door.

"Where's Castle?" Grady called to the deputy.

Malden shrugged as the two men walked to the door of the diner. "He wasn't at the station and I tried raising him on the radio but got nothing."

Grady sighed and shook his head. "I've put up with this crap long enough. I'm going to have to do something about him. I guarantee you he's getting plastered at The Grotto."

"I don't think he's there, Jim. I drove past there and didn't see the cruiser."

"Well then he's probably at Sullivan's drinking with old man Norwood." Grady sighed again as he opened the door. "I hate to let the man go, Bill, but I just can't keep putting up with this."

Grady and Malden crossed to their usual booth, the sheriff grabbing a toothpick from the shot glass on the counter. The sheriff waved Donna over and she arrived with two cups of coffee.

"You want to see a dinner menu, boys?" she asked.

"Nope. Ate supper at the station tonight. Just a slice of apple pie for me. Bill, you want anything?"

"Coffee's fine for me, thanks." Bill leaned back in the booth and adjusted his Sam Browne belt and holster. "I don't want to get into this again with you, Jim, but I haven't trusted the guy since he started. There's just something about him. I can't put my finger on it but I don't think he's always square with us."

Grady put his hand up. "I know, I know. I'm beginning to think you may be right. I've talked to him about these disappearing acts before but there may be more to it than just cutting out for the occasional nip at The Grotto." Grady paused while Donna slid the slice of pie in front of him. Once she had walked back to the counter, he continued. "You know that he and Larry McConnell served in the same unit in the Pacific?"

Malden shook his head as he raised the cup of coffee to his lips. "I knew they were both in the Army, but didn't know they served together."

"Yeah, I didn't know either. Charlie was originally from somewhere in Indiana but when he was discharged he came here, bounced around a little and I finally hired him when Woodruff retired. It was only recently that Charlie told me that he and McConnell were Rangers. I guess they both took part in some raid in the Philippines. They helped rescue a bunch of POWs but according to Charlie both he and Larry racked up a lot of Japanese kills in the process. Charlie was pretty proud of it. Apparently Larry urged him to come here after he got out."

Bill took another sip of coffee and held his cup with both hands. "You know, Charlie always seemed a bit of a loose cannon. He was too quick to shove someone around when they weren't cooperating rather than calm the guy down with words. Maybe he enjoyed the killing a little too much over there."

The sheriff was finished with his pie and pushed the plate back, sticking the toothpick in his mouth. He raised his eyebrows. "I don't know—that seems to be a stretch. Besides, you saw action in France and I've never seen you get violent with anyone."

Bill laughed. "You're right. There goes my theory."

\* \* \* \*

Deputy Charlie Castle tucked in his uniform shirt and zipped up his pants. He grabbed his gun belt from the floor and swung it around his waist, fastening it in the front. He patted the revolver that hung from his belt and winked at Brenda. "Not a word now, darlin'. You know the rules."

"Of course I'm not going to say anything. How stupid do you think I am?" Brenda focused on buttoning her blouse, her chin pressed against her neck as she looked down. "But what if Larry finds out?"

"My god, Brenda, you really are stupid aren't you? Larry is dead. Has been for almost three years now."

Brenda shook her head from side to side, her blond hair trying to keep pace with her head as it swung back and forth. "I know he's alive. He promised me. Promised we'd be together."

Charlie grinned at her and rubbed the stubble on his cheek. "Well, dead men's promises don't mean much do they?"

"But he had a plan. He told me. He even took some money from the office of the cannery when no one was there one night. I've—I mean, Larry's—been holding onto it all this time." She finished with her blouse and looked up. "I probably shouldn't say anything else. If you arrest him, you'll charge me too as an accessory after the fact. I learned that from listening to *Perry Mason* on the radio."

"Don't worry, honey, I won't arrest you." Castle took the handcuffs out of their leather pouch and swung them around his finger. "I might lock you up though unless you tell me the rest of this grand plan of Larry's. And how can I arrest a dead man?"

"Okay," Brenda said, "but pour me another drink."

\* \* \* \*

Margaret and George ran up the stairs the instant they heard Davey screaming. Margaret raced to the landing, her feet a blur up the steps, George right behind her. She grabbed the door frame to Davey's room, whirled inside and hit the overhead light switch. She took two steps into the room and gasped.

Crayons were scattered in the bed and the empty tin lay next to Davey's face. A thin line of blood traced down Davey's cheek and two spots of red stained the soft flannel sheet. Margaret overcame her brief shock and crossed to his bed, scooping him up in her arms and stroking his head.

"Shh, shh, it's okay, Davey. You're okay." She rocked him gently in her arms for a few minutes until his cries quieted. Margaret twisted her head around to get a better look at the cut on her son's cheek. She licked her thumb and rubbed the blood off. It was a superficial cut and the blood clotted quickly.

While Margaret was calming Davey down, George gathered up the crayons from the bed then picked up the tin. Examining it closely, he saw a burr in the metal on the side of the box. He rubbed his finger over it and felt that it was quite sharp, easily sharp enough to cut Davey's skin.

Davey was finally relaxed and quiet. Margaret had moved to the rocking chair and was rocking softly, cradling her son against her shoulder. She looked at George with eyes wide and mouthed, "How did this happen?"

George shook his head slowly, unable to fathom this new turn of events. He reached in his jacket pocket for his pipe, but felt nothing. He had thrown it on the sofa when they heard Davey's screams. Fearing that some embers may have spilled onto the sofa, he turned and walked quickly down the stairs. The pipe was sitting sideways on the cushion, but no tobacco had escaped. He picked it up and lit it, gently puffing some mushrooms of smoke into the room. He could hear Margaret putting Davey back in bed and walking carefully down the stairs.

Margaret stood in the middle of the living room with tears welling in her eyes. In her cupped hands she held the crayons and the empty tin. She silently placed the crayons and box on the coffee table and sat gingerly in the chair. "How could this happen?" she repeated.

"I don't have any earthly idea," George said, wrapping his suddenly cold hands around his warm pipe. He held up the tin of crayons and examined it. "Is he going to be okay?"

"Yes, it was just a small cut. It was just the shock of it I'm sure that made him scream."

George handed the tin to Margaret. "There's a small but sharp piece of metal on the edge of the box. That's probably what cut him. But how in the world did it – and all the crayons – end up back in his bed?"

Margaret took a couple slow steps to her chair, then whirled around to face George. "Remember the doorbell ringing by itself earlier today? And now this? This is going to sound silly, but what if there's a..." She stopped herself and rubbed the tears from her eyes, and with a quick laugh continued. "What if it's a ghost?"

Another person, Larry most likely, would have laughed at her but George smiled a kind smile. "Well, I'm not sure I believe in ghosts, so why don't we leave that for the last explanation. Let's try to rule out other possibilities before we give the supernatural too much credence."

Margaret laughed again, feeling much calmer. "Perhaps you're right."

"Besides," George added, "that would make you Mrs. Muir and your ghost Captain Gregg. But who would I be, Miles Fairley? I'm not that much of a cad!"

George was such a gentle man, Margaret thought. With just a few gestures and some kind words, he had brought her back from the brink of hysteria. Even got her laughing at the reference to *The Ghost and Mrs. Muir*, one of her favorite movies.

She pushed her hair back and wiped her eyes for the last time. "I just don't understand it. It doesn't make any sense."

"I agree, Margaret, but there must be an explanation. The doorbell and the crayons are not connected, of that I'm quite sure. Even though I couldn't find it, there must be a short or some frayed insulation in the wiring to make the doorbell go off. I'll have to think a little harder to explain the crayons though."

## Chapter Four
## Thursday, June 10

THE NEXT MORNING at the station, Deputy Castle stood in sharp contrast to his boss, the sheriff. Grady's uniform was always crisp and neat, while his junior deputy's shirttail typically sneaked above his belt, even first thing in the morning. Castle never pressed his shirt or pants, never shined his shoes. But that was the least of his problems today.

"Charlie, I barely know where to begin with you. Neither Bill or I could raise you on the radio last night. I wanted to meet at the Wadsworth to discuss coverage on the west side. Sheriff Rauber's going to be down a man and has asked if we could expand our patrols into some of the eastern areas of Wyoming county. I wanted to discuss it with you and Bill before I made an assignment, but guess what? You've got the job." Grady took the toothpick out of his mouth and pointed at Castle. "Extra patrols, more hours. I don't want to hear any griping about it either. You start tonight."

"But Jim, something's wrong with my radio, I swear. I never heard you calling. I was in my car the whole night. Honest." Charlie balled his fists as the dressing down continued.

"Deputy, I don't believe you for a second," Grady said, pointing again with his toothpick. "And another thing. I've been doing a lot of thinking. Consider this your last chance. If I catch you drinking on the job again, or even hear about it, or if I catch you in a lie, you're out. Now make your rounds and take the time to think about if you want to stay employed." Grady softened his voice a little. "I'm willing to forget your screw ups in the past, but I've got to see you making a solid effort. Act like a professional lawman and you'll have a long career here." He nodded toward the door and Charlie turned on his heel and stormed out.

Grady's senior deputy came out of the back office after the front door closed. "You think he'll change, Jim?" he asked.

"I'm not sure. I don't think he's suited for a job at the cannery or the lumberyard. If he can just stay on the straight and narrow, he'd make a decent cop. Like I told him, I'll give him one more chance. Keep an eye on him when you have time. Don't crowd him though."

Before Deputy Malden headed out to his car, the office phone rang. Sheriff Grady picked it up and listened to the operator for a moment. He glanced at Malden, "Long distance call coming from State Police Headquarters in Albany. Wonder what this is about."

Grady returned his attention to the phone when the call was connected. "Yes, hello Investigator, what can we do for you?" Grady listened for a few moments, nodding occasionally, his eyes widening at one point. "Of course, we'd be glad to see you, Ted. A couple days you say? All right, I'll call over to the Starlight Motor Court and arrange a room for you. You'll see it on your right as you're coming into Kingsbridge. You'll like it, all the comforts of home." Grady rolled his eyes at Malden who let out a quick laugh. "Okay, thanks Ted. We'll see you tomorrow."

Sheriff Grady put the phone down and ran his hand through his thinning hair. "That was Ted Perkins with BCI in Albany. He's re-opened the Larry McConnell case. Technically, I guess, he never closed it. But he wants to re-interview Slim and a couple others. And he wants to question Charlie Castle."

"Castle!" Bill exclaimed. "What for?"

"I don't know. He wouldn't say."

"I can't remember, was Castle on the force then or was Woodruff still here?"

"I think he was. I can't remember exactly when he came to town, but I think it was a month or two before McConnell drowned," Grady said.

Malden leaned against his desk, facing Grady. "By the way, did Perkins say why he was looking into the case again?"

"Said he got a tip. Just a typewritten note in the mail. Didn't come to him specifically, but was addressed to the State Police in Albany and ended up on his desk. He said he was going to bring it with him tomorrow." Grady twirled his toothpick around in his fingers. "Remember at the time, I thought there might be something more to it than just an accidental drowning. And you didn't believe me. You need to respect your elders, Bill!"

Bill laughed and turned to the filing cabinet in the office, digging out the McConnell case file. "So Perkins wants to re-interview Slim. Does he want to talk with everyone?" Grady nodded his head. "Should we start lining them up? We've got Mrs. McConnell, their neighbors the Silvas, Brenda at The Grotto, Norwood at the marina, and a couple others to work through," he said, running his finger down the list of names.

"No, I don't want to get the word out until Perkins actually gets here. Especially if he wants to talk with Castle."

\* \* \* \*

Deputy Castle didn't know he was being talked about the moment he was arriving at The Grotto. He was still steaming from the lecture Grady had given him and threw the door open, startling Brenda and her uncle. He marched to the bar and growled through clenched teeth, "Set me up. And when I'm done we're going to talk about Loverboy Larry and your plans to live happily ever after."

Brenda swallowed, seeing that he was not in a mood to joke or flirt with. "Charlie, I can't. We don't open for another few hours. I only had the door unlocked because —"

"Give me a god-damned drink now!"

As Brenda's uncle started to walk over, she said, "Charlie, you know we can't serve 'til one o'clock. If the State Liquor Authority finds out we served before one, they'll fine us. Even Sheriff Grady could make trouble for us."

Charlie slammed his hand down on the bar. "I don't give a damn about the SLA and I sure as hell don't give a damn about Grady. Now pour!"

Brenda stood back, unsure of what to do. She looked at her uncle who approached from her left. He said in a quiet voice, "I'll take over here. Why don't you finish unpacking the new glasses in the back." Brenda glanced at Charlie and quickly walked to the stockroom.

Brenda's uncle poured Charlie a shot of rye which he emptied in one gulp. He banged the shot glass onto the bar and pointed to it with his finger, glaring at The

Grotto's owner. He poured another and set the bottle down next to the glass.

"Charlie, what's gotten into you?" he asked.

"Shut up, old man, and keep pouring." Castle gulped down another shot and pointed again to the empty glass.

Charlie looked around the bar while the older man splashed more liquor into the glass. A flash of yellow through the window caught his eye. He leapt from the bar stool and ran to the door to see Brenda easing her Buick from the gravel parking lot onto the blacktop.

"Brenda!" Charlie yelled angrily. He screamed her name again as the car accelerated around a bend in the road and disappeared from sight.

Charlie ran to the bar and clenched Brenda's uncle by the collar and pulled him in close, over the bar, his breath dripping with the sour smell of rye. "Where the hell is she going? She better not be going to get Grady."

"I don't know, Charlie. I don't know." The deputy released the man, pushing him backwards. He ran out of the bar and threw open the door to his cruiser. Charlie wrenched the key and mashed the gas pedal to the floor, speeding onto the blacktop after Brenda.

Brenda pushed the accelerator harder once she saw Charlie's cruiser lights in her rearview mirror. The Buick's engine was screaming as it hit its top end. She figured she had only a minute or two lead and hoped she could get a call in to the operator by the time she made it to her house. She shouldn't have told him Larry's plan the other night. Shouldn't have told him she's been receiving letters from Larry. Sure, Charlie laughed at her, but she knew the truth. Larry was out there, arranging everything so they could be together.

Larry couldn't wait to get away from Margaret, Brenda knew. All her nagging, no man could put up with that. It wasn't Brenda's idea for Larry to kill his wife—she didn't like that part of the plan and didn't think he was serious about it anyway since Margaret was still alive. Disappearing from the boat in the middle of the lake was a stroke of genius though. Once all the pieces fell together and he sent her the final word, she'd pack up and head to wherever he told her.

Brenda's focus zeroed in on the road as her tires slipped onto the shoulder. She let off on the gas slightly and righted herself, then pressed on the pedal harder to keep her distance from Charlie.

She never should have gotten mixed up with Charlie, she thought. But it had taken Larry far longer to call for her than he had promised. And she missed being with a man. She missed Larry so much. Charlie had a far worse temper than Larry ever did. She could handle Larry, but once Charlie got going, look out. It was like sticking your hand in a hornet's nest. She wasn't sure why he was so enraged this morning, but right now he was chasing her and she was afraid of what he would do if he caught her. She had to get home and call for the sheriff.

Brenda hit the brakes and swung the wheel to the left, the car's back end coming around as she steered right to correct, then straight into the driveway. She jumped out of the car and ran inside her house to the living room. She could hear Charlie's car approaching as she stuck her finger in the 0 and spun the dial on the phone.

Please hurry, she pleaded, bouncing on the balls of her feet. Finally the operator picked up and she was put through to the Sheriff's office just as Charlie raced into her driveway.

* * * *

Fran made the short walk from her house to Margaret's with her daughter Caroline by her side. The June afternoon sun was warmer than usual for this time of year and she adjusted her hat to block the glare. Margaret's flowers surrounded them with color as they walked up the side of the house to the kitchen door. Fran knocked and was pleased to see Mr. Carmichael open the door for them.

Once they were inside and Caroline had run off to play with Davey, the three adults sat at the kitchen table, sipping lemonade. Margaret told her neighbor what had happened the night before with Davey's crayons and the small cut on his face. George maintained that there was an earthly explanation for it all, Fran was convinced that there was a ghost in the house, maybe more than one, and Margaret was somewhere in the middle.

Fran took a long swallow of lemonade, pushed her glasses farther up her nose and turned to Margaret. "Honey," she said, "my oldest sister in Rochester sees a fortune teller every month." She lifted her eyebrows and looked over the tops of her glasses at her friend.

"I'm not sure what your sister seeing a fortune teller has to do with anything," Margaret said with a laugh.

"Well, I think we could use some of her expertise in a case like this. You know, to solve the mystery of your ghost."

"What case? There is no case here, Fran!"

"You said yourself you had a ghost. We need to find a way to talk with it and find out if it's friendly or not."

Margaret narrowed her eyes at her neighbor. "No, I didn't say I had a ghost. I said we *might* have a ghost. I'm leaning toward George's explanation."

George put his glass down on the table and shifted in his chair. "I still don't really have an explanation, I'm afraid. I'm just not ready to start blaming the spirit world." He paused to open his pipe case, selecting a particularly shiny billiard shape and began to fill it with tobacco from the pouch. "I am inclined to believe it might have something to do with the wind. It was quite breezy last night and the windows are drafty. Who knows? Perhaps a freak wind blew in and caught the corner of the coloring books. They acted like a sail, picking up the box of crayons and sending them to Davey's bed. The full tin struck Davey and broke open, scattering the crayons around him."

"Oh, come now, Mr. Carmichael," Fran said. "Do you really believe that? Margaret, what do you think? It couldn't possibly be the wind. Was anything else in the room disturbed?" When Margaret shook her head no, Fran continued. "So, what do you think it is—the wind or a ghost?"

Not wanting to choose between her best friend and George, Margaret stood up, "I don't know, Fran. Why are you making me choose?" She reached toward the pitcher next to the sink. "Now who would like more lemonade?"

When everyone's glasses were filled, Fran said, "I'm going to call my sister tonight and get the name of that fortune teller. I heard the woman even helped the State Police find a missing boy in Elmira a couple months ago. She's very perceptive."

George had lit his pipe and coils of smoke were rising to the ceiling. "I don't have much faith in fortune tellers and the like, I'm afraid. No offense to your sister, Mrs. Silva, but I think most of them are charlatans, preying on vulnerable people who are anxious for answers that they could probably find within themselves. For free."

"Don't be so quick to judge, Mr. Carmichael," Fran replied. "The first time my sister went to the palm-reader, shortly after her husband died, the woman told her what her husband had died of. And my sister never even told her she was widowed."

"Did your sister make an appointment with this fortune teller before she went to see her?" George asked.

"Of course, she wasn't going to take the bus all the way across town without an appointment."

"Is it possible then that with the name of her newest client, the fortune teller just did a little research to find out some background information on your sister? A quick call to the newspaper's obituary department would reveal that your brother-in-law had recently died."

"Well…" Fran said, not liking the direction the conversation was taking.

George winked at Margaret and said in a low voice, "Now, let's try something. On occasion I too am touched by some unknown psychic powers." He puffed a large volume of smoke above the kitchen table and swirled it around with his hands. "I'm going to try and uncover your late brother-in-law's name." He peered intently into Fran's eyes. "I'm getting a certain sound, a *J* sound, was his name John, or perhaps James?"

"No, smarty pants! It was Gene," Fran said with a snort.

George didn't break character, but did wink again at Margaret. "Ah, but I was getting a *J* sound, and the soft *G* sounds like *J*. So I wasn't far off. But let's continue. Gene sadly died of some sort of malady of the abdomen." He moved his hand slowly from his chest down toward his stomach and continued to speak as Fran nodded her head. "It would appear that he had a cancer. Stomach cancer, I believe."

Fran and Margaret both gasped. "How did you know that?" Fran asked breathlessly. "That was never in the obituary. And how did you know his name?"

"Now, remember, I *didn't* know his name. You told me

his name after I guessed that it began with a *J*. And I started with James and John because they are extremely popular names for people roughly our age. As is George, both starting with the same sounding letter. Just a lucky break that his name wasn't one of those three, but still started with a *J* sound."

Now it was Margaret's turn to comment. "How very clever," she said. "But how did you know that Gene died of stomach cancer? There's no way you could have known that. Another lucky guess?"

George sat back in his chair and tamped his pipe. "More of an educated guess and a little luck. First of all, unless someone dies in an accident or from wartime injuries, most people die of something...here," he said, indicating his midsection. "Heart attacks are the most common in the upper chest area, but when I moved my hand down my chest earlier, you didn't have any reaction. When I got to my stomach, your eyes widened a bit. I took a guess and said stomach cancer. It could have been liver failure or a couple other common ailments, but I guessed and went with the stomach."

The two women laughed. "You'd be great at a party, Mr. Carmichael," Fran said.

"Oh, I don't know about that. But it does make for a spot of fun. I hope I didn't offend you with my criticism of fortune tellers."

"No, not at all. I still believe in their powers but I think you have some powers of your own." Fran smiled at Margaret and got up to fetch her daughter from the living room where she and Davey were playing with some marbles.

* * * *

Deputy Castle threw open the front door of Brenda's house and raced in. "Brenda!" he bellowed, running from the living room to the kitchen and finally the bedroom, stopping in the door frame. Brenda was sitting on the bed, clutching the letters Larry had sent her over the last couple years.

Charlie was breathing heavily, staring at Brenda, who said nothing. He then heard a voice, small and tinny, coming from the living room. He noticed the phone's receiver hanging by its cord from the table, slowly scraping the hardwood floor. "Who the hell did you call?"

"I, I was just calling my mother when I heard you roaring up here. You're scaring me."

"You're a liar! If I pick up that phone right now, whose voice am I going to hear?" Brenda shifted her gaze downward but didn't say anything. Charlie took a step toward her. "Who's on the phone?"

"Bill Malden," she said quietly, her lips quivering.

Charlie took another step at her, but then quickly turned around and strode to the phone. He picked up the dangling receiver, took a breath and spoke in an even voice. "Hey Bill, this is Charlie. Everything's okay here. Brenda just thought she had a burglar. No, no, you can call Grady and tell him to stand down. Everything's fine. Yeah, she's okay. All right, thanks." He hung up the phone carefully and walked into Brenda's bedroom.

Charlie was squinting at Brenda, the outline of a vein in his forehead visible. He sat down next to Brenda on the bed. "Now why don't you tell me what this is all about, sweetheart?" His breath stinking of rye, he leaned in closer. "And why did you run off from The Grotto? You could have killed someone driving like that, you know. I should run you in right now, you're a menace to the public."

"I don't know. I've just never seen you so mad. I was

afraid."

"Oh, and what do you have there?" Charlie said, looking at the envelopes in Brenda's hand. He tore them from her and sneered. "Aw, love letters from a dead man. How romantic."

"He's alive!" Brenda said, snatching the letters back from him. "Who else would be sending me these letters?"

Charlie laughed out loud. "Who indeed? Now, how much money did you say he 'borrowed' from the cannery?" Charlie unsnapped his holster and drew his revolver out, idly spinning the cylinder back and forth.

Brenda stiffened at the sight of the gun, its long barrel being pointed occasionally at her as Castle loosely swung the weapon from side to side. "Um, it was only a few hundred dollars, he said. Maybe a thousand at the most."

"Hmm...just a couple hundred dollars. That doesn't sound like a lot to run away on. Are you sure it wasn't more than that? Maybe a few thousand? Or more?" He swung the gun towards Brenda and kept it trained on her.

"No, just a few hundred. That's all he said, I swear it!" Brenda was shaking, silently praying that Deputy Malden had been able to radio the sheriff.

"I don't like when you lie to me, Brenda. You lied to me just now about who you were talking to. And you're lying about how much money old Larry has socked away. I also need to know where exactly the money is. Where have you hidden it?"

"Honest, Charlie. He has the money with him, that's how he's able to be hiding out for so long. And he has to be real careful with it 'cause he only has a couple hundred."

Charlie let out a deep sigh and stood up. He crossed to the nightstand, his revolver still in his right hand, aimed to the floor. Charlie flung the drawer out of the table, its contents spilling out. Seeing nothing, he kicked over the nightstand itself, the lamp falling onto the hard floor. Brenda screamed as the bulb shattered. Charlie grabbed the leg of the nightstand with his free hand and yanked it upward, examining it on all sides for an envelope taped to the underside.

Enraged, the deputy turned to the other wall and began flinging out dresser drawers, disgorging clothes and make up. Finding nothing, he upended the dresser but still found no money.

Brenda sat on the bed and tried to make her body as small as possible, hunching down while Charlie's rage surrounded her like a tornado. In the distance she thought she heard a siren. She straightened slightly and turned her head to hear it better.

Charlie caught her movement and ran to her. "It looks like my boss is going to interrupt our little party." Charlie brought his revolver up and thrust it under Brenda's chin, pulling her hair back and pointing her face upward. "Now let me tell you something. When he gets here you're going to tell him you thought there was a burglar in the house. You'll point to this mess and say when you came in you thought you heard someone in the bedroom. I'm going to open that window so he thinks someone crawled out of it when they heard you coming. You got that?" He pushed harder with the gun.

Brenda nodded her head as much as she could and mumbled her agreement.

Charlie released the gun from her chin and opened the window. He saw Sheriff Grady's car pulling next to his in the driveway. He nodded toward Brenda. "If you say anything at all, I'll kill you both." Castle holstered his gun as Grady knocked on the front door.

Brenda stood up and sucked in some air as she realized she hadn't been breathing. She smoothed her hair and walked into the living room to let Sheriff Grady in. Brenda jumped when the screen door slammed behind him.

"Sorry about that," Grady said, reaching behind him to ease the door shut before it bounced and slammed again. "Everything okay, Brenda? Where's Charlie?"

"Yeah, I came in and thought I heard someone in my bedroom. That's where Charlie, er Deputy Castle, is."

"You sure you're okay? You don't look so good."

"Yes, I'm just a little nervous. Mind if I sit down?"

"No, no, go right ahead," Grady said. "Let's see what my deputy has found." Grady left Brenda in the living room and entered the bedroom. Castle was next to the window, peering outside.

Castle turned to the sheriff as he walked in. "Take a look at this. I think he must have jumped out of the window when Brenda came home. According to her, nothing was taken, but she doesn't know what he could have been after. Probably just a random thing."

Grady took off his hat and stuck his head out the window, looking at the ground below the window. He leaned out the window and turned his head to the left and right, then to the ground again. After a second, he eased his large frame back into the house and put his hat on. "Hmm...I don't see any footprints down there. It's about a four foot drop and the ground is probably still soft from the rain we've had. Surprised there's no footprints."

Charlie stood behind the sheriff as he continued to look through the still open window. Charlie's right hand rested on the wooden butt of his Smith & Wesson revolver as he listened carefully to the sheriff's next words. If Grady wasn't convinced that there had been a burglar who escaped from the window, Charlie might have to—

"He must have lowered himself very carefully to the ground," Grady said, after he shut the window. He turned around to face his deputy who relaxed his right hand slightly. "Nice work, Charlie. Getting here so quickly, you may have saved Brenda's life. Especially if the guy was still hanging around. Once you pulled up, I'm sure he ran off."

Grady looked around the bedroom. "Wonder what he was looking for? He called out to the living room, "Brenda, can you come in here, please?"

Brenda entered, her face no longer ashen and her breathing now steadier. "Charlie will help you put the room back together. You're sure you don't see anything missing?"

Brenda looked around at the remnants of Charlie's rage and shook her head. "You're not leaving, are you Sheriff?"

"No, I just want to take a look around outside." He stopped and looked at the papers in her hands. "What are those?"

Brenda looked up and shot her hand to her pocket, stuffing the letters deep inside. "Oh, nothing. Just some letters from my mother I came across when I was cleaning."

Grady tilted his head. "Wait, I thought you had just come home and heard something. You had been cleaning?"

Brenda caught some movement behind Grady. Charlie was looking directly at her and quietly unsnapping his gun holster.

"Yes. I mean, no. I mean I was cleaning out my car and

found these letters. I was bringing them in to put them away." Brenda could feel the blood draining from her face again. She swallowed hard but was relieved when Grady put his hat on and started toward the door.

"Okay. I'll be right outside if you need anything or think of something. Charlie, you don't mind helping Brenda get her room back in order, do you?"

"No boss, I'll be glad to help her. Won't take any time at all." Charlie tipped up the dresser he had thrown to the floor ten minutes prior as Brenda slowly began picking up her clothes. Grady let himself out of the front door and was making his way around the side of the house.

"Nice job, Brenda," Charlie whispered in a sinister tone. "You played that pretty cool."

Brenda was still trembling when Charlie finally finished picking everything up. He breezed past her exiting the bedroom, sliding his hand around her back. "Take care now, sweetheart. I'll be back and we'll talk some more about our mutual dead friend."

She shuddered as he released her. He walked out the front door, letting the screen door slam. Brenda walked to the door and watched the two men talking. Charlie got in his car and gave her a quick salute through the windshield. Grady started to get in his car and as Charlie was backing up, he changed his mind and got out. He waved to Charlie and walked to Brenda's front steps. He could see Charlie twisting in his car as he drove away, desperate to know what the two of them were talking about, but unable to come up with an excuse to turn back.

Brenda let Sheriff Grady in and he immediately asked to use the phone. Brenda pointed to it on the table and stepped a few feet away. What she heard startled her.

"Bill, it's Jim. I don't know if he's headed there now, but if Charlie shows up at the office in the next few minutes try and keep him there 'til I get back. Don't raise his suspicions. I'm at Brenda's—yeah, she's fine—but I'll be back soon. Charlie was here when I got here, stinking of booze. At the least, I'm going to fire him, and I might end up arresting him, depending on what Brenda tells me. Okay, see you in a few minutes."

Grady turned to Brenda. "Why don't you tell me what happened here? Bill got your call and radioed to me that you were in some sort of trouble, but that's all he could understand. And I know Bill wouldn't have called Charlie, so how did he end up here?"

Brenda felt her knees give way and with Grady's help, she made it to the sofa. Her tears came easily and she burrowed her face in her hands for a few minutes before looking up at Sheriff Grady. Brenda explained what had happened at The Grotto, and how Charlie gave chase when she fled to her house. She didn't say anything about the letters. It was a mistake telling Charlie about them and she sure wasn't going to tell Sheriff Grady about letters from a man everyone thought was dead.

"So you never heard anything when you came in?" the sheriff asked. "You were just trying to get away from Charlie and when he ran in, he tipped over the furniture to make it look like a burglary?" Grady spoke softly, careful not to be too intimidating. He had a feeling Brenda wasn't telling him everything, but he didn't want to frighten her. "Was he looking for anything here? Why did he follow you in the first place from the bar?"

Brenda shook her head. She had to think of something to keep Sheriff Grady in the dark, especially about Larry. It had to be something believable, something with a kernel of truth. She ran the back of her hand under her nose and said quietly, "Last night I told Charlie I wanted to break it off between us. He got pretty sore about it and came into The Grotto this morning demanding a drink and to talk about it. He was yelling and getting so mad that I got scared and just took off. When I realized he had come after me, I didn't know what to do. If I had been going in the right direction, I would have just drove right to your office, but instead I went home. I called just as he came in after me."

She wiped her eyes and blinked a couple times. She hesitated, but decided to tell Grady how Charlie had pulled out his gun and threatened her with it and how he said he would kill them both. "I think he meant it too, Sheriff."

## Chapter Five
## Friday, June 11

IT WAS JUST AFTER NOON when Sheriff Grady returned to his office in downtown Kingsbridge. He saw Deputy Malden's patrol car parked in back, and was hoping to see his soon-to-be-ex deputy's car as well, but Bill's car was the only one in the parking lot.

"Has Charlie shown up here at all?" Grady asked as soon as he opened the door.

Bill looked up from his desk and said no and that he hadn't heard from him either. "You want me to call him?" he asked, gesturing to the radio set on top of the file cabinet.

"No, not yet. I don't have time to mess with him right now. Perkins from BCI should be here soon." He turned abruptly and looked at his senior deputy. "Actually, yes, let's get him in here. The State Police want to question him, so we'll have him right here waiting. If Perkins isn't ready just yet, Charlie can rest quietly in the tank. I have some questions of my own for him."

Grady went to the radio and raised Charlie, asking him to come in because Sheriff Rauber had some extra areas he needed him to patrol. Castle said he'd be there in about fifteen minutes. Perfect, Grady thought. He would need to get Charlie's weapon away from him and he didn't think he would give it up willingly. He may also have to forcefully put him in the jail cell.

Grady was forming a plan in his mind when the front door opened. Grady whirled around to see a man in a slightly crumpled brown suit and hat standing in his doorway. Grady smiled and stood up from his desk to meet the BCI detective. "Ted! Nice to see you again. It's been a couple years."

Perkins smiled back and the two shook hands. He leaned out the door and pitched the stub of his cigar into the street before closing the door behind him. He greeted Bill with a wave and hello but Grady stopped him by placing both hands on his chest. His face was serious.

"Hey! What gives, Sheriff?"

Grady nodded toward the door. "No littering in my county." He then broke into a wide grin and patted Perkins on the shoulder, leading him into the office.

"You all settled into our version of the Waldorf Astoria?" Bill said with a smile.

"Yeah, I just came from there. It's not too bad. Two years ago you had me staying in Avon. How come I get to stay in town this time and not ten miles away?"

Grady spoke up, "Back then the Starlight was still cleaning up from some flooding we had in the area. We had a bit more snowmelt than usual that spring and the Genesee just didn't want to stay in her banks. Avon wasn't affected, but we caught the brunt of the flooding here upriver. Fortunately it crested and receded quickly. Now the Army Corps of Engineers has just begun building a dam at Mt. Morris. It should be completed—" Grady stopped and looked sharply at the front door. "Did you park out front, Ted?"

"Yeah, is that a problem?"

Grady ran to the door and threw it open. He ran to the curb and looked quickly to the left and right. All he saw of Charlie's patrol car was its tail end as it whipped down a side road.

"Damn!" Grady ran back into the office and grabbed the shotgun from its rack.

"What's going on?" Ted asked at the same time Bill jumped up from his desk.

"We're having a problem with Charlie Castle. The guy you want to interview. I hired him as a deputy not long after the McConnell incident and he's gone off the deep end." The three of them were running through the back room toward the parking lot. "I wanted him here when you got here but he must have spotted your car out front. I'll bet it spooked him and he's on the run."

When they reached the back lot, Grady quickly explained the layout of the town to Perkins. "Basically three ways out of town on the main roads, Ted. Route 63 north or south, or 408 to the west into Mt. Morris, then south."

Grady jogged to his patrol car as Malden was getting in his. "Bill, if he took Groveland Rd, he might be going south on 63. I'll head that way. You take 408 and stay on it along the edge of the park." Perkins started around the building toward his own car and Grady called after him. "Ted, take 63 north into Geneseo. I'll call Sheriff Rauber and have him keep an eye out if he heads west. If anyone spots him, let me know." The three cars sped off in different directions.

\* \* \* \*

Minutes after he raced west on New York State Route 408 in pursuit of Castle, Deputy Malden came to the intersection of Routes 36 and 408 in downtown Mt.

Morris. Traffic was relatively light and he skidded to a stop in the middle of the road. Castle's patrol car was nowhere in sight. Malden took a quick guess and spun the wheel to the left. Accelerating quickly, he turned sharply right and continued on Route 408, heading southwest.

The area consisted of mostly farmland and also roughly paralleled Letchworth State Park, offering many places in which to hide. Malden knew that as soon as he rounded the slight curve just a mile or so out of town, the road would be straight. If he had chosen correctly, he would be able to see Castle's car and hopefully catch up to it.

Malden hadn't heard anything on the radio yet about Castle being spotted, so he had a good feeling that he might have headed west out of Kingsbridge. As soon as he rounded the bend, he accelerated to top speed, siren screaming and light flashing. He slowed slightly at each side road, just enough to glance quickly left and right to see if he could spot his target. Ridge Road, nothing. Frost Road, nothing. Hoagland Road, nothing. At Guile Road, he screeched to a halt. He made another quick decision and turned right again, heading west. After a couple turns, he made his way to River Road where he turned back to the north. This time he drove more slowly, convinced that if Castle was hiding somewhere, it would be to his left, in the nearby woods and brush of the state park.

He passed the occasional farmer's field and copse of trees on the right, but he was mostly interested in the dense woods on the left. That would be the place where Castle could easily drive off the road and stash the car behind a grove of trees. If he was smart, he would hide the car and lay low until dark. Much easier to flee the area at night than in the daytime.

Malden was looking not only for the car but tell-tale tracks in the grass. He glanced left and right as he idled— there! Facing southward, tucked behind some trees on the left Malden could make out the front grill of Castle's patrol car, probably a hundred yards away.

The deputy tensed as he pulled over to the side of the road, keeping his distance. He rolled to a stop and looked in all directions to see if Castle was on foot. Only the grill and one headlight were visible, so he couldn't tell if he was still in the car or not. Malden called to the others and reported his location. Grady began coordinating with Perkins over the radio as they reversed their respective directions and began closing in. Malden then pulled his revolver from its holster and double-checked the cylinder.

Occasionally swiveling his head from side to side, Malden sat mostly still, focused on Castle's car. He listened as Sheriff Grady reported getting closer and gave directions to Perkins. It was obvious that Castle was on the run. They were pursuing a trained killer armed with a revolver, multiple rounds of ammunition, and probably the shotgun stored in the trunk of the cruiser. And, Malden now realized, a man who had been listening to every word that was being transmitted over the radio.

* * * *

Fran and Caroline had left and George was in his room, writing out his first report for the home office on the cannery. He had just made his first visit and introduced himself to the plant manager, who was relatively new on the job. Everything had gone well and George was now fully engrossed in his initial assessment.

He could smell the ham that Margaret was baking and his stomach grumbled a bit in anticipation. He opened a tin of biscuits he had brought over from England and bit a corner off. George found himself quite taken with the little burg of Kingsbridge. It reminded him of some of the smaller hamlets between Birmingham and Stoke-on-Trent. Even the name, Kingsbridge, had a royal feel to it.

Margaret was a lovely hostess, as well, George thought. So very welcoming and kind, going to great pains to make him comfortable in his new home. And Davey was such a joy. He reminded George of Ian, but he acknowledged the possibility that any little boy would remind him of his beloved son.

He missed them both terribly and had been relieved when his company suggested he relocate, at least temporarily, to the States. The terrors of the war had been over for a couple years but George was finding it difficult to overcome the grief of losing fellow RAF pilots and the ultimate grief of his wife and son gone. He had had no trouble finding a job after the war ended, working for a U.S.-based food company that was expanding overseas. George was named acquirements manager in the company's only British office, in London. But working and living so close to where his family had perished made it hard to focus so he welcomed the move to New York. And he was actually glad it wasn't New York City. This small town, rural environment was perfect for him.

From his room on the third floor of Margaret's older, but still tidy, clapboard house, George paused to listen to Davey clang some pots and pans in the kitchen while his mother prepared dinner. He smiled as he heard Margaret urging him to be quiet. He remembered that Ian often banged on an upturned pot with Maureen's wooden spoons. George closed his eyes to bring the memory into focus.

Another sound soon interrupted the pot banging.

George flicked his eyes open and cocked his head. It was a clicking sound, a rhythmic clicking, or tapping. He looked around his room, expecting to see maybe a bird pecking at the window. Seeing nothing he stood up slowly.

The sound wasn't coming from his room. He stepped slowly to the doorway. It was definitely emanating from below, but closer than the first floor where Davey and Margaret were. He could still hear Davey striking the pots and Margaret sliding dishes in or out of the oven.

George took another couple steps into the small hallway. It definitely wasn't coming from this floor. His bedroom was not the source, nor the hallway, nor the small storage closet at the end of the hall. The tapping sound was coming from the floor below him.

Click–click, click–click, click–click.

George started down the stairs slowly, the wood creaking in protest beneath his feet. He reached the midpoint of the stairs and saw a light from Davey's room off to the right. It was hard to see at first because, though it was late in the afternoon, there was still sunlight streaming in. But a lamp was flashing.

On–off, on–off, on–off.

Click–click, click–click, click–click.

*What the devil?* "Davey?" George asked quietly, not moving. He still heard what he assumed was Davey banging on the pots and pans in the kitchen. *Had Fran's daughter Caroline come back, and Davey was in his room? If that was the case, Davey shouldn't be playing with the light switch like that.*

Click–click, click–click, click–click.

George moved down the stairs more purposefully, calling to the boy. "Davey, you really shouldn't—"

Davey's room was empty.

On–off, on–off, on–off.

Click–click, click–click, click–click.

George stood in the doorway to Davey's room watching the lamp on the little boy's dresser flash on and off. He blinked his eyes and blinked again. *I don't understand. How can this be? There's obviously something wrong with the lamp, some defect to make the switch turn 'round and 'round like that. Still…*

The light continued to flash on and off steadily. George prided himself on being a sensible, practical man, and felt no fear. *Most curious.* Although he'd never seen or heard of lamps malfunctioning like this, he was sure that's what it was.

At the same time, he recognized the impossibility of what he was seeing. An electrical switch is a simple device. The switch is rotated by one's fingers, which either blocks the electricity or allows it to flow to the light bulb. There must be some mechanical force on the switch for it to rotate. The electricity can't act on the switch, though, causing it to rotate.

Click–click, click–click, click–click.

George shook his head slightly and blinked again. After another moment, he crossed the room to the dresser and looked under the shade. Sure enough, it was rotating on its own, the light flashing on an off in a regular pattern. Completely impossible, he thought.

He reached toward the switch to stop it from turning but paused. *What if the house was…?* No, Fran's ideas were just too fanciful, reassured himself. He grabbed the switch between his thumb and forefinger. He held his fingers there for a moment, not able to comprehend what was happening or how. The switch continued to rotate. He snatched his fingers back but then gripped the switch more firmly. Still the switch rotated and the light continued to flash on and off.

George tried again to grab the switch, this time with an iron grip. In response, the lamp itself twitched back and forth on the dresser.

George released the switch. He stood up straight and pursed his lips tightly. Determined now to end this impossibility, he knelt at the side of the dresser, looking behind it for the plug. It was too shadowy to really make out where the switch was, but he could probably just reach his hand back to feel for it.

George stretched his arm to reach for the plug and he grasped it firmly with his fingers. The black circular plug must have had a crack in it, exposing him to the wall circuit's full current. For George, his fingers gripping the plug tightly and unable to let go, it felt like an eternity until the fuse downstairs blew with a loud pop.

* * * *

Brenda needed to calm herself with a drink before she started her shift at The Grotto. She sat at her small kitchen table and sorted through the letters that Larry had sent her during the last two and a half years. She didn't care what Charlie Castle told her. Larry was alive and putting the final pieces of his plan in place. She ran her fingers over the smudged postmark on one of the envelopes and wondered what he had in store for her in Alexandria Bay. This town was in the heart of the Thousand Islands, where Lake Ontario met the St. Lawrence River.

He wrote about all the islands and how there was actually almost two thousand of them, big and small, and how some even had large mansions on them. She couldn't imagine living on an island, but had gone to the library and looked up Alexandria Bay and the surrounding area. Sure enough, palatial homes, mansions and even castles! Larry had joked in the letters that they'd be living in one of the mansions. She didn't think he had stolen enough money for that, but she couldn't wait to see them just the same.

Between the money that he had been able to take from the cannery office and the tips she earned from the bar, and maybe the occasional five spot she took from the till, they would easily have enough money to start their life together. Alexandria Bay sounded wonderful, she thought, and she was bursting to get away from here and be with Larry.

She thumbed through the envelopes, more than thirty of them, and watched how the postmarks danced along the edges, like a cartoon. As they flipped past, one of them stood out from all the others. Brenda went back through them slowly and fished it from the pile. She took it out and stared at the postmark. All the envelopes had an Alexandria Bay postmark on them, except this one. How could she have missed this when she opened it? It was postmarked Kingsbridge, NY.

Brenda jammed her finger into the ragged top of the envelope and slid out the folded paper inside. Had Larry come back from Alexandria Bay and mailed her a letter? Why did he risk being seen here and not at least called her? She opened the letter and read his now familiar penciled scrawl:

*October 12, 1947*
*Dear Brenda,*
*I've been thinking about you so much. The leaves are really pretty here. They've finally turned to their fall colors. I know you would like them very much. Hopefully by next fall I'll be able to bring you up here so you can see how beautiful they are yourself.*

*Everything is coming together nicely. We won't be living in it, but remember I told you about that big mansion here in Alex Bay? Well, the owners of Prescott's Palace want me to be their cook and maintenance man as soon as the house is complete. The job pays real good and I'll keep on the lookout for things I can pinch that they won't notice.*

*Don't forget to keep your part of the money safe. It might not be safe for me to wire you money when I'm ready for you to come, so make sure you have enough.*

*Love,*

*Larry*

Brenda remembered thinking that last part about the money was a little odd when she read it in October of last year, and it still didn't make sense. She only had about a hundred dollars saved (or taken) from her job at The Grotto. Not that she was going to spend it frivolously, but it was a pittance compared to what Larry said he had.

What really confused her now was the postmark. It was mailed from here in Kingsbridge! Alexandria Bay was two hundred miles from Kingsbridge. It was easily a four hour drive. Maybe five. It just didn't make any sense. All the letters before that and all the ones after were mailed from Alexandria Bay.

Brenda downed her drink and decided she needed to make a trip to the library. When she arrived, she asked the librarian for any books on Alexandria Bay and this Prescott's Palace that Larry had mentioned. She was given three books on the area and she took them to one of the long tables and sat down.

When she was done with her research, she was more confused than ever. Nobody lived in Prescott's Palace. Nobody had ever lived there. In fact, only the foundation was ever built and most of the locals called it Prescott's

Folly because the developer, William Prescott, had conned some pretty big society folks out of a lot of money with the promise of building a large hotel on one of the islands, but instead ran off with the funds.

*So who was hiring Larry, and why was* this *letter mailed from Kingsbridge? Nothing makes sense.* Brenda slowly returned the books to the librarian and got in her car. She tried to make sense of it all as she pulled into The Grotto's small parking lot.

She didn't want to get him involved, but maybe she should ask Charlie about this the next time she saw him. Once he cooled off about whatever it was he was so mad about earlier. *What am I thinking? He stuck a gun to my face and threatened to kill me. No, I can't ask Charlie about this. I never want to see him again.*

Slim was a good one to ask. He was quiet, but he seemed real smart. And he never tried to make a pass at her. She was so used to men trying stuff with her that it was kind of nice just to have a drink with Slim when he came into the bar. Yes, she decided, she would ask Slim. Of course, she couldn't say anything about Larry. She had foolishly confided in Charlie that he was still alive and she wouldn't make that same mistake again. But she could ask him if he knew anything about this palace in the Thousand Islands.

## Chapter Six

SHERIFF GRADY PULLED IN behind Deputy Malden's car. He slid over the seat and got out the passenger door, keeping his car and Bill's between himself and Castle's patrol car. He kneeled down at the right window of his deputy's car as Investigator Perkins pulled up. Ted slid over and got out of the car through the passenger side as well, then went to the trunk and retrieved his shotgun. Crouching low, he trotted up the side of the cars and joined Grady at Bill's car.

Castle's car was still facing the opposite direction on the other side of the road, hidden partially behind a line of trees just off the shoulder. "No movement," Malden reported to the other two. "If he's in the car, I'm sure he's spotted us. And heard us."

"All right. Let's fan out over to the right, through that field and just over that rise," Grady said, indicating a farmer's soybeans to the east. "We'll move north, parallel to River Road so we're behind his car, and then cut back across the road and come in at the edge of the tree line."

Malden exited his car and the three lawmen hustled over the slight elevation then made their way north about five hundred feet. They trotted over the road, the rear end of Castle's car barely visible in the trees. After just a few feet inside the tree line the temperature dropped and although the sun was high, shadows prevailed amid the dense summer foliage.

The three men approached the car slowly, unsure if it had been abandoned or was occupied by Castle. When they were within about a hundred feet, Grady indicated to Malden and Perkins to go deeper into the forest and come at the car at an angle while he approached directly from behind. The car looked empty, but Castle could have been lying down in the seat waiting for them. He also could have been some distance away, watching all three of them approach, waiting.

Grady looked in all directions but saw nothing. He could see Malden and Perkins through the trees working their way toward the car. The ground was relatively flat, but sloped gently toward the river and cliffs which were about a thousand feet to Grady's right.

They were close now, maybe twenty five feet. Grady crept forward, gun drawn, keeping his body behind trees as he moved forward. Malden and Perkins did the same as they approached from the side. Perkins had his shotgun at the ready.

Malden was fifteen feet now from the open passenger window of Castle's car. He peered out from behind a tree but saw no one in the car. He crouched down and scooted to the next tree. Turning sideways to keep a small profile, he rose up slowly and glanced out again, now less than ten feet from the car. The car looked empty.

Grady was five feet behind the rear of the car, cautiously looking in the back window. He could see nothing as well. The trunk appeared to be latched but, taking no chances, he stayed behind the relative safety of a mature oak tree.

With the barrel of his shotgun aimed in front of him, Perkins took a deep breath and came out slowly from behind his own oak tree. Trying to keep his footfalls as quiet as possible, he approached the right side of the car, finger poised on the trigger.

The car was empty. Perkins ducked his head in completely and checked both the front and back seats to confirm his hopes. He let the air out of his lungs and said, "All clear."

Grady and Malden breathed normally again as well. Grady walked to the trunk but before he tugged on it, he moved around to the side of the car, just in case Castle was hiding inside and ready to shoot. The sheriff reached over and pulled on the trunk. It was secure. Malden even looked under the car before all three of them relaxed.

"So, the question is…where is he?" Grady asked. "I don't suppose the keys are in the car?" Perkins glanced in and shook his head. Grady fished in his pocket for a toothpick but found none. "Kind of a strange place to just park the car. Did he ditch the car here and take off across the field? He might be holed up in that barn, waiting 'til nightfall," Grady said, pointing to the farm across the road and a half mile across the soybeans. "He could have planned to come back for the car or steal the farmer's truck to get out of the area."

Perkins spoke up. "I think he could have done a better job of hiding the car. If he had driven another fifty feet, there's a bigger opening in the trees. He could have really buried himself in here and not been visible at all." The State Police investigator was suddenly on the alert, swiveling his head in all directions. "Maybe he meant for us to see his car."

The moment the three men realized that it was a trap, a high-powered rifle round slammed into the thigh of

Deputy Bill Malden. He cried in pain and crumpled to the ground. The other two crouched low. Grady pulled the handkerchief from his pocket and pressed hard on Malden's leg to try and stop the bleeding. As he bent down, another round from Castle's rifle screamed past Grady's head and into the side of the car.

"We're sitting ducks here!" Perkins yelled. "Let's get to the other side of the car." As Malden writhed in pain, Grady and Perkins pulled him along the ground toward the front of the car. Another round hit a tree two feet in front of them. Perkins whirled around and loosed a blast from his shotgun. They continued to pull Malden toward the left side of the car as another round slammed into the front fender.

"He can't be too far away from us and still have a clean shot. But there's too many trees in the way. I can't see him," Perkins said after taking a quick look over the hood of the car. He handed his handkerchief to Grady whose own was saturated with blood.

Grady pushed the new handkerchief into the hole in Malden's leg. "I can't get the bleeding to stop!"

"Better use a tourniquet," Perkins said. He started to remove his belt but Malden shook his head.

"No, I don't want to lose my leg," he said, through gritted teeth.

"I think it hit your femoral artery. You'll be dead in five minutes if we don't." Perkins wrapped the belt around Malden's thigh cinching it tight, just above the wound.

Grady continued to put pressure on the bloody hole until the bleeding slowed. Perkins raised his head up just above the car's roof but saw nothing. A bullet from Castle hit the tree behind them, just over Perkins' head. He ducked back quickly.

"Ted," Grady said, "let's pull him back a little so I can

try and get in the car and radio for help." They dragged Malden back a couple feet and Grady pulled open the door from his crouched position. He shut it after a couple seconds.

"What's wrong?" Perkins asked.

"Castle took the microphone with him. We can't call anyone."

Despair passed between the two men before Perkins spoke up.

"We have to get help for your deputy. I'll run to your car and radio for help. Can you keep Castle at bay?"

"I don't know for how long. He's probably already circling around."

"It's our only hope. It's *his* only hope," Perkins said, nodding at Malden, who had grown quiet. "You've got your revolver and I'll leave you the shotgun. I fired once, that leaves you five shells."

Perkins handed his shotgun to Grady and started to turn. "Wait—you don't happen to know what kind of rifle this guy of yours is using, do you?"

Grady turned, unsure of why Perkins had asked. "Yeah, it's probably his M-1 from the war. He was proud of the fact that he somehow held onto his Army issue rifle. Why?"

"Perfect! The M-1 magazine holds eight thirty-aught-six rounds. I don't remember how many shots he's taken at us, but when the last round is fired, the clip ejects with a distinct metallic 'ping' sound. With luck, that's his only clip, although he still has his revolver with him, I'm sure. That might give you a chance to rush him. Hold the trigger down on the shotgun. As fast you can pump the action, another shot will fire. The challenge now is figuring out where he's hiding."

Grady looked down at his stricken deputy. "I don't

want to leave Bill, but I can't just let Castle finish us off. Go! I'll figure something out."

Perkins nodded and practically crawled on all fours toward the road to keep his head out of Castle's line of sight. He was only six feet from the car when two shots rang out chewing up the soft ground beside him. Perkins rolled forward and darted to the side behind a large oak tree.

"Grady! Castle has to be up a tree!" Perkins pointed upward as he called to the sheriff in a hushed voice. "If he was standing on the ground, there's no way he could have seen me. The car would block his view of me. I'm going to make a run for it. Cover me with a blast from the shotgun – aim high! He can't have too many shots left, remember to listen for the 'ping.'"

With that, Grady whirled upward swinging the shotgun above the roof of the car and fired. The blast echoed through the woods as branches and leaves fluttered to the forest floor. Grady was disappointed he didn't hear a body landing hard on the ground when he crouched back down behind the car. He felt a bit hopeful seeing Perkins halfway across the road at a full sprint.

His hopefulness vanished when he heard an ominous sound. Footfalls approaching slowly, the occasional twig snapping. Castle might have been in a tree taking potshots at them but now that Perkins was gone, he was on the move.

The ringing in his ears from the shotgun blast was making it difficult to tell where the movement was coming from and he couldn't risk peering over the car to look. Grady would have to take a chance. No, maybe an educated guess. Earlier, when he was approaching the empty car from the rear, he noticed that the woods were denser toward the front of the car. Castle had wedged the car in and stopped when the trees became too close together. He was probably approaching from the left to give himself as much cover as possible.

Grady looked beyond the hood of the car but could see nothing. He could still hear Castle coming closer and it *did* sound like he was coming from that direction. But how far away? Impossible to tell with his ears still ringing.

Bringing up the shotgun would be difficult from this position, but he could use his pistol and take a shot in the general direction, if only to cause Castle to waste another round.

Grady slowly drew his revolver out of its holster and transferred it to his left hand. He rested the gun on the front roof post of the car and, unable to really aim it, pulled the trigger.

Grady's shot was met with a close-sounding rifle shot that shattered the left headlight of the car. The sheriff ducked down instinctively, but knew that Castle was getting closer. He brought his revolver up again but didn't have time to pull the trigger as the spotlight mounted on the side of the car exploded with a .30-06 cartridge. Shrapnel from the spotlight embedded itself into Grady's hand and he dropped his revolver in pain.

Wait! Before the spotlight was hit, wasn't there a "ping" sound? Yes, Grady thought, it's hard to tell for sure, but there may have been.

Without hesitating, he grabbed the shotgun from the ground and bolted out from behind the car. If Castle had another clip, he would just be inserting it now. And if he didn't, he would be drawing his revolver. This was Grady's only chance. He came up firing, furiously pumping the action on the shotgun.

He ran fast and laid down a swath of 12-gauge shot

ahead of him in a wide arc. When the gun was exhausted he stopped and crouched low behind a tree. Grady heard nothing, partly because his ears felt like they were filled with cotton. But even beyond that, he heard no movement.

Grady looked around and saw nothing but trees. He looked up half-expecting to see Castle aiming his rifle at him from above, but only saw the green canopy. When he looked ahead again, he spotted a glint of metal lying on the ground about twenty feet away, just to the left of a hemlock tree.

The tree didn't look large enough to hide a man but, still wary of another trap, Grady cautiously made his way toward the tree. He looked around—and up—aware that Castle was still armed, but saw nothing.

Convinced he wasn't about to be ambushed, he stood straighter and arrived at the tree. The clip from Castle's M-1 Garand rifle lay in the leaves and tufts of grass at the base of the tree. Grady also noticed a few drops of fresh blood on the bare earth. Castle had been hit! If he had another man, or a dog, and more firepower, he would go after him. But he also had a man in critical condition. Grady picked up the clip and looked around one last time before running back to the car to tend to Malden.

Deputy Malden was lying on his back on the ground, not moving, eyes closed. "Bill. Bill!" Grady shook his deputy but got no response. "Bill!" he shouted again. Still no response. Grady shook him again and this time felt Malden's body tense slightly. "Bill! Come on! Open your eyes." Malden's eyes fluttered a little and he took a shallow breath. "That's it, you can do it! Help's on its way. Stay with me buddy."

Grady jerked his head up as he heard footsteps approaching from the roadway. Perkins crossed the grass at the edge of the woods and weaved effortlessly through the trees. "Is he okay? Where's Castle? I heard gunfire and was afraid…"

"Bill isn't doing so hot. I ran after Castle and when I got back he was unconscious. Were you able to call for help?"

Perkins was bent over, hands on his knees catching his breath. "Yeah, I called Sheriff Rauber's office and they're sending men. There's also an ambulance on the way." He knelt down and patted Malden's face. "Hey Bill! Wake up, c'mon. Medics will be here soon. Stay alert."

After a few minutes the wail of a siren could be heard screaming south on River Road. "They're almost here, Bill. Stay with me," Grady said, shaking his friend gently. Perkins ran to the road to flag down the ambulance.

Grady and Perkins returned to the abandoned patrol car after Malden was secured in the ambulance and headed to the hospital in Dansville. "Hey, you should have that hand looked at, Jim," Perkins said, noticing the blood on the sheriff's left hand. "What happened? I heard a lot of shots."

The sheriff and the State Police investigator stood just inside the woods at the hemlock tree where Grady had found the clip. Grady explained what happened and finally pointed deeper into the trees.

"I hit him, or you did, but once he fired that last round from the rifle, he must have run. He may have known I had heard the clip ejecting. Probably ran toward the cliffs. "They're pretty high along this stretch of the river, but plenty of places to hide. It's getting a little late in the day to be mounting a full search, I'm afraid. I would need to get quite a few men together, and at least a couple dogs. By the time we got everyone together it would be nightfall and I don't want men traipsing around the woods in the dark with flashlights advertising their position, just waiting to be picked off. No, we'll wait 'til morning."

They turned back toward the road. "I'll call for a wrecker to tow the car back to the office. Then I'll let Rauber know to hold off for now, but see if he can't put some men together first thing tomorrow. I want to hang around until the tow truck comes, then we can head back to my office. I'll call Dansville later and see how Bill is doing." Grady took a deep breath and dug his right hand into his pocket, feeling around for a toothpick that wasn't there.

"Hell of a thing, Ted. I've never fired a gun at a man before. Never served in the war—wanted to, but couldn't leave the county without a sheriff—but only one thing was on my mind and that was to kill Charlie Castle."

\* \* \* \*

Margaret had just closed the oven door after spooning some juice over the ham when she heard a loud pop. She jumped and dropped the ladle on the floor. Davey ran in from the living room to investigate. Margaret paused for a moment then walked to the foot of the stairs.

"George?"

When she didn't get a response or hear anything from upstairs, she headed up the steps. She got to the landing and something caught her eye off to the side, in Davey's room. She gasped when she saw George's body lying still next to the dresser. She ran to him and knelt down beside him.

His body was lying on its side, most of his arm behind Davey's dresser. "George! Mr. Carmichael! Are you okay?" She grabbed his shoulder and he groaned slightly. "George. You've fallen. Are you hurt?" George started to rise from his prone position but fell back. He let out a long breath and slowly opened his eyes.

Regaining his strength, he sat up. He blinked a few times and opened and closed his fist. He spoke slowly. "I tried to unplug the lamp and there must be a short in it. I remember an intense tingling and then, then nothing." He shook his head and opened his mouth wide. "I've gotten shocked before, but nothing like that."

"I'm going to call for a doctor. You've taken a bad jolt."

"No, no. I'll be all right. I just need a few minutes."

"Are you sure?"

"Yes, quite. Help me up if you would, please."

After a moment, George was sitting on Davey's bed with Margaret beside him. She cradled his hand in hers, examining the burn marks on his fingers from the plug. "We should at least get some butter on those before they blister too badly."

She ran down the stairs, checked on Davey who was playing again in the living room, and returned with a stick of butter. Margaret unwrapped the wax paper and took George's hand in hers again, rolling the butter around his thumb and fingers.

"Feel better?" she asked.

"A little."

"George?" She paused. "Why were you trying to unplug the lamp?"

George took in a quick breath and looked at Margaret. "I was in my room working on a report and heard an odd clicking sound. I got up to investigate, and found Davey's lamp…"

Sensing his hesitation, Margaret stayed quiet, not wanting to press him.

George furrowed his brow a little and continued. "Davey's lamp was turning on and off by itself. The switch was rotating, on-off, on-off."

Margaret sat up straight and stared at her new tenant. "How is that possible?"

"It isn't, not as far as I know. But that's what it was doing. I reached up and tried to turn it off but it kept twisting between my fingers."

Margaret realized that she had been holding onto George's hand for some time now and his fingers were more than covered in greasy butter, so she slowly released it and folded the wax paper over the butter.

"That's when I knelt down and tried to unplug the lamp. The whole thing was impossible, as you say. I still don't understand it. We'll definitely have to replace the plug though, as it may be a fire hazard."

Margaret stood up from the bed with a start. "Oh my, I forgot about the ham. I hope I haven't burned it." She turned to George, "Are you sure you're okay? I can still call Doctor Gilger."

"No, really, I'm fine." George grasped the bedpost to steady himself as he rose slowly from Davey's bed. "I'll be down in a second."

Margaret turned and left her son's room, looking back to make sure he was truly okay. Satisfied, she descended the steps to the living room, thankful that Davey was still quietly playing with his toys. Once in the kitchen, she opened the oven door and was equally thankful that the ham was just a little charred in places, but not too badly. She turned the oven down and started preparing the side dishes.

She heard George coming downstairs and Davey greeting him when he reached the bottom step. She was still amazed at how well her son had taken to George. Davey was open around strangers most of the time anyway, but not like this. She knew she had made the right decision about her new tenant.

Margaret leaned out of the kitchen to find Davey sitting next to George on the sofa "reading" his favorite book to him. "Is he bothering you, George?"

"Not at all, don't be silly! You have quite the lover of literature here, you know."

"Oh, I know. One of his favorite trips is to the library." She glanced back at the pot of green beans boiling on the stove. "Are you well enough for our game of bridge at Fran and Dick's tonight? We can call it off if you're not up to it."

"Wouldn't dream of it. I'm feeling better by the minute."

A little over an hour later the Silvas were welcoming Margaret, George, and Davey into their house. Davey didn't waste any time darting through the kitchen to find Caroline while George introduced himself to Fran's husband.

"Dick, it's a pleasure to meet you," George said, shaking his hand.

"Likewise, George, I've heard a lot about you. You've reduced my wife to a babbling lunatic ever since she laid eyes on you."

Fran gasped. "Dick! I have not. Why would you say something like that?" She half-smiled, half-smirked. "I just want our English friend to feel welcome here in Kingsbridge. We were allies in the war, you know."

"Yes, dear. I'm aware that we fought on the same side," Dick said, chuckling. "Now then, let's have a drink and then we'll get down to some serious card playing. George, what's your pleasure?"

"I'll have a Manhattan please."

"Good choice, George, good choice." Dick ran his hand through his black hair and looked to Fran and Margaret. "And for the ladies?" Dick prepared the drinks and directed them to the sofa and chairs in the living room.

"George, Fran tells me you were RAF? I'm sure you got to know some of our flyboys over there. A couple fellows from this area were in the Army Air Corps, some of the wildest ones you'll ever meet, too. Made it back alive, that's what counts. One of 'em even flew a plane under the train bridge at Letchworth. Can you believe it? Have you been to Letchworth, George? It's a beautiful park, they call it the 'Grand Canyon of the East'. You need to go sometime. Heck, I'll go with you, show you around."

While Dick took a breath, Fran interjected. "Dick, please. You're overwhelming our guest." She turned to George with a warm smile. "You'll have to forgive him, George. Dick can get a little excited at times." That earned a playful scowl from Dick.

Their drinks finished, Dick arose and unfolded the legs of the card table. "George, grab those chairs over there and we'll get set up." He pointed to the hutch and continued, "You'll find a brand new deck of cards in the first drawer on the left."

Margaret helped George with the chairs and leaned in close, "Sorry, I should have warned you about Dick. Sometimes he's a little much to take," she whispered.

"Oh nonsense. I like him. I like them both," he replied, clearly enjoying himself.

The four of them gathered around the card table as Dick pointed to the chairs. "Boys against the girls," he said. "We could make it Yanks versus Brits, but that'd be three against one and hardly fair."

Fran rolled her eyes. "Dick, the game's not even possible to play that way. It has to be partners, two and two."

"I know that, Fran. I was just joking. C'mon, give a guy a break." He looked at George and winked. "We always kid like this." Dick grabbed the deck of cards and broke the seal on the pack. He emptied the cards out, removed the jokers, and began shuffling.

"This must be an American custom. I always played where partners were determined by cutting," George said wearing a teasing grin.

"Right you are, George!" Dick said. "But my house, my rules! We will cut to see who deals first, though. High card deals." He laughed and finished shuffling, setting the deck in the middle of the table.

"Margaret," Dick said, "Would you be so kind as to cut to a card?"

After the cutting, Fran picked up the deck and gave it a final shuffle. She dealt the deck and they settled into the first round. Ten minutes later, she and Margaret were smiling. "All that and a small slam," Fran said happily writing down their score and handing the deck to George on her left.

George picked up the deck and split it into two halves. He grasped the ends with his thumbs and prepared to riffle the two sections together. As soon as he put pressure on the right hand packet with his thumb, he winced in pain and dropped the cards.

"What's the matter, old boy," Dick asked, affecting a British accent.

"Oh, nothing, I foolishly burned my fingers earlier today trying to unplug Davey's lamp. There must be a split or crack in the wiring but it got me good." He held his hand out to be examined.

"It was the strangest thing," Margaret said. "George said that the lamp kept turning on and off by itself. He couldn't stop the switch from turning so finally tried to unplug it. Blew a fuse and everything. I was quite worried about him, but he seems fine now."

"It doesn't hurt as bad as it looks. Florence Nightingale came to my rescue with a stick of butter," he said with a flourish, looking at Margaret. "I'll take a look at the lamp tomorrow and see if I can't replace the old cord with a brand new one."

Dick tilted his head to the side slightly. "Shouldn't need a new wire. We gave that to Davey on his first birthday. Bought it brand new." He paused and rubbed his chin. "You say the lamp was turning on and off by itself? Never heard of that. Isn't possible. Don't know how—"

"Dick! Give George a moment to tell us what happened," Fran said, glaring at her husband.

After George explained everything that happened, and Margaret described what she heard and did, both Fran and Dick sat back in their chairs.

"Well, that settles it," Fran said. "I'm calling my sister and getting the name of that fortune teller she saw in Rochester. Margaret, your house is obviously haunted."

"You will do no such thing, Frances! My house is not haunted and I do not want some silly tea leaf reader stomping around it. Plus, it will frighten Davey." Margaret was adamant, although she knew that Fran would eventually talk her into letting the woman from Rochester come, if only to get Fran to quit nagging her about it.

## Chapter Seven

MOST OF THE REGULARS at The Grotto were already in their usual places that evening when Slim found his seat at the bar. He nodded to Brenda and she placed a beer and a small container of peanuts in front of him. Patti Page's soft tones were rolling out of the Wurlitzer in the corner. Billiard balls were being knocked around the slate table by the window.

By the time Slim was ready for his second beer, Brenda had had enough drinks to no longer be nervous about asking him about the palace. "Slim," she said, handing him another tray of peanuts, "Have you ever been to the Thousand Islands?"

Slim's hand froze over the peanuts and he turned his head slowly to Brenda. "Why do you ask?"

"I don't know, just curious. Been thinkin' about taking a trip there some day."

Slim stared at Brenda for half a minute before he gradually picked a peanut from the tray and cracked the shell in his hand. "Yeah, I've been there a few times. Got to make another run up there on Monday."

"Are there really a thousand islands?"

"I guess. I've never counted them." Slim wore a small,

cautious smile on his face.

"I hear they have big mansions up there, too. Even a genuine palace." Brenda said, her eyes big.

"Yeah, Prescott's Palace, if you can call it that. It's a little west of Alexandria Bay."

"Who lives there?"

"Nobody."

"You mean it just sits there?"

"Nothing there but the foundation." Slim cracked another peanut shell and worked on prying the nut out. "It's a big basement, but still just a basement."

"Is there a caretaker or anyone that makes repairs?"

"Not that I know of. I think you can catch a boat over to the island and go exploring." Slim sipped his beer and put it down. "Why so much interest in Prescott's Palace?"

"I don't know. It's just so romantic. Plus I've never seen a real palace before. Even one that hasn't been built yet." Brenda started to turn around to mix another Tom Collins for herself but stopped. "Slim, can I come with you next week when you go to the islands?"

"Uh, no. I'm afraid not."

"Oh, please, Slim. I'd love to see all the islands and the palace. Please?"

"No, it's simply out of the question. Plus there's no palace. You'll be disappointed."

"Well, what are you doing up there?"

Slim took a long pull from his beer before he responded. "Not that it's any of your concern, but I'm, um, meeting with someone. It's kind of a business meeting."

Brenda laughed as she wiped the bar with a towel. "Slim, you're not a businessman. You work at the cannery stuffing beans into tin cans. Now c'mon, why can't I go with you?"

Slim frowned and finished his beer in one swallow. He simply shook his head and started to get off the barstool.

"Wait, Slim! I'm sorry about what I said. Really. Here, let me get you another beer, on the house." Brenda quickly grabbed another bottle and set it in front of him. "Listen, I won't be any trouble to you at all. I just want a ride up there. I don't want to make that drive by myself. Once we get there, you go to your meeting and I'll go over to the palace."

"I don't know, Brenda," he said. "It's a long drive and I'll probably spend the night there. You have to work."

"We're closed on Mondays and I can get my uncle to come in early on Tuesday. It will all work out, I promise. You won't even know I'm there. Please?"

Slim sighed and drank his beer. "All right, you can come. But no more questions about what I'm doing up there. It's a business meeting, that's all."

"You're a peach, Slim! Thank you so much." She reached across the bar and squeezed his hand.

She would definitely poke around Alexandria Bay while she was there, Brenda thought. At the least she would find someone to take her to the island where the palace was, maybe talk to someone who knows Larry. What if she could actually see him, and talk to him? She would have to make sure Slim wasn't around, of course, make sure he went off to his meeting.

Brenda fought hard to contain her excitement about going to the Thousand Islands. She couldn't let Slim notice how overjoyed she was that she might actually see Larry after two long years. Letters just weren't enough. And boy, would she give Larry a piece of her mind about mailing a letter from here in Kingsbridge, but not even coming to see her while he was in town that day.

She was also going to get to the bottom of this palace.

Larry made it sound like it was almost built while Slim said it was barely started. Why would Larry lie to her, she thought as she wiped down the bar.

\* \* \* \*

Sheriff Grady and BCI Investigator Ted Perkins returned to Kingsbridge and sat in the sheriff's office. Grady plugged in the coffee pot and began brewing some coffee. Perkins lit a cigar and pulled some files from his briefcase.

"When you called," Grady said, "you said you wanted to interview Charlie Castle, and I couldn't figure out why. I'm still not sure of his connection with the Larry McConnell drowning, but it wouldn't surprise me now if there was one."

"It all started when I received this letter," Perkins said, pulling an envelope from the file and handing it to Grady.

"Hmm...postmarked from here," Grady said, turning it over and examining both sides of it. "And the letter?"

"Here," Perkins said, puffing on his cigar. "Typed, no signature or name, of course." He handed the white paper, folded in thirds, to Grady who opened it and read in silence.

*To: State Police, Albany NY*

*Re: Disappearance of Larry McConnell, Kingsbridge NY, April 1946*

*Larry McConnell was reported drowned in Baylor Lake. Body never found. Witness reports say his boat tipped and he never surfaced. This may not be full story. Please investigate more fully.*

*Focus on Charlie Castle.*

"That's it?" Grady said. He turned the page over but it

was blank on the other side.

"That's all, I'm afraid. I typically wouldn't put much stock in an anonymous tip like this, but it mentioned Castle and before I came out here I did some checking on him. Not a nice fellow."

"I'm beginning to see that. He seemed very well qualified when he approached me for a job as a deputy. Honorable discharge. Showed me his WD AGO form."

"Well, he certainly served, but he altered his discharge papers. He was court-martialed shortly after the raid in the Philippines in which he—and Larry McConnell—took part. Turns out on the march to the POW camp, he killed two Filipino guerrillas who were helping our guys get to the prison. Killed them in cold blood. During the raid he went beyond killing a Japanese soldier. He and McConnell were spotted beating the hell out of a wounded guard at the camp. Moments later he pointed his rifle at the lieutenant who saw them and threatened him over something, never found out what. He left the army with a dishonorable discharge.

"He bounced around California for a month or so," Perkins continued. "Later Indiana, and finally here. I was surprised when I learned that he became a deputy. Last job I thought he would try for."

"I'll take the blame for that," Grady said. "He checked out fine. I interviewed him several times, as did Bill. He seemed like he would fit in nicely. Guess I read him wrong."

"Don't beat yourself up. He's basically a conman, a violent one, but a conman nevertheless. And conmen are slick, they're charmers, they'll tell you want you want to hear. And he's smart. Don't forget that. He knows how to get what he wants."

Perkins pulled some more papers from the file while

Grady poured another cup of coffee. "I'd like to re-interview some folks here that we talked to the first time around. We can work the Castle angle with them, see if that stirs anything up."

"Understood. My first priority now though is capturing Castle. I need to make some phone calls and get some men together for tomorrow morning."

"Okay. If you don't mind, I'll head over to Mrs. McConnell's and talk to her. It shouldn't be too late to call on her."

A few minutes later, Ted Perkins parked his car in front of the McConnell household just as Margaret, George, and Davey were walking back from the Silvas. Ted trotted up the walk and waved to them.

"Mrs. McConnell? May I have a word?"

They stopped as Ted approached. He fished his wallet out and displayed his badge. "I'm not sure if you remember me, Mrs. McConnell, I'm Ted Perkins with the State Police Bureau of Criminal Investigation. I spoke with you a couple years ago about your husband's apparent drowning."

"Yes, I remember you," Margaret said, eyeing his badge.

"This must be your son. I recall you were almost due when I first met you."

Margaret gripped her son's hand a little more tightly, unsure of why this detective from almost three years ago was suddenly back in her life. "Yes, this is Davey. And this is George Carmichael, a friend—a tenant—of mine."

"Mr. Carmichael, very nice to meet you," Ted said. They shook hands and Ted asked if he could come inside. "I just have a few questions for you regarding your husband's case. We never really closed it and there's been some new evidence."

"Yes, you can come in. Let me get Davey off to bed before we talk though."

"Of course," Ted smiled. "Thank you for seeing me."

Once inside, Margaret got Davey changed and tucked in. He was always worn out from playing with Caroline and didn't resist going to bed. Back downstairs, Margaret offered to make some coffee for George and Ted, but they both declined.

George started toward the stairs. "Margaret, I certainly don't want to intrude while you and the detective talk. I'll head up now."

"Please stay. You're not intruding at all, George. I might need someone to lean on depending on what Mr. Perkins has found."

The three of them sat down in the living room and Ted removed a small notebook from his briefcase. "Mrs. McConnell, I'm sorry to rehash something that I'm sure was quite painful for you, but—"

Margaret interrupted, "Did you find his body? Just tell me."

"Well actually, no, we didn't. But we've come across some evidence that has us believing that your husband's death was not an *accidental* drowning like we originally concluded."

"I don't understand." Margaret shook her head from side to side as she tried to process this information. "Are you saying that Larry was killed?"

"We don't have any definitive proof yet. But we're moving away from our original findings that he drowned. Not finding his body wasn't indicative of anything at the time, but the new evidence that has come to light suggests that he may have been..."

"Murdered?" Margaret said quietly. Perkins nodded. They sat in silence for a few moments until Margaret took a deep breath and spoke. "Mr. Perkins, do you have an idea of who may have killed him? And what is this new evidence you have?"

"We don't have a suspect at this time, although we are actively checking a few leads." He flipped through his notebook. "Now, when we spoke the first time, you said that you and Mr. McConnell didn't get along, is that right," he asked, deflecting the question about the new evidence.

"Yes, Larry and I had our usual marriage ups and downs at first, but then he suddenly turned very mean."

"And this was around the time you became pregnant with Davey?" Perkins asked.

Margaret nodded her head. "It was a few months after. At first, he was excited. He painted Davey's room and even built him a beautiful dresser." Margaret pulled up the dresser's key she wore around her neck and spun it between her fingers. "He was always good with tools and such. Then, practically overnight, he changed. I would ask him what was wrong, but he would never tell me."

Margaret grew quiet, but continued after a pause. "He even accused me of being with someone else. Claimed that Davey wasn't his." She stared at the floor while her eyes filled with tears. "He had such a quick temper, too. If I said the wrong thing, he'd yell at me and even..." She rubbed her cheek with her hand.

"I'm sorry to have to put you through this again, Mrs. McConnell, but can you at all pinpoint when your husband began to change towards you?"

"Not exactly, but it was about six months before Davey was born, so that would make it probably October or November of 1945."

"Interesting." Perkins wrote down the dates in his notebook.

"Mr. Perkins," George said, "you had mentioned some new evidence. What is the nature of the evidence?"

Perkins looked up and responded, "I'm sorry Mr. Carmichael. I can't reveal that at this time. But it was strong enough for me to examine the case again. We are re-interviewing all the witnesses and involved parties and, frankly, looking at some of them as possible suspects, something we hadn't done two years ago."

George sat up from his spot on the sofa and leaned towards the detective. "Surely you don't suspect Mrs. McConnell of anything?"

"No, of course not. Mrs. McConnell wasn't anywhere near the lake at the time. We have a witness who saw Mr. McConnell fall out of a boat on Baylor Lake but there are some unanswered questions.

"Then I'm curious, Mr. Perkins," George said, "why do you believe that he was murdered? A man falling out of a boat seems pretty straightforward."

"It's been my experience that sometimes witnesses aren't always truthful, or perhaps the witness made a mistake."

Margaret looked up, wiping her eyes. "As I understood it from Sheriff Grady, Slim was on the shore waving to Larry and saw him fall in." She looked at George, "Slim was one of Larry's friends. One of his few male friends."

"That's right," Perkins said. "We'll be interviewing him as well. As the lone witness to the incident, Mr. Estancia's account of what happened is critical to the investigation. Please understand, nobody suspects you of anything. I just wanted to talk to you about the incident and see if, perhaps, there was anything else you remember about the days surrounding Mr. McConnell's death."

Margaret looked puzzled. "Who's Mr. Estancia?" she asked.

Perkins flipped through his notes. "Bertram Estancia. That would be Slim, as you call him."

Margaret smiled. "How funny, I don't think I ever knew him as anything other than Slim. Never knew his last name. Or his first. He always seemed like such a nice man. Quiet, but very nice. Don't know how he put up with Larry toward the end. Larry wasn't just mean to me."

Perkins nodded, made some more notes, then looked up. "Anything else about that day you can recall?"

"I don't think so. I told you and Sheriff Grady everything at the time. Larry and I had gotten into a fight when he was going fishing. I asked him when he would be finishing up Davey's crib and he got quite upset with me for asking. He said he and Slim were going fishing. It was supposed to be him and Slim and Charlie, but Charlie couldn't make it."

Perkins looked up from his notebook. "That would be Charlie Castle? You didn't mention Mr. Castle the first time."

"Oh, yes, the three of them were supposed to go fishing, but something came up and Larry said it would just be him and Slim."

"Mrs. McConnell, you said that your husband's demeanor toward you changed about six months before your son was born, is that correct?"

"That's right."

"Is that also around the time that Charlie Castle came into town?"

Margaret paused, her eyebrows furrowed while she put the dates together in her head. "Yes, probably a month or so after Charlie called Larry from Indiana. They had served together in the Pacific and Charlie had looked Larry up. He said he was looking for work. Larry invited him to Kingsbridge. Larry had heard that the sheriff had an opening for a deputy. He stayed with us for a couple days. I didn't like him, to be honest. He seemed very... shady. I don't know, I just didn't get a good feeling from him. He and Larry drank a lot, something that Larry usually didn't do. He would have a couple beers now and then, but once Charlie showed up, they drank and caroused a lot.

"I was glad when Charlie found a room to rent. Those few days he spent with us were very 'dark'. I don't how else to explain it. It was as if a dark cloud came into the house with him, and stayed, even after he left. Larry was never the same after that."

Perkins finished writing in his notebook and looked at Margaret. "Anything else about Mr. Castle or your husband?"

"Yes, Charlie seemed to have this 'control' over Larry. Just like the drinking, he could make Larry do most anything. I don't think Larry believed a hundred percent that I had cheated on him. I think Charlie suggested it, and he went with it. He was furious about it. I kept telling him that I would never be with someone else, that I loved him. The more I told him I loved him, the madder he got." Margaret hung her head and wiped her eyes again. "I just wanted a happy home for our baby."

Margaret ran her hand through her hair and continued. "I think Charlie even got Larry to steal money for him."

Perkins stopped writing in his notebook. "When was this?"

"A couple months after Charlie arrived in town."

"What do you remember about that, Mrs. McConnell?"

"Well, I found an envelope stuffed in one of Larry's boots one day. It contained cash, lots of it. I asked him about it and he got very angry, accusing me of snooping through his things. I said I was just straightening up our closet, but he didn't believe me."

Perkins was listening intently and asked, "Did you ask where he got the money?"

"I did, and he said that he was holding it for Charlie. I asked him why Charlie couldn't just hold his own money, but he got even angrier and I was afraid he was going to hit me, so I left it alone."

"What made you think he stole the money?"

"Because Dick Silva, our next door neighbor, worked at the cannery with Larry. His wife, Fran, said that money came up missing from the office. Over two thousand dollars." Margaret paused and said in a lowered voice, "And that's how much money was in Larry's boot. There were rumors that some of the plant manager's personal money had been stolen, but I don't know if Larry was involved with that."

"What became of the money?" Perkins asked.

"I never saw it again. And I never asked him about it again, either."

"Did you ever report it to Sheriff Grady?"

Margaret turned her eyes downward and shook her head slowly. "I know I should have. But I was so afraid of Larry. I was afraid of what he might do to me if I told the sheriff. Frankly, I've forgotten all about it until now. I can try to replace the money."

Perkins smiled. "I don't think that will be necessary. You're not the one who stole it. We should probably tell the manager at the plant what happened to it, at least to square their books if they haven't written it off entirely by now."

The phone rang, startling all three of them slightly. Margaret answered it on the third ring. "Yes, Sheriff, he's here. I'll bring him to the phone." She called to Perkins who took the receiver from her. After a minute, he hung up the phone.

"I need to go, Mrs. McConnell. You've been very helpful. Thank you for speaking with me." He shook hands with both Margaret and George and left through the front door.

* * * *

Slim sat in his car, a Hudson coupe, eating a sandwich and waiting. Baylor Lake was quiet at night with just the sound of an occasional fish leaping out of the water. The trees he had parked under blocked the full moon. He was across the lake from Sullivan's Landing, the dock light reflecting in the water. It was just after midnight when the car approached from the other direction and parked next to him. The driver killed his lights and rolled the window down quickly.

"Slim! Did you bring the needle and thread? Can you do it? This hurts like a son of a bitch. It took me forever to stop the bleeding."

"Yes, I can do it, Charlie," Slim said, swallowing the last bite of his sandwich. "Come on over, we'll get you patched up."

Castle slid out the passenger side of a beat-up old brown Nash and got into Slim's car. Slim turned on a large flashlight and positioned it on the dashboard toward Charlie. Slim looked over at the car to his left and asked, "Is that new? I mean I know it's not new. It looks like it's been sitting in a field since before the war. I've just never seen you drive it."

"Never mind about the car. Just sew me up."

"Okay, okay, don't get jumpy," Slim said while he unraveled some thread. "So what happened anyway? How'd you get shot? And why didn't you just go to the hospital? They've got specialized needles and sutures, far better and safer than what I've brought."

"Never mind about the hospital. And never mind about how I took a bullet in my arm." Charlie was getting agitated and the smell of liquor filled the car. "I pay you well enough not to be asked questions."

Slim held the needle up and began to thread it when he stopped. "About that, Charlie. Monday is going to be my last trip to Alexandria Bay, I'm afraid."

"What!" Charlie whipped his head to the left and glared at Slim. "You're going to keep going there as long as I tell you to."

"Charlie, I haven't felt right about it from the beginning. I don't like deceiving her like that. What could you possibly be writing in those letters that you can't mail them from here? It doesn't make sense."

Charlie's voice was firm. "Listen, what's in those letters is my business. I pay you ten dollars plus gas for every trip you make. And part of the deal was no questions. Now you're asking questions. I don't like it." He looked at Slim's hand holding the needle. "Now get me sewed up."

Slim sighed and licked the end of the thread, inserting it carefully through the eye of the needle on the second try. He held together the skin on Charlie's right arm and worked the needle back and forth over the wound.

"You're lucky it only grazed you."

"Well, it grazed deep enough to hurt like crazy. There was blood all over the place."

"I still think you ought to have a doctor look at it." Slim was closing off the makeshift suture.

"I don't care what you think. Just finish the job." Charlie winced as Slim pulled the thread tight against the skin. "And don't ever let me hear you talk about not going to Alex Bay. Remember, I call the shots."

Charlie got out of the car and threw a twenty dollar bill on the seat next to Slim. Next he tossed a sealed envelope on the seat. It had a 3-cent stamp in the corner and was addressed to Brenda Singer in Kingsbridge, New York.

* * * *

Sheriff Grady looked up as Perkins walked in to his office. "News on your deputy?" he asked.

"Nothing yet. I got a call a little while ago from just north of Portageville. Woman said her husband's car has disappeared from the barn he was keeping it in. He's still over in Europe and not expected back for another couple months. She said she knows it was taken sometime tonight because she was in the barn earlier in the day and nothing was out of place. The keys were hanging just inside the door. Saved Charlie from hot wiring it."

"You think there's a connection between the missing car and Castle?"

Grady nodded. "I'm positive. Portageville isn't too far from where he ambushed us. Easy to imagine Castle checking garages and barns and finding an old car and taking off with it."

"What kind of car?"

"1936 Nash. I've called the neighboring counties and told them to be on the lookout for it." Grady twirled a toothpick between his fingers. "I'm headed to the hospital in Dansville to see Bill. I can't just sit here waiting for the phone to ring. Why don't you head down with me."

A half hour later they were standing at the nurse's station on the surgery wing of the hospital waiting for the doctor, the smell of antiseptic and other assorted chemicals swirling like a fog. A few minutes after their arrival, a tall man dressed in white and wearing glasses met them. The front of his surgery gown was covered in smeared blood.

"Sheriff Grady?" the surgeon said, looking at Grady. "Your deputy is going to make it. Whoever applied that tourniquet knew what they were doing and saved Mr. Malden's life."

Grady and Perkins both let out a deep sigh. "What about his leg?" Grady asked.

The doctor reached over the top of the nurse's station and grabbed a pack of cigarettes from the desk. Fishing one out of the pack, he struck a match and lit it, nodding. "He'll definitely keep the leg. There won't be any need to amputate. That doesn't mean he's out of the woods. There is some nerve damage and the bullet tore up quite a bit of muscle but the sooner we can get him back on his feet and walking around, the quicker he will heal. At this point, I can't say for sure if he will make a full recovery. He'll be able walk again, but maybe only with a cane. Or he could surprise us and, with a lot of hard work, be back to a hundred percent. In any case, it will take several months."

"Thank you, Doctor. Can we see him?" Grady looked past the doctor toward the hallway.

"I'm afraid not, Sheriff. He's still in recovery and pretty groggy."

"I just need two minutes with him. Please."

The doctor inhaled deeply from his cigarette and exhaled through his nose. "All right. One minute. No more." He turned toward one of the nurses seated at the desk. "Kay, would you escort the sheriff to Recovery Room Three? He has one minute."

Once in the room, Grady pulled up a chair to Malden's bedside and squeezed his hand. "Bill, can you hear me?"

Deputy Malden opened his eyes slightly.

"Bill, it's me, Jim." He squeezed his deputy's hand a

little firmer to bring him through the morphine fog. After a moment, Malden opened his eyes a little wider. "You're going to be okay. The doctor just gave me a full report. You'll be back to work in no time."

Bill labored to take a deep breath. "You okay? Perkins?"

"Yeah, we're both fine, Bill." Grady tried to sound as upbeat as possible. "Listen, the doctor said you'll have to work at it, but he's confident you'll be back to full strength in just a couple months. Your leg's going to be okay. I need you, Bill. Stay strong. You can get through this."

Bill nodded and took another breath. "Castle. Did you…"

Grady paused, unsure if whether he should tell his deputy that the man who almost killed him was still at large. The sheriff shook his head. "No, we didn't get him. But he stole a car and I've alerted the other counties. We'll find him. Don't worry about him though. Your job is to get better. I'll let you know—"

The nurse standing in the doorway cleared her throat.

"Bill, I have to go. I'll check in with you tomorrow." Grady stood up and squeezed the deputy's hand again. He looked at Malden. "We'll get him, I promise." He watched as Bill nodded his head again and slowly closed his eyes, sleep overtaking him.

## Chapter Eight
## Saturday, June 12

FRAN OPENED HER DOOR and ushered in Margaret and Davey, both shivering from the downpour. Margaret held the kitchen door open and shook her umbrella outside, propping it besides the frame.

"Gracious! Where did all this rain come from?" Fran exclaimed, leading them up the half flight of stairs to the kitchen. "You could have waited 'til it stopped."

Margaret smiled and looked down at Davey. "*Someone* wanted to play with Caroline, and didn't care if he got wet." She bent down and took his shoes off and patted him on the head as he ran off to find her.

Margaret sat at the kitchen table while Fran brewed some coffee and put a few freshly baked brownies on a plate. Fran shared some gossip from the neighborhood while they ate and, unable to wait any longer, asked about the car she saw parked in front of Margaret's house the night before.

"You are a nosey one, aren't you?" Margaret said.

"Well, it's not every day the State Police come calling. What *was* that all about last night? Dick thinks it's about Larry and I suspect there's more to your new friend

George than meets the eye."

"George? Why would the police want to talk to him?"

"So, it *is* about Larry," Fran said with a satisfied smile. "What did they have to say? Did they find his body?"

"No, I asked him—Investigator Perkins—that right away. He said that they haven't found him yet. But the case was never closed and they have new evidence. They want to interview everyone again because they think Larry was—"

"Murdered?!" Fran blurted.

"Yes, murdered," Margaret said, trying to keep her voice calm. "Fran, can you not be so excited about this? It's still rather difficult for me. I mean, I know Larry was tough to be around and I haven't exactly played the part of the grieving widow, but it's still not easy sometimes."

"I'm sorry, Margaret. I should be more sensitive. Please, go on."

Margaret recounted the conversation with Perkins, including the part about the stolen money, while Fran refilled their coffee cups.

"Do you think Larry stole that money from the cannery?" Fran said, returning the coffee pot to the counter.

"I don't know for sure, but where else would he have come up with it? However he came up with the money, I'm sure Charlie was mixed up in it somehow." Margaret took a bite of her brownie and swallowed hard. "He was pure evil, Fran. And his presence in our house was the start of the troubles between Larry and me. I have no doubt Charlie was the cause."

Fran sat back in her chair, thinking. "Maybe Charlie's the cause of your troubles now."

"What troubles?"

"The haunting."

"Oh Fran, not this again. My house is not haunted."

"How else do you explain the things that go bump in the night over there?" Fran said, taking a sip of coffee.

"Well, even if it is haunted, Charlie's not responsible for it. He only lived here a few days plus he's still alive. If anything, it would be Larry who's causing—" Margaret put her hand to her mouth.

"Now do you see why I want to get that psychic to do a reading in your house?"

Margaret sighed and stared at her cup of coffee. "All right. Go ahead and call her."

\* \* \* \*

Sheriff Grady and Investigator Perkins arrived at the spot where Castle ambushed them the day before. It was just before noon and the rain had intensified. Both lawmen checked their guns and ammunition before stepping into the dense woods.

"Assuming Castle's responsible for that stolen car out of Portageville," Grady said, "I doubt we'll run into him out here. But there might be a reason he chose this particular place to set his trap."

The trees didn't block the falling rain and before long both men's raincoats were doing little to block the dampness and cold. Dirt had turned to slippery mud, and wet grass and leaves made for a slow and slick advance.

"Should we get more men out here?" Perkins asked. "There's a lot of ground to cover."

"No, Rauber is keeping an eye out for the second stolen car. Plus, I don't think he's here. I think he *was* here though, so right now we're just looking for some pieces of evidence. Maybe we can figure out what he's up to."

"How far back do these woods go?"

"The road parallels Letchworth State Park, and the

edge of the gorge is probably a mile in this direction. Maybe a little less."

"How high is the gorge?" Perkins asked, pausing to light a cigar.

"At this point, it's probably two or three hundred feet."

Perkins whistled. "Wow! That's quite a drop off."

"Yeah, definitely not someplace I'd want to be exploring in the dark," Grady said.

Perkins puffed on his cigar, the smoke drifting past him. "I've lived in New York all my life, but never visited the park."

"It's a beauty, that's for sure." Grady glanced over at Perkins who was puffing harder on his cigar. "You going to be able to keep that lit with this rain?" he said with a laugh.

"Not to worry. I can keep these things going in rain or snow, even a blinding blizzard."

They came across a small trail and stopped, looking left and right. "Probably a game trail," Perkins said, kneeling down to examine the matted grass. "Not to say that Castle didn't use it either though. Looks fairly wide in spots, like deer have used it." They took the path to the right, toward the gorge.

"Your wife mind those things?" Grady asked, pointing to Perkins' cigar.

"Joyce? Doesn't mind a bit. She's a real peach." Perkins flicked some ash on the ground. "My corporal at the Schenectady lab not only introduced me to these fine Cubans, he introduced me to Joyce as well."

"Really? How did that come about?"

Perkins stopped on the trail, looking down and slightly to the left. "Wait a second. Are those tire tracks?" he said. Looking ahead, he shook his head. "Definitely tire tracks, Jim." Perkins turned around and looked back the way they had come, through the tall grass. "This is more than a game trail. I bet if we head that way, we'll eventually come to the road."

They turned back and headed toward the gorge. A few minutes later they came to a crude, dark structure in between two trees, about ten feet off the trail and through the trees.

Grady and Perkins left the trail, making their way through the trees and undergrowth. They broke through the trees into a small clearing to find a lean-to between two birch saplings. A sturdy oak branch stripped of its leaves was secured with rope between the two birches. Oak and other branches were used as a base layer and pine branches on top created a one-foot thick roof.

A few feet away were the remains of a campfire and some food wrappers. Examining the inside of the lean-to, which was surprisingly dry in spite of the rain, they found a ragged blanket and an empty whiskey bottle. Looking closer at the blanket, they discovered that parts of it were caked in a dark red, brownish substance, which Perkins was certain was blood.

"Definitely Castle's handiwork," Grady said, looking around at the shelter. "With his military training, he knows how to survive in the wild. This isn't so far from civilization that hunters would have built it and it's a little too sophisticated for kids."

"And the blood," Perkins said, "is probably his. We found fresh blood in the woods yesterday. He must have been hit, ran back here, and patched himself up, or at least stopped the bleeding."

They looked around the campsite some more but found nothing of interest. The rain had slowed to a steady drizzle, dampening the sounds of the forest.

"What about the tire tracks?" Grady asked. "That has

to be connected somehow."

"Let's head toward the cliffs. Maybe he stashed the car deeper in the woods," Perkins said, taking a final puff of his cigar and throwing the butt into the pile of burnt wood and ash.

A half hour later they reached the top of the cliff. It was a sharp drop off, a clear boundary between densely set trees, grass, bushes, and the layers of shale that the Genesee River had cut through over tens of thousands of years in its journey north.

The river was higher than normal for this time of year and running more swiftly than usual. A winter with almost sixty inches of snow combined with a wet spring, plus the rains of the day, saturated the ground. Grady and Perkins approached the edge, moving from tree to tree, trying to keep a safe distance from the precipice. The tire tracks led directly to the edge of the cliff, but no car was in sight.

"Could he have done us a favor and driven off the cliff?" Perkins said, looking around. "The tracks lead right to the edge and they look fresh." They were standing two or three feet from the edge, each holding onto a tree, trying to peer over.

"I don't see a car down there," Grady said, "but it's too steep to see the base of the cliff."

Perkins moved to a tree closer to the rim. Grady motioned him back, "Ted, it's too dangerous. We'll drive over to the other side of the river and see what we can find from there."

"Jim, that'll take at least two hours. If I can just get a clear view past some of those outcroppings." Perkins slid his feet over the wet leaves with a firm grasp on the tree, straining to look down.

The Genesee raged below them, three hundred feet

down, along a rock-strewn river bed. Rivulets of water rained down from the rim all along the seventeen-mile gorge, slowly swelling the river to heights it hadn't seen in fifty years.

"I think I see a car down there, Jim." Perkins eased himself over the edge of the cliff a final time to confirm what he was seeing. With his left foot planted against the tree and his left hand gripping it tightly, he saw the car. "Yes, definitely a—"

Perkins felt his foot slip on the wet leaves as a piece of shale gave way underneath him. He clung to the tree as he slipped downward, desperately trying to grab it with his right hand. As Grady sprinted across the path to the tree, Perkins managed to swing his hand up and grab the trunk, his legs scrambling underneath the tree for the now-exposed roots.

Grady thrust out his hand around Perkins' wrist and held fast. "Got you!"

Perkins was breathing hard, but wasn't panicking. His feet had found the roots and he was stable. Grady maintained a constant pressure on his friend's wrist while he slowly climbed upward, and finally rolled over the edge of the cliff and to safety.

\* \* \* \*

Grady and Perkins met Sheriff Rauber in Mt. Morris. The neighboring county's sheriff had received their call and brought a small motorboat on a trailer so they could investigate the fallen car.

The rain was still coming down as mid-afternoon approached. They gunned the motor upriver, fighting the current as the rain pelted their faces. Finally, after three hard miles of the motor straining against the downstream flow of the river, just around the sharp bend in the river called the Hogs Back, they spotted the car. Completely demolished, parts and body panels strewn everywhere along the bank, the 1936 Nash 400 de Luxe had suffered a violent and calamitous end.

Grady drove the boat onto the sloping, rocky shore while Perkins jumped out and tied the boat to a large boulder near the car.

Both men made their way toward the car, on its roof, two of its wheels still intact, a third several yards downriver, the fourth nowhere to be seen. Grady looked inside, hoping to find Castle as dead as the car.

"Nothing!" he called to Perkins, above the noise of the rushing water.

"A couple doors are open and the windshield is broken out. Could he have been thrown clear?" Perkins asked, looking around the wreckage.

"It's possible," Grady replied. "If he ended up in the water, I'm sure he got swept downriver. No telling where he ended up if that happened."

Perkins ducked his head inside the car. "No keys!" he shouted back to the sheriff. "He didn't drive over the cliff. He pushed it over."

"Why would he have done that?" Grady asked, pulling a toothpick from his pocket and setting it between his teeth. "He's on the run. Surely he needs a car to get away."

"He can always steal another. Plus, how much time have we spent just today tracking his movements from yesterday. The point of his attack, his little campsite in the woods, the tire tracks that lead to the cliff, and now this. We've spent all day on a wild goose chase." Perkins paused. "Unless this is another trap for us. Maybe he knew we'd end up here today and he's waiting to pick us off from above or, more likely, from over there." Perkins pointed toward the top of the opposite river bank.

"That M-1 rifle of his would have no problem with the distance, would it?"

"No. Let's get the hell out of here," Perkins said, untying the rope to the boat.

* * * *

The rain had slowed a little when Margaret and Davey made the quick dash back home from Fran's house. They hung their jackets inside the kitchen door and Davey bounded into the living room.

"Davey!" Margaret called. "Mr. George is probably working upstairs. Let's be quiet for him, okay?"

Davey slowed his movements to a crawl and carefully pulled his collection of toy cars from its box. Margaret smiled as she pulled a pan from the cupboard. Dinner tonight would be a shepherd's pie, something to remind George of home. She'd never made one but found a recipe in one of Fran's magazines.

The leftover pot roast would be very tasty along with the peas, onions, and mashed potatoes. Fran had said that corn would be good as well, but it would be another month or two before the crops would be ready for harvest. Margaret wasn't sure if this was how shepherd's pie was prepared in England, but hoped George liked it just the same.

As Margaret was pulling the leftover meat from the refrigerator, the phone rang. She set the pan on the table, made her way to the living room and picked up the receiver. "Hello? Oh, hi Fran." She paused, twirling the phone cord between her fingers. "Tonight? I don't know. I'm just getting dinner ready and I won't have time to clean the house. Are you sure she can't come any other day?" Margaret let out a deep sigh. "All right, if you think it's best. I'm still not sure about this whole thing, you know."

Margaret hung up the phone, smoothed out her apron, and returned to the kitchen. As she returned her attention again to the leftover roast, she heard George coming down the stairs. She glanced out from the kitchen and saw him tussle Davey's hair as he walked past. George dug a small pipe from his pocket as he looked at Margaret.

"Do I have time for a pipe before dinner?"

"Yes, it won't be ready for another hour or so."

"Splendid. Is there anything I can do to help?" George struck a match and lit his pipe, coils of smoke reaching upward. "What are we having, by the way?"

Margaret looked at him with raised eyebrows. She bit her lip and replied. "Shepherd's pie. I've never made it before, but I thought I'd give you a taste of jolly old England!"

"Shepherd's pie?! Boy, I haven't had that in years. Maureen made the best—" George stopped when he saw Margaret's face drop. "Oh dear, look what I've done." He approached her slowly.

"George, I'm sorry. I didn't mean to bring up sad memories."

"On the contrary, Margaret. Nothing sad about it. I love shepherd's pie and I can't wait to give yours a try." George puffed on his pipe and looked around the kitchen. "Now is there anything I can help with?"

"Nothing at all. You can have a seat and keep me company. Are you all done with your work?"

George pulled out a chair at the table and settled in. "Done for the day, at least."

Margaret began peeling the potatoes, then turned to George. "I should probably tell you. We're going to have company tonight."

"Oh? Dick and Fran?"

"Um, no, although probably Fran will be here." Margaret peeled some more. "I let her talk me into calling that fortune teller in Rochester her sister uses. She'll be here around seven-thirty."

George struck another match and put it to the bowl, smiling. Margaret looked at him expectantly and when he was finished lighting his pipe he winked at her. "I'll try not to cause too many problems tonight."

* * * *

The dishes were washed and Dick had fetched Davey for the evening next door. George was in the living room cleaning his pipes and Margaret was tidying up in the kitchen when she heard a car pull in to Dick and Fran's driveway.

"Well, it won't be long now and we'll get to the bottom of all this," Margaret said, turning to George. "Remember, you promised to be good."

"Hmm...I think I said I would *try* and be good," George said. "Actually, I think I'll rather enjoy this." He got up and joined Margaret in the kitchen. "Don't worry. After that magnificent dinner, how could I do anything to embarrass you tonight?"

"You really liked it? You're not just saying that?"

"On my honor. You Colonists know your way around the kitchen."

A few minutes later there was a knock at the kitchen door. Margaret turned to George and nodded her head. "I'm glad you're here." She opened the door and greeted Fran and their guest for the evening.

Once inside, Fran made the introductions. "Irene, this is Margaret McConnell and her houseguest, George Carmichael. Margaret and George, please meet Irene Adler."

Irene was tall with short, dark hair that fell just below

her ears. She wore a lily in her hair and her eyes were an endless coffee brown color. In one hand she carried a bag, not unlike what a doctor brought on house calls. In the other, she held an orange and white striped cat close to her side, whom she introduced as Winston.

"I hope you don't have any vicious dogs about," Irene said as she let Winston slip from her arm.

"Uh no. No pets," Margaret said, staring after the cat as it trotted into the living room.

"Excellent. Let's get started then, shall we?" Irene sat at the kitchen table, and the others followed. "Fran tells me you have a haunting."

"Well, I'm not sure if the house is actually haunted. I'm not sure if I believe in ghosts anyways."

Irene waved her hand and shook her head. "I didn't say you had a ghost, or ghosts. I said that you have a haunting. We're not sure yet what has taken up residence here, if anything. Now why don't you tell me everything that you've experienced. Fran already has, but I want to hear it from you. Leave out no details."

While Margaret was describing the incident with the tin of crayons, she saw Winston the cat walk slowly up the steps to the second floor. "Excuse me, your cat just went upstairs. He can't be after mice. I'm sure we don't have any."

Irene glanced through the archway to the living room and turned back. "He'll be fine. Please continue." Even Irene was startled when Winston raced back down the stairs. She looked at the cat and motioned him to lay down, which he did on the floor of the living room.

Margaret finished telling Irene about the crayons and began to tell her about what George experienced with the lamp. Irene held her hand up. "Let's hear it from Mr. Carmichael, as he was the one who received the shock."

George leaned forward and looked at Irene. "Well, as Margaret said, I was working in my room when I heard this clicking sound." He stopped and tilted his head slightly. "Miss Adler, are you acquainted with a Mr. Wilhelm von Ormstein, by chance?"

Irene blinked twice and folded her hands in front of her on the table. "No, why do you ask?"

"It's nothing," George said. "I must have you mixed up with someone else." He continued with the story of his encounter with the lamp in Davey's room.

Margaret and George had recounted everything to Irene and she finally sat back in her chair. She snapped her fingers twice and Winston came padding back into the kitchen. He jumped into her lap and she stroked the fur on his head while he purred. Fran had a wide grin on her face, clearly enjoying the entire proceedings.

"Mrs. McConnell," Irene began. "May I call you Margaret?" Without waiting for an answer, she went on. "I don't think you have a straightforward haunting. That is to say, that even though you are the widow of the late Mr. McConnell, I do not think he is the cause, or at least the sole cause, of what you have been experiencing. Before I present my theory, I should like to examine the house. Winston has made his rounds, and I would like to do the same."

As Irene backed her chair from the table and the rest of them stood, George asked, "Miss Adler, if I may be so bold, I think it only fair that you give Margaret, er, Mrs. McConnell, an estimate of the cost of your services before you go any further."

George wasn't sure who took the most offense. Fran, whose grin was suddenly gone, or Irene who stood even straighter, or Winston who had leapt from Irene's lap when she stood and had stopped purring.

"Mr. Carmichael, I do not gaze into crystal balls or read tea leaves for tips at carnivals. I am a professional. I am a published investigator of the supernatural. A well-regarded and respected spiritist. As strange as it may sound, I communicate with the dead. And I am here tonight as I was under the impression that Mrs. McConnell was concerned about unexplained happenings in her home. I am here to provide answers to her and make my recommendations. I do not *charge* people for this service. I possess a gift, and I give of myself freely in this capacity."

Irene turned and walked into the living room while George stammered an apology. Margaret and Fran headed out of the kitchen and George followed. Winston darted in front of George at the doorway and promptly lay down, forcing him to step over the cat.

Irene Adler stood in the center of the living room and slowly turned around, gazing on every square inch of furniture, lamps, tables, carpet, pictures, even the ceiling. She took a deep breath and held it. The other three stood at random positions in the room, not quite knowing what to do. Winston weaved lazily in between Margaret's and Fran's legs. He ignored George entirely.

Irene walked slowly down the hallway toward the front door while the rest watched her. Winston followed closely behind. After reaching the front door, she turned left into the dining room and repeated what she had done in the living room. A few minutes later, she walked silently through the living room and up the stairs.

Margaret, George, and Fran looked at each other and followed Irene. Winston, however, stayed in the living room, even after Irene repeatedly snapped her fingers. When they got to the hallway on the second story, Irene went to the top of the stairs and called to Winston who slowly crept to the bottom of the staircase and looked up at her.

"Winston, come here. Now." Irene snapped her fingers and pointed to the cat. Winston's ears were pinned back against his head and he gradually made his way up the steps, finally reaching the top. "Most peculiar, him acting that way."

Irene chose the first room, Margaret's, and entered, standing at the foot of the bed, and slowly turning around, examining everything. She touched a few pieces of furniture, but said nothing. Winston entered the room leisurely and left when Irene did.

The rest of them moved aside for Irene as she walked into the bathroom. Neither she nor Winston stayed long and they were back out in the hall.

Davey's room was next. Irene stepped in. The others stayed in the hall, along with Winston. Irene snapped her fingers, but Winston wouldn't budge. "Winston, here," Irene said curtly, snapping her fingers again. The cat stayed put. Sighing, Irene walked over to him and picked him up, his claws digging into the thin carpet in the hall. Finally she had him in her arms and walked back into Davey's room.

The moment Irene crossed the threshold into the bedroom, Winston exploded out of her arms, thrashing his legs and claws, hissing and screeching up and over her shoulder. Fran screamed as Winston jumped from Irene's bloodied arms and onto the hall floor. He scurried through their legs and tore down the stairs.

Bits of orange and white fur were floating in the hall as Irene whirled around and yelled, "Winston!" She ran after him, stumbling down the steps and almost falling. Margaret and the others trailed along. Winston was cowering between the sofa and an end table, while Irene knelt down and stroked his head.

"Miss Adler, are you all right?" Margaret asked softly.

Irene stood slowly and took a breath. "Yes, although I'm sure I look a fright."

"Oh dear," Margaret said, while Fran and George gathered close. "Your neck and arm are bleeding quite a bit."

Irene touched the palm of her hand to her neck, under her right ear. "I've never seen him act that way. Do you have something I can wash up with?"

"Of course. Here, let's go back up to the bathroom." Margaret led Irene up the stairs.

Irene turned to Fran and George. "I'll be back down in a minute. I would just leave Winston alone 'til he's had a chance to calm down."

Fran, still shaken, looked at Winston. "Don't worry, he can have the whole room to himself. We'll be in the kitchen. Come on, George, I'll make us some coffee. Or maybe something stronger."

Margaret took Irene upstairs to the bathroom where she helped her clean the cuts from Winston's claws. A portion of the cut wouldn't stop bleeding on its own, so Margaret dug out a bandage from the medicine cabinet. After Irene was cleaned up, she straightened her hair and smoothed her blouse.

"Thank you, Margaret. I have no idea what came over Winston. He's never done anything like that. He even stands up to neighborhood dogs, puts them in their place every time. That's why I asked if you had any dogs in the house, because if so, you might want to put them outside while Winston's around. He's not afraid of anything."

Margaret walked down the hallway from the bathroom to Davey's room. "The cat went crazy just as you entered my son's room."

"Yes, I felt him tense up as I turned around toward the bedroom. And as soon as I entered, he just went berserk." Irene touched the scratches on her neck and face.

Irene crossed into the room and stood in the middle of it. Margaret stood in the doorway watching her, intrigued. Irene walked to Davey's bed and ran her fingers over the coverlet.

Irene then went to the dresser and stopped. She stared at it and felt her throat closing. She was thirsty for air. A small gasp escaped her mouth as she turned to Margaret for help.

"Miss Adler?" Margaret rushed to her side. She led the trembling woman to Davey's bed, sitting her down on the edge. She held Irene by the arms and sat beside her. "Miss Adler, Irene, relax. Just breathe. Are you okay?"

Irene Adler was finally able to take a deep breath. Her legs still felt weak and she wasn't sure if she could stand up. She pointed to the dresser and asked, her voice quivering, "How did you know?"

"Know what?" Margaret said. "What are you talking about?" She stood up, looking at Davey's dresser. On the top were deep, crude gouges in the wood, as if made from a large knife or chisel. But they weren't random scratches. They formed distinct letters: L I L Y

Margaret's eyes grew wide and she threw her hand to her mouth. She staggered back toward the bed, her head shaking from side to side. She wanted to scream but nothing came out.

**Chapter Nine**

THE SUN WAS STILL BELOW the horizon when Slim pulled in front of Brenda's house. He tapped the horn a couple times and waited. In the three minutes it took for her to finish getting her things together and lock up, the sky had gone from a deep red to a pinkish color. High, wispy clouds became visible in the distance.

She pulled open the rear door of the car and threw her suitcase on the seat. "Slim, thank you so much for letting me hitch a ride with you. I'm so excited!"

"Yeah, don't mention it." Slim's voice didn't hold nearly as much enthusiasm as Brenda's. He started the car and it lurched on to the roadway with a start. Before long, they were up to speed and headed north.

* * * *

They chatted about the weather, and how much it had rained over the last couple days. Slim commented that the red sky meant more rain to come. Once they reached Avon, they took Routes 5 & 20 to the east. The sun was completely up now, but denser clouds were pushing in. Brenda tried to make conversation but after the weather topic had run its course, it was evident to her that Slim wasn't in a talkative mood.

The green, rolling hills spread out before them as they made their way east. Slim and Brenda stopped at a roadside park shortly before noon and ate the ham and cheese sandwiches Brenda had prepared. Brenda cracked open a bottle of root beer and handed it to Slim.

"How long 'til we get there?" Brenda asked.

Slim took the roadmap from his back pocket and spread it onto the weathered picnic table. "We're almost to Watertown." He pointed out the small city on the map. "We'll pick up Route 37 from there and be in Alex Bay in about a half hour."

Brenda finished drinking her root beer and started gathering up the sandwich wrappers. "Thanks for letting me tag along, Slim. I really appreciate it."

They got back in the car and a short time later Slim pulled into a parking spot on James Street in downtown Alexandria Bay. He pointed down the street and Brenda followed his gaze. "There's a small marina there. You should be able to find a boat to hire to take you Prescott's Palace. Remember, you're not going to find much. I'm not sure why you want to see it in the first place, but it's your time you're wasting, not mine." Brenda opened the passenger side door and stepped out. "I'll meet you back here in an hour, okay? Don't be late, we got an early enough start that we can make it back tonight without spending the night."

"Only an hour? Oh Slim, I was so hoping I would have more time to explore. This looks like such a beautiful little village. Won't your business meeting take more time?"

Slim sighed. "I could maybe stretch it to two hours, but not any longer. Let's meet back here at two o'clock."

Brenda frowned as she gathered up her purse, but nodded her agreement. "Okay Slim. See you later!" She shut the door and walked toward the marina as Slim grabbed his briefcase from the back seat and walked in the opposite direction.

Brenda arrived at the marina a few minutes later and walked into the office. The small quarters gave her a respite from the smell of dead fish and gasoline. The man behind the desk looked up as she entered. His eyebrows raised slightly as he didn't recognize her as a local.

"Hello, my name's Brenda Singer. I'm from Kingsbridge. It's south of Rochester."

"And what can I do for you Brenda Singer from Kingsbridge, south of Rochester?"

Brenda couldn't tell if he was flirting innocently with her or being a typical lecherous old man. "Well, I'm wondering if I can hire a boat to take me to Prescott's Palace. I understand it's on one of the islands."

"Prescott's Palace?" The man behind the desk sat back in his squeaky office chair and lit a Pall Mall. "Why in the world do you want to go to Prescott's Folly?"

"My, uh, husband is going to work there. He's going to be the groundskeeper and cook."

The man squinted at Brenda and took a drag from his cigarette. "Honey, ain't nobody working at Prescott's. There's nothin' on the island 'cept for part of a foundation."

"But that can't be. Larry wrote me several times that he was getting a job there." Brenda was clinging to a rapidly fading hope that Slim—and her own research at the library—was wrong.

"Look, Brenda from Kingsbridge," he said, flicking a bit of ash into an empty coffee can, "the island is only three and a half acres. There's a half-dug foundation, a dozen or so pine trees and some rocks. There is absolutely nobody living or working there. Ole' Prescott took a lot of people for a ride ten years ago and I think the bank now owns the whole island. Now I'll take you out there if you want, but it's going to cost you." He paused to leer at her. "Maybe I'll fire up my boat anyway and you and I can do some sightseeing. I won't charge you anything…any money that is."

Brenda took a step back toward the door. "That's okay, sir. You've answered all my questions. Thank you." She turned and quickly left the office, the door closing on the man's laughter.

Brenda walked slowly back along James Street, catching glimpses of the St. Lawrence River through the buildings. She just couldn't figure it out. She had planned on asking the man at the marina if he knew Larry, but was feeling too uncomfortable in his office to stick around for more questions.

She walked past Slim's car and turned right on Church Street, down a slight hill toward the water. She walked amongst the motels and resorts on the river, wondering which of the half dozen or so small islands she could spot was the home of Prescott's Palace. She didn't see anything remotely resembling a palace. Brenda sat on a waterfront motel's dock and watched the boats coming and going along the river.

Her eyes welled up out of frustration and for missing Larry so badly. She was so close to him, she could feel it. Alexandria Bay was such a small town, not much bigger than Kingsbridge, and perhaps if she asked around someone might recognize his name or description. Brenda got up and wiped her eyes, feeling a newfound sense of confidence and hope.

She walked back to James Street, where the concentration of shops, diners, and taverns seemed to be the highest. Again she walked past Slim's car parked at the curb, but this time she noticed something strange. Slim's briefcase was in the backseat, the one he had taken with him when they each got out of the car. She looked around but didn't see any sign of Slim.

It was only just one o'clock and they weren't supposed to meet again until two. Slim must have brought the briefcase back and went back out, maybe to another appointment. More likely, she thought, his appointment was over and he didn't need the briefcase any longer, dropped it off at the car, and headed to a nearby bar.

Brenda looked around again. Trying to put everything together, she gasped. *What if Slim was with Larry right now?* Slim's occasional drives to Alexandria Bay *must* have something to do with Larry. Larry must be planning some big surprise, and that's why Slim was so reluctant to have me come along, she thought.

She hesitated, then looked around again. If Larry is having Slim drive up here for something, then perhaps that briefcase contains a clue. Brenda knew she shouldn't, but she slipped into the passenger seat and reached into the backseat. She brought the briefcase forward and set it on her lap.

At that moment, Slim was getting up from his stool at Captain Miller's, a small bar located a few storefronts from where his car was parked. He downed the last of his three beers and put a dollar bill on the bar. He nodded to the bartender and exited the tavern.

Brenda positioned her thumbs on the brass buttons at the front of Slim's briefcase. She gripped the sides with her fingers and slid the buttons outward, releasing the latches. She took a breath and lifted the lid carefully. There was a single item in the briefcase, which Brenda removed slowly.

Brenda held a white envelope in her hands. It was

addressed to her. As she sat staring at the envelope, reading her name over and over, a shadow appeared at her door.

* * * *

Obsessed with securing the money that he was convinced was hidden in Brenda's house, Charlie Castle was crouched behind the trees lining her road. Her car was in the driveway but there was no activity evident in the house. It was too early in the day to have lights on, but he saw no movement at all from inside.

He sat still for over an hour, watching, cursing the rain that had begun falling again. A few cars had passed and the mail truck stopped momentarily with a quick delivery, but Castle remained unseen.

Finally, with no vehicles in sight and still no sign of Brenda in the house, he darted across the road and to the back door. He rapped on the door and waited. He knocked again, harder and louder. Convinced that Brenda was not inside, Castle unsheathed his combat knife and in a matter of seconds had unlocked her door.

He swept into the house, keeping his knife drawn and looked quickly in each room of the small house. Satisfied that he was alone, Castle began a methodical search for the cache of money. He started in the kitchen, pulling drawer after drawer out, emptying the contents onto the floor. When each drawer yielded nothing, he threw them into a heap in the corner. Dishes and glasses were thrown from the cupboards.

His rage growing, Castle pulled the range from the wall and looked behind it. He yanked the small icebox away as well after examining the inside. There had to be thousands of dollars hidden somewhere and he was going to find it.

Castle stepped over the broken dishes and into the

living room. He grabbed the stuffed rocking chair and tipped it over, thrusting his knife into the back of the upholstery. With a downward strike, he ripped open the back and pawed through the batting but found nothing.

He stabbed the sofa and cushions. He overturned side tables and lamps, pulled up the area rug and tossed it aside in a fury. Castle stalked into the bedroom, intent on giving it a much more thorough search than before.

Flinging open the nightstand drawer and dumping the contents, the bundle of letters he had written to Brenda landed at his feet. He picked them up and flipped through them, laughing to himself. She was so gullible, believing that Larry was still alive.

He paused on a particular letter, staring at it. He ripped it out of the bundle and inspected the postmark. *The letter was mailed from here in Kingsbridge! Why didn't Slim mail it from Alexandria Bay? This could ruin everything.* Brenda was supposed to believe that Larry was preparing for their life together in the Thousand Islands. Castle rifled through the remaining letters and was glad to see that all the rest had the proper postmark, but Slim was going to pay dearly for disobeying him.

Castle had originally thought to start writing her as Larry in the hopes that she would write back. He would concoct a story that Larry was going to leave his wife and they would run off together. There had been rumors that McConnell had stolen a sizable amount of money from the cannery and Castle thought letters from Larry might loosen Brenda up about where the cash was. He couldn't be too obvious about it though, so he made vague references to the money in every second or third letter.

And having Slim mail the letters from upstate was a particularly brilliant touch. Castle just picked a point on a map and sent Slim on his way once or twice a month with a new letter penned from a dead man. But this charade was getting tiring. Brenda never wrote back with any information about the money, only her stupid dreams of living happily ever after with Larry.

Unless...during Slim's first trip to Alexandria Bay, he rented a post office box for the return address and he was to check it each time he mailed a letter from the Islands. Slim had been sloppy once and mailed a letter from Kingsbridge, maybe he neglected to give him some of return letters Brenda had written. Oh yes, Slim was going to be begging for mercy when Castle was done with him.

* * * *

Brenda flinched when Slim appeared at the open passenger window. She looked up just as he snatched the letter from her hands.

"Slim! What is that? Is this what you came up here for? I don't understand what's going on." Brenda's eyes searched Slim's for answers but he simply stood there, gripping the envelope.

Finally, Slim let out a deep breath and his shoulders slumped. He walked around the front of the car and got into the driver's seat. As he turned the key, he handed the letter to Brenda.

"Open it."

She slid her fingernail underneath the flap and tore the envelope open. She pulled out the letter and unfolded it. Tears filled her eyes and dripped a path down her cheeks as she read the letter from Larry, still not understanding why Slim had it.

"Slim, did you write this?"

He shook his head and looked over his shoulder. Traffic was clear and he put the car in gear and pulled away.

"Then why are you mailing it for Larry? Where is he?

Did you meet with him here?"

Slim pursed his lips and looked at Brenda as they stopped at the first intersection. "I'm sorry, Brenda. I just can't do this any longer. It's not fair to you."

"What's not fair?" She wiped her tears with her fingers and stared at Slim. "What are you talking about?"

Slim sighed and began his story as they made their way south out of Alexandria Bay. "I didn't write the letters. I'm only the deliveryman. I drive up here every few weeks, drop a letter off at the post office, check for any mail, then drive back to Kingsbridge. I've been doing it for two years now. I've hated every minute of it, I'm sorry for what it's doing to you and I'm not going to do it anymore."

"But why in the world would Larry have you drive up here to mail a letter?" They picked up speed as they left the edge of town. "It just doesn't make sense. Tell me the truth, Slim. Larry doesn't live here in Alexandria Bay, does he?"

"No, Brenda, he most definitely does not."

"Well, he can't be living in Kingsbridge. It's such a small town, I would have seen him."

Church Street became Route 26 and they passed farmers' fields punctuated by small groves of trees. By the time they reached Hyde Lake and had turned south on Route 37, Brenda was crying again, begging Slim to tell her where Larry was.

"All right. I'll tell you everything. But you're not going to like what you hear." A copse of trees flew by the window on Brenda's side as she looked at him.

"I don't care, Slim. I don't understand anything that's going on and I just want the truth."

"Like I said, I haven't been writing the letters, but neither has Larry." Slim paused. "Charlie's been writing them. He pays me ten dollars to drive up here and mail them, so it looks like Larry's living in Alex Bay."

"Charlie? Charlie?!" A mile's worth of telephone poles whisked by as Brenda sat silently. "I should have known he was mixed up in this somehow." Now tears of anger filled her eyes and she quickly wiped them away. "So where is Larry if he's not writing the letters. Surely he doesn't know that Charlie's been writing to me. I know they were friends but—"

"Brenda," Slim interrupted and breathed in slowly. "Larry is dead. I saw him drown in Baylor Lake just like I told you at the time. Charlie has been writing the letters to you, but I have no idea why."

Brenda's voice caught in her throat. "Why would he do something like that?"

"I don't know. But there's something more, just a hunch I have." Slim glanced over to Brenda and then back to the road. "I think Charlie is somehow responsible for Larry's death. I even wrote a letter to the State Police urging them to reopen the case."

"But how can that be? You said yourself you saw Larry fall out of that boat and he never came back up."

"I don't know, I'm trying to piece it all together. Trying to re-live everything I saw from the shore that day. If Charlie hadn't had me running these letters up here every month, I wouldn't have suspected him of anything. And I really don't have anything to go on other than that, but I just feel like he's involved."

They were almost to Watertown when Brenda twisted in her seat to face Slim. "Damn you! Why did you mail the letters to me in the first place? Just for a measly ten bucks? I've been believing this whole time that Larry was alive and loves me. We were planning on getting away, just the two of us. He had the money that he took from the—"

"What?" Slim asked, looking away from the road.

"Nothing. Just that Larry had saved some money and we were going to use that to run away together."

"Did Charlie know about the money?"

Brenda frowned and nodded her head.

"That's it! That's why he's been writing you. He wants that money. I'm tellin' you, I think he killed Larry."

* * * *

Slim and Brenda drove the remaining hours back from the Thousand Islands in relative silence, finally arriving at Brenda's house around dinner time. Slim helped Brenda with her bag and followed her up the steps to the front door.

Brenda unlocked the door and turned the knob. She pushed the door open but it struck something hard with a bang and Brenda let out a small gasp. The door was only partway opened but revealed a living room in complete disarray.

"What's wrong?" Slim asked from behind her.

"Oh no. Not again." Brenda pushed on the door and was able to slide the heavy coffee table across the hardwood floor. She and Slim stepped into the room and saw the furniture upended, lamps smashed, picture frames broken. Their shoes crunched over shattered glass as they made their way further into the room.

"This happened before?" Slim asked, looking around.

"Charlie chased me here a couple days ago from the Grotto. He tore up my bedroom looking for Larry's money. He thought Larry had hidden it in my house. If Sheriff Grady hadn't shown up, I don't know what he would have done with me."

They walked through every room in the small house. Furniture had been ripped apart, holes punched in the walls, floorboards pried up, kitchen appliances tipped over. Brenda slowly picked up an overturned dining room chair and sat down. She buried her head in her hands and sobbed.

Slim began picking up furniture that could be salvaged and placing the chairs and tables where he thought they belonged. After a few minutes Brenda quieted and he said softly, "We should probably call the sheriff."

Brenda stood and wiped her tears away, nodding her head. She moved from the dining room into the kitchen and glanced out the window to her car. She slumped when she saw the doors hanging open and the upholstery ripped. "Slim, look!" she said, pointing out the window.

Brenda opened the kitchen door and they both descended the wooden steps to the back yard. The car was parked on a gravel path that led from the road to the garage. Brenda had never parked her car in the small structure, instead using it as additional storage since her house did not have a cellar. The garage door hung open. Boxes, some small furniture and framed pictures were scattered around the floor. Behind the garage and the small yard, there was nothing but dense woods.

Both doors, the hood and trunk of the car were open. The spare tire had been thrown to the ground and the jack and other tools strewn on the gravel. The cushions in the front and back seat had been ripped open, the stuffing hanging out of the tears.

Brenda was sitting on the edge of the passenger seat slowly shaking her head as Slim was bent down, examining the engine compartment.

"I don't think he did any damage to the motor, Brenda. Nothing looks out of place here." Slim waited for a reply, then stood up and shut the hood. He walked over to where Brenda was sitting. "We really should call the sheriff. He needs to know about—"

"What does the sheriff need to know about?" A dark, growling voice said from the open garage door.

Slim jumped and whirled around, startled to see Charlie leaning against the frame of the garage. Brenda stood up, her hand covering her mouth in a gasp.

"Now don't you two just make the cutest couple," Charlie sneered. He strode over to the car, covering the distance in a few long, angry steps.

"What the hell have you done?" Brenda screamed.

"Shut up!" Charlie yelled. He raised his hand to slap her, but Slim reacted in time. Slim grabbed Charlie's wrist and forced it almost to the ground. Brenda stepped back and Charlie wrenched his arm free.

In one quick motion, Charlie drew his combat knife free from his belt and pointed it at Brenda and Slim from waist-level. "Brenda, you're going to get me that money now. I don't know where you and Larry have it hidden, but I'll tear this house down to find it. Oh, and don't bother calling the sheriff. Your phone doesn't work anymore."

Charlie lunged for Slim and drew him in close with one hand, spinning him around. He pressed the knife against Slim's throat. "Your friend and I have some things to discuss. Now run along like a good girl and get me that money."

"Charlie, let him go. Don't hurt him. I swear there's no money here."

"Last chance, Sweetheart. And whether you get me the money or not, I am most certainly going to hurt dear Slim. You see, I discovered that he has a hearing problem. He had very explicit instructions from me, and he didn't listen." Charlie's arm tightened around Slim's chest as he moved the knife from his neck to his ear. Slim squirmed but was unable to get free.

Castle slid the arm that was pinning Slim against his own body up and bent Slim's ear outward. The razor edge of the knife was pressed against the back of Slim's ear.

"Slim, you were supposed to mail those letters from Alexandria Bay. Why did I find a letter here that was mailed from Kingsbridge?" Castle's voice was filled with a simmering rage. "Now you've spoiled everything." He looked up at Brenda, who was still standing next to the car. "Why haven't you gotten my money yet? *Go!*"

"I'm telling you, there is no money here. You've destroyed my house for nothing. The money was never here."

"Then where the hell is it?"

Brenda paused and in that moment, Charlie sliced through Slim's right ear. He flung it to the ground as Slim screamed in pain. He writhed and tried to bring his hand up to his head but Castle held him tight. Blood spurted out, spattering the white gravel.

Brenda shrieked in horror as Slim continued screaming. Charlie glared at Brenda as he twisted his knife in his hand and aimed it inward toward Slim's stomach. Slim struggled but was no match against Castle's strength and training.

"He has three seconds to live. *Where's the money?*"

"It's at Larry's house. He hid it there, but I don't know where. I swear. It's somewhere in his house. Now please, for God's sake, let him go."

Castle tightened his grip on the knife and thrust it inward and up, just below Slim's sternum. Slim's screams echoed through the woods as he crumpled to the ground.

A delivery truck speeding by slammed on its brakes,

the driver unsure of what he had witnessed as he approached. The truck skidded to a stop on the wet pavement and the driver jumped from the cab.

Brenda's hysterical shrieks convulsed through her body as Charlie ran past her and around the house, away from the hulking driver who was sprinting toward him.

Brenda was panicked as she ran to Slim whose blood was pooling around him. The truck driver stopped his pursuit of Charlie and knelt at Slim's side. He wrestled his jacket off and pressed it against the wound in his chest.

Tears streaked down Brenda's face as she watched Slim become pale. He blinked and opened his mouth, but no sound came out.

Brenda looked up briefly when Charlie sped past in Slim's car and when she looked back to Slim, he was gone.

## Chapter Ten

MARGARET STARED AT THE gouged letters on the top of the dresser. The raw wood was exposed and slivers lined the edges. It was unmistakable. The name "Lily" had been crudely carved into the dresser.

Margaret regained her composure and turned to Irene who had just arisen from the bed and stepped forward shakily. "Why did you have such a reaction to seeing this, Miss Adler?"

Irene paused and looked downward. "'Irene Adler' is not my real name. I was born with the name...Lily Langtry." Irene looked up and into Margaret's eyes. "Does that name mean anything to you?"

Margaret shook her head. "No. Should it?"

Irene smiled slightly. "Probably not. Unless you're a fan of British theater."

"Oh! I had no idea you were famous. I mean, you know what I mean. I'm sorry," Margaret stammered. "I thought you were just a spiritualist. Oh, I don't mean *just* a spiritualist." She laughed, "I should probably just let you explain."

"Not to worry, Margaret. I am *just* a Spiritist. Lily Langtry was a famous English actress who died in 1929.

My family name happens to be 'Langtry' and my father was a big fan of the Sherlock Holmes books."

"I don't understand – what's the connection between Lily Langtry and Sherlock Holmes?"

"As I mentioned, my father was a big reader of the Sherlock Holmes mysteries. Obsessed with them, you could say. In the first story, *A Scandal in Bohemia*, Holmes is outwitted by a woman. The woman's name in the story is Irene Adler. That character is thought to be based on the actress Lily Langtry. My family name is Langtry so I think my father felt compelled to name me Lily when I was born. It was his connection to his hero, Sherlock Holmes, however tenuous."

Margaret tilted her head slightly and asked, "Why did George ask if you knew Wilhelm von somebody-or-other when you first arrived?"

"Your houseguest is quite perceptive. He must be a fan of the Sherlock Holmes books as well. Wilhelm von Ormstein is the central character in *A Scandal in Bohemia*. He is, in fact the king of Bohemia and is engaged to a Scandinavian princess. But, in the story, he has a scandalous dalliance with Irene Adler."

Margaret looked at the deep scratches in the dresser and shivered. "Why did you change your name?"

"My father was involved in a financial scandal in Boston during the Depression. He bilked a lot of people out of substantial amounts of money. He ended up going to prison and I did what I could to distance myself from him. I still loved him, of course, but the Langtry name was not held in good stead. I moved to Rochester just before the war and changed my name to Irene Adler. He understood and was pleased that I had picked a new name with another, even stronger, connection to Sherlock Holmes."

Margaret nodded her head and looked again toward the dresser. "So someone carved your real name in Davey's dresser. Who knows that you're actually "Lily Langtry" around here?"

"That's just it. Nobody knows. I've gone by the name Irene Adler for over ten years now. I had the name legally changed in Boston before I moved here. I mean, I suppose it's possible to search the court records and come up with it, but I just don't see someone going to all the trouble. And then carving my name into your son's dresser."

"Then what's the explanation?"

Irene turned to the dresser and laid her hands on it for the first time, tracing the letters of her name with her fingers. She closed her eyes and gently moved her hands across the top and fronts of the drawers. After a few minutes, she jerked her head back briefly and lifted her hands from the dresser. She took a deep breath and faced Margaret.

"Would you mind if we went downstairs?" Irene asked. "I'd like to check on Winston."

"Of course. Is everything okay?"

"Yes, I'm fine. Let me just see Winston. And maybe get something to drink."

"Certainly," Margaret said, leading the way out the door and down the stairs.

George was sitting on the sofa puffing his pipe and Fran was in the chair absentmindedly stroking her brown hair. They were talking about the incessant rain when they were joined by Irene and Margaret. Irene knelt down next to the side table where Winston was lying. She petted him and whispered something to him, then rose and sat on the other end of the sofa from George.

Margaret looked at George and Fran enjoying their

scotches and asked Irene if she would like one as well.

"No, thank you. Just some water would be fine."

Margaret went to the kitchen and filled a glass with water and returned, handing it to Irene.

Fran sat forward on her chair and looked to Irene and Margaret. "What do you think, Miss Adler? Is the house haunted?"

Irene took a sip of water and held it in her lap. "There is something certainly…unnatural in this house." She paused and took another drink. "I should probably talk it over privately with Mrs. McConnell."

Fran frowned but cheered up when Margaret replied. "No, these are my friends. I don't mind if you speak in front of them. I'd like to get their opinion on what you think is happening, especially letters carved into Davey's dresser."

"What?!" Fran practically leaped out of her chair.

George removed his pipe from his mouth and sat up straighter. "What's happened to Davey's dresser?"

Margaret explained about the crude letters and their significance to Irene. Fran wasted no time running up the stairs to see them for herself. While Fran was still upstairs, Margaret looked hopefully at George, wishing he could provide an answer.

Fran returned and looked at Irene, "So your real name is Lily?" Irene nodded and Fran continued, "And nobody knows this? I mean, I remember reading in *Movie Life* a couple years ago that Cary Grant's real name is Archibald Leach. Can you imagine? Archibald?"

Irene looked at Fran and shook her head, "Only a handful of people in my family know my real name."

Fran's eyes darted to George. "So, smarty pants, who carved her name into Davey's dresser?"

"I'm afraid I can't offer an explanation," he said. "I am

rather curious about it though." George stood up from the couch and excused himself as he went to investigate.

George returned after a few minutes. "Miss Adler, I'm at a loss. Do you have an explanation? Bear in mind that I'm a skeptic, but I'm certainly open to hearing what you have to say."

By this time, Winston had jumped up next to Irene and she was petting him while he purred. "I know you don't believe in my powers, Mr. Carmichael, and that's okay. I know what I am able to perceive, or tap into, and I will tell you that in the twenty five years I've been doing this, I've never encountered anything so...malignant, so evil."

Fran glanced at Margaret and raised her eyebrows, smiling a wide grin.

Irene turned her head toward Fran. "Mrs. Silva, this is not a game. I know you think I'm here to provide an evening's entertainment with some parlor tricks, but this is real." Her voice was low and determined.

Margaret shot Fran a look and urged Irene to continue.

Irene patted Winston on the head and resumed. "I have encountered many ghosts and spirits through the years. Most have been human and exactly what is depicted in popular books and the movies. They have lost their way, sometimes as a result of a sudden death. They are in a state of shock, so to speak, unable to complete their passage to the other side. But they are equally unable, of course, to return to the world of the living. The ghosts live in a sort of limbo, usually occupying their dwellings. Many of them interact with the physical world in harmless ways, and some try to communicate with the living.

"Occasionally I encounter a ghost who was not particularly likeable when they were living. As a ghost, their baleful side is magnified. At the residents' request, I will attempt to communicate with the wraith and help him find his way completely to the other side. It's like they're wearing blinders and are unable to see their way through. I'm usually successful in helping them."

"How exactly do you accomplish this?" George asked.

"After I enter a deep trance and make contact with the ghost, I can usually persuade them that their entire life, from birth to death and beyond, is a journey. A journey that must be completed. It does no one any good if they stay about a place haunting it, least of all them. Even the not so pleasant ghosts usually have people that they loved and want to join on the other side. It doesn't happen right away but, after a while, they eventually make their way through and the hauntings cease."

George relit his pipe, a plume of smoke drifting upward. "Miss Adler, how is Margaret's case different?"

"I'm not entirely sure, but I don't believe this is a straightforward haunting, such as a ghost in the traditional sense of the word." She paused while she scratched Winston behind the ears. His purring grew louder as he padded his paws on her legs. "The key is Davey's dresser. The rest of the boy's room is fine, but when I touched his dresser, I felt a, a shock almost. No, more than that, it was a darkness, an entity of some sort, and I felt it practically pulling on me."

"Are you saying that something is *living* in Davey's dresser?" Margaret asked.

"In a sense," Irene replied. "Spirits, and sometimes ghosts, can inhabit pieces of furniture. Usually they—"

"Wait a minute," George interrupted. "What's the difference between ghosts and spirits? Aren't they the same thing?"

Irene smiled and answered patiently. "Ghosts are just what you think they are. They are the souls of the dead.

They haven't completed their journey to the afterlife and are stuck here in this realm. Spirits, on the other hand, include a whole family of unseen beings, mostly of the lower classes. Sprites, or fairies, are the most innocent, but some spirits can be quite threatening. Demons are most mischievous and, depending on their level, may often be violent."

She took a drink of water while the others waited expectantly for her to continue. George was puffing on his pipe a little more vigorously when she spoke again.

"But we're not dealing with ghosts here. Or the usual spirits. Definitely not the fairies and I'm doubtful that this is the work of a demon. This is something beyond demonic. As I said, spirits will sometimes occupy an inanimate object like a piece of furniture. Poltergeists will often be drawn out of such an object with the appearance of a baby or small child. When your friend called me and explained what was going on in your house, Mrs. McConnell, my assumption was that it was a poltergeist. Almost always harmless and something that goes away in time. Poltergeists are below even sprites in the kingdom of spirits. They are mere elements, but are attracted by the incredible energy pent up inside an infant or toddler. Drawers will open and close, chairs and other objects can slide across the floor, doors will swing open or shut seemingly by themselves. It's usually the work of poltergeists and nothing to worry about.

"But no, we are dealing with something quite different here. And, I must tell you, for the first time in doing this, well, frankly I'm afraid."

Irene finished her glass of water and Margaret stood to take it from her. "Miss Adler, what can be done about it? Is it safe to stay in the house?"

Fran looked at her friend and answered before Irene

could say anything. "Margaret, you know that you and Davey are welcome to stay with us." She looked at George. "And, of course, George, you would be most welcome as well," she said with a smile. "We have plenty of room."

Irene stood up from the couch and addressed Margaret. "I don't think it's necessary to move out. But I would probably avoid Davey's room. You saw Winston's reaction when I brought him into the room but, as you can see, he's quite comfortable in other parts of the house. So it might be best to have your son sleep elsewhere at night, perhaps your room, or here on the sofa."

"Miss Adler," George said as he rose. "I'm still skeptical, of course, but what is the next step? What is your course of action here?"

"Normally I conduct a séance and attempt to communicate with the spirit. I can often help them find their way to the other side. If they're not lost but simply recalcitrant, I usually persuade them to complete their journey. But this case is different. I'm not ready to begin a séance and I'm not even sure I should. I need to do a little research before I can make a proper recommendation." She turned and looked at Margaret. "With your permission, I'd like to enter Davey's room again and look at the dresser one more time before I leave."

Margaret agreed and Irene started for the stairs. Winston had taken Irene's spot on the sofa and curled into a tight ball.

"May I come with you?" George asked.

"Of course, be my guest."

Several minutes later George and Irene returned to the first floor. Margaret and Fran were in the kitchen, having collected the glasses from the living room. Irene gathered up her black bag and called to Winston who slowly uncoiled himself from the sofa, arched his back and yawned. He jumped down and walked to the kitchen, then leapt into Irene's arms.

"Mrs. McConnell," Irene said, "my second examination of your son's dresser was most illuminating. Something I've never encountered before, but I think with some research I may be able to identify exactly what it is that we're dealing with. If you would let me have a couple days, I should like to call you and make a follow up appointment."

"Yes, that would be fine, Miss Adler. Can you tell me what you found so interesting?"

"I took the liberty of opening the drawers of the dresser and found a small, black stone, egg-shaped, in the top right drawer. Do you know anything about it?"

"Nothing really. It's just a rock that my husband brought back from the war. Larry said that he found it in the Philippines on his march through the jungle. Does it have something to do with what's going on in the house?"

"I think so. When I picked it up I felt distinctive pulsations from it. Physical vibrations."

Margaret looked to George who shrugged his shoulders. "I took it from Miss Adler and handled it quite extensively, but felt nothing. It is remarkable in that it is completely smooth with no bumps or ridges. It's entirely black with no discoloration or streaks of any other color."

"I guess I really never paid it much attention," Margaret said.

"As I said, now that I've seen the house, the dresser, and this remarkable rock, I should like to conduct some research and come around in a few days to see you." Irene said goodbye and left out the kitchen door, leaving

Fran and George and Margaret looking at each other for a moment before Fran spoke.

"Are you convinced now, Margaret, that you have a real, live haunted house? And what about you, George? Surely you mustn't have any doubts now?"

"I don't know what to think," Margaret said, "but I do need to go get Davey and put him to bed. I'll have him sleep with me for now."

George just shook his head in response and relit his pipe, moving to the sofa. Margaret looked over her shoulder at him as she and Fran moved through the kitchen and out the door.

"I'll be back soon, George."

George nodded and puffed on his pipe, deep in thought.

Upstairs, the vibrations of the black egg-shaped stone in Davey's dresser became more pronounced and knocked quietly against the inside of the drawer.

* * * *

Sheriff Grady had changed out of his wet clothes hours before but still felt chilled from the incessant rain and the sloshing around on the banks of the Genesee. Perkins had headed back to his motel room for the night and the sheriff was just closing up the office when the phone rang.

"Sheriff's Office," he said, hoping whoever needed him could wait until morning.

"Sheriff, this is Brenda Singer. Slim is dead. Oh my God, come quick, Sheriff. Charlie stuck a knife in him. Right in front of me."

"Slow down, Brenda, slow down. Where are you and is Charlie still there?"

Brenda took a deep breath and spoke again. "I'm at home and no, Charlie isn't here."

"Okay, I'll be there in five minutes. Lock your doors until you see me pull up."

Grady hung up with Brenda and called the hospital for an ambulance, giving them Brenda's address just outside Kingsbridge. The rain had stopped for the most part but as the sheriff arrived at Brenda's, a slow drizzle started again.

Brenda came out and ran toward him, the front of her yellow blouse stained a deep red. She circled her arms around Grady, crying. He let her sob, then gently took her arms and pushed her back. "Where's Slim, Brenda?"

"Over there," she said, pointing up the gravel driveway beyond the house. "That truck driver saw what happened and tried to save Slim but it, it was too late."

"Are you okay to walk with me and explain what happened?"

She nodded, wiping the rain and tears from her face. "Slim and I had gone up to Alexandria Bay."

"In the Thousand Islands?"

"Yeah, we came back about an hour ago. Slim helped me with my bag to the door and when I got in the house, it was a mess. Just like last time but much worse. There was furniture everywhere, dishes smashed, lamps broken. I knew it was Charlie." They arrived at Slim's body. Brenda looked at Sheriff Grady, not wanting to look at Slim's lifeless form. "We looked out the window and saw my car doors open." She sniffed and continued to wipe stray tears away. "We walked out and saw that he had been in the garage. The door was open. All of a sudden, he just appeared, demanding to know where..."

"Demanding to know what?"

"Oh Sheriff, there's so much to tell you. I found out everything from Slim on our drive to Alexandria Bay." She paused. "Larry McConnell is dead."

"Uh, yes, I know. He drowned in Baylors Lake. But why don't you tell me what happened tonight and we can talk about Larry later."

Brenda finished recounting what happened when the ambulance arrived. Sheriff Grady guided her inside the house and asked her to wait. She changed out of her blood-soaked clothes while Grady examined Slim's body.

The ambulance loaded Slim's body and left. Grady interviewed the truck driver and dismissed him, then met Brenda inside to get her story.

"I should never have gotten involved with Charlie, Sheriff," Brenda said. "Or Larry, for that matter. I've messed up everything."

"It's all right. Just tell me what happened."

She started at the beginning, telling him everything about her affair with Larry, the money that he stole from the cannery, their plans to run away together, the letters and who had really been writing them, everything.

## Chapter Eleven
## Sunday, June 13

"GEORGE," MARGARET CALLED from the kitchen, "I need to drive over to Dunkley's Market and get eggs and butter for some baking. Would you mind watching Davey for me?"

George looked up from his ledger and glanced at Davey asleep in the easy chair. "Not at all. Or if you want to stay, I'd be happy to go instead. You'll just have to let me know where I'm going."

"No, I don't mind. Plus, you're busy. I'll only be a half hour or so—it's just on the other side of downtown."

Margaret smiled at him as she gathered her purse. What a remarkable man, she thought. If only she had met him instead of Larry, her life would have surely turned out differently. But that's water under the bridge now, she said to herself. Other clichés came to her mind as she left quietly out the kitchen door and pulled out of the driveway.

Margaret was lost in thought and didn't notice the black Hudson coupe sitting on the curb across from her house. Even if she had, she probably wouldn't have seen the driver who was slouched down in the seat.

From the car, Castle watched her get in her car and drive away, but there was no sign of her son. Maybe a friend or neighbor was babysitting. It was daylight anyway, and he might be too easily seen breaking in. No, he would wait. And watch. Or perhaps a more direct approach was in order, he thought.

In the kitchen of Margaret's house, George was going over the cannery's books from last year, calculating which of the dozen or so vegetables the factory processed were the most profitable. His papers were spread out on the table and he puffed his pipe slowly, reaching for a pencil. Davey stirred briefly from the living room but was sound asleep.

George was moving his pencil along a line in the ledger when there was a knock at the kitchen door. He stood up quickly, dropped his pencil on the table, and strode to the door, fearful that the knock would wake up Davey. He moved the curtain aside and saw Fran at the door. He opened it and put a finger to his lips.

"Davey's sleeping."

"Oh, I see," Fran said, her voice low. "Listen, could you come over for just a minute? The pilot light is out on the stove and I need to get Dick's dinner started. I've tried several times to get it lit, but it's a little tricky."

"Dick's not home?"

"No, they called him for a shift this morning at the cannery. He gets double-time since it's a Sunday. But he'll be home in a couple hours and I want to have dinner ready for him. He can always get it started, but it's a trick I've never learned"

"I really shouldn't leave Davey alone." George looked over his shoulder. Davey was still curled up in the chair. "Can it wait 'til he wakes up or Margaret gets home? She shouldn't be long."

"Oh, he'll be fine, George. It'll just take a minute. Please?"

George took another look through the kitchen and saw that Davey was still. "All right. But if I can't get it lit I'll have to wait until later to fix it."

"Thank you, George, you're such a dear." Fran held the door open for him as he stepped down onto the side steps and quietly closed the door.

Castle was still slouched down in Slim's car when he saw the neighbor walk over to Larry's ole' lady's house, stand at the door for a minute, and then return with a man in tow. Good-sized fellow, nicely dressed. Looks like Margaret is well past the mourning stage and has a new husband, Castle thought. That could complicate matters a bit, but nothing he couldn't handle. Still no sign of the kid, though, so waiting some more made sense.

After just a couple minutes, George walked back to Margaret's house, the burners on the stove fully lit and Dick's dinner started. He opened and shut the door softly and was relieved to see Davey in the same position as when he left. He returned to the sofa and resumed examining the ledger.

Overall, the profit margin was good at the cannery and, at least initially, he didn't see any obstacles in the way of his company buying the outfit. He still had quite a bit of work to do before he drew up his recommendations but, George thought, he was feeling quite at home in Margaret's house and in Kingsbridge.

George was making some notes when he heard a car drive up next to the house. He stood and headed to the kitchen to help Margaret in with the groceries. She waved as she was getting out of the car. He took the bags from her as she came in.

"A half hour on the dot, Margaret!" he said to her with

a grin.

"I got lucky. Sometimes Mrs. Dunkley will talk your ear off. Davey still sleeping?" She glanced into the living room as she put away the eggs and butter.

"Not a peep out of him. By the way, I did leave him for just a minute or two. Fran needed me to fix her pilot light."

"Oh, that's fine," Margaret said. "He's a sound sleeper, and probably has another fifteen minutes or so before he wakes up." She grabbed her apron from the hook in the pantry. "Now then, how about I get started on a chocolate cake?"

\* \* \* \*

Sheriff Grady and Inspector Perkins pulled up outside Castle's apartment on the east side of Kingsbridge. It was the small upstairs unit of a duplex, with a staircase running up the side of the house. They exited the car and made their way up the steps softly and without speaking. As they reached the top, they both drew their revolvers. Grady stood to one side of the door and Perkins the other.

"Sheriff's Department!" Grady boomed as he pounded on the door. "Open up Castle! We've got a warrant."

Grady and Perkins paused, straining to hear anything inside. Another rap on the door was met with silence. Grady stood in front of the door, leaned back against the railing and kicked it hard with his boot. The door held but finally yielded after a second kick, swinging open to reveal a sparse, dimly lit apartment. Both men went in swiftly but a quick check of the rooms confirmed that Castle wasn't there.

"Too much to hope for him being home," Perkins said.

"Let's look around. Put that warrant to good use. Judge Morse wasn't too happy with me disturbing him on a Sunday morning."

Grady started searching in the living room while Perkins headed to the bedroom. "Ted, anything specific we should be looking for?"

Perkins called from the bedroom where he was looking through dresser drawers. "Anything that we can use that would tie him to the McConnell drowning—like a written confession!" Perkins laughed, then continued. "I'm not sure what it would be, but we also want to look for any information that leads us to where he's hiding out. Address book, letters, receipts, anything like that."

Sheriff Grady went through the drawers of the small kneehole desk in the living room below the front window, but found nothing of interest. The magazine rack revealed nothing more than some *Spot* magazines and other men's periodicals. As he moved to the kitchen, he called to Perkins, "Any luck, Ted?"

"Nothing so far," he replied. Perkins had searched the dresser and nightstand, but found no clues. He opened the closet to find about two dozen shirts on hangers, several pairs of pants and a deputy sheriff uniform along with some shoes. The shelf above the rack held some boxes, which he started to bring down.

Moving the boxes to the bed, he sat down and started going through them. After several minutes of fruitless searching, he gathered them up and replaced them in the closet. He stood back and noticed something peculiar about the shirts. Studying the row of shirts, he called for Grady to come in.

"Jim, what do you make of this? See anything odd?"

Grady stood for a moment looking at the clothes. "Not really. What am I supposed to be noticing?"

"Every shirt is a solid colored shirt." Perkins pointed to the corner of the closet. "Except that one. It's been thrown on the floor, and it's plaid."

"Hmm…" Grady mused, retrieving a toothpick from his pocket and placing it between his teeth. "Let's take a look." He reached down and grabbed the red flannel shirt. He held it front of him by the shoulders, its long and wrinkled sleeves drooping down.

Perkins had taken a step toward the closet and grabbed one of the solid colored shirts from the hanger. "What size is that?"

Grady looked at the tag. "Seventeen, thirty-four." He looked up at Perkins. "What are you getting at?"

The inspector flipped through several of the shirts hanging up. "These are all eighteen, thirty-six."

"This isn't Castle's shirt," Grady said.

"All the short-sleeved shirts have an eighteen inch collar, too."

Grady turned the flannel shirt over in his hands. "So whose shirt is it, and why does Castle have it in the corner of his closet?" The sheriff flipped the shirt back so it was facing him and reached into the front pocket. Feeling something at his fingertips, he reached a little further and came up with a crumpled piece of white paper.

Tossing the shirt to the bed, Grady went to the dresser and gently unrolled and smoothed out the piece of paper. It was small, washed out, about twice the size of a business card, with some faded blue ink barely visible in places.

"Looks like it's gone through the wash," Perkins said.

Grady turned the note paper over and back again. "Or a lake."

Perkins looked at the sheriff. "This is Larry's shirt?"

"I think so. Look, I've never seen Castle wear anything but his uniform or one of these shirts," Grady said, waving at the shirts in the closet, "and the sizes aren't the same. And all I ever saw Larry McConnell in were plaid, flannel shirts." He looked back at the note on the dresser. "I can't make out what this says, but that looks like an $M$ at the bottom."

"For *Margaret*."

"That's my bet. There's not much here, but let's get it into some better light." Grady and Perkins walked to the bedroom window and the sheriff held up the paper to the sunlight. The morning was bright, but there were already some high clouds gathering which meant more rain on the way.

"Looks like a list of some sort," Grady said. "Is that second word 'garbage'?"

Perkins leaned in to get a better look. "I think it's 'cabbage'. And that's definitely 'apples'. It's a grocery list, stuff for Larry to pick up at the store."

"That's what it is all right. If Charlie killed Larry, why in the world would he have kept his shirt?"

"Who knows? Maybe as a trophy of sorts," Perkins mused. "I investigated a case in Binghamton last year where the killer kept the shoes of his victims. Very strange. One for the shrinks to explain."

"Let's show this shirt and the note to Mrs. McConnell. Get her to confirm it was Larry's." Grady looked around the room. "I think we're done here anyway."

\* \* \* \*

Margaret was putting the finishing touches on her cake, spreading the frosting into little swirls with her spatula. George had bundled up his ledger and other papers and retreated to his room while Davey was "helping" his mother in the kitchen.

Davey reached on his tiptoes and reached across the table with his finger toward the cake. Margaret turned around from putting the spatula in the sink just in time to take him gently by the hand and steer him away. "No, no, Davey. That's for later when we get back from the park."

Margaret turned her son around and led him into the living room where he climbed up on the sofa to look at one of his books. Margaret climbed the stairs to the second floor and called to George from the landing. "George, Davey and I are going to the park in a few minutes with Dick and Fran. There's a concert at the bandstand at three o'clock. Would you like to come?"

George folded up the ledger and walked to the top of the stairs. "You know, I could use a little break. That sounds like a wonderful idea. I'll be down shortly."

"Oh good. I'm so glad," Margaret said, her eyes bright.

\* \* \* \*

The circumstances couldn't have been better for Charlie Castle. He watched as Larry's widow, her son, and her new man got into a car and drove away, followed closely by the next door neighbors. He waited ten minutes to make sure they hadn't forgotten something and returned prematurely. He exited the Hudson and walked in the opposite direction of Margaret's house, went a few blocks, crossed the street, then walked leisurely toward her house.

He looked casually from side to side to make sure no one was watching him. Satisfied that nobody was, he turned up her driveway, walked past the side kitchen door and into the backyard. It was a deep backyard, with a row of tall hedges separating Margaret's lot from the one behind her.

Castle still wasn't entirely happy about breaking into the house during the day, but figured the risk would be worth it, now that he was positive the house was empty and should be for a while. He reached up and grabbed the frame of the window. The unlocked window slid open easily. Castle hoisted himself upward, swung his leg around and dropped into the living room of Margaret's house.

Castle was focused in his search for the money, but not reckless. He did not want signs of his presence known so he was careful when going through drawers and cabinets. He started in the living room, searching behind pieces of furniture, in and under and behind side table drawers. He moved to the kitchen and opened all the cupboards, pulled open all the drawers, even checked the refrigerator and freezer. In the front hallway, he checked the coat closet and the pockets of the hanging jackets. He jammed his fingers into the toes of shoes and boots, but found nothing.

Getting more frustrated by the minute, Castle reminded himself not to be careless. Ripping everything apart, no matter how satisfying, would create alarm when Margaret and her man came home to an obviously burglarized house.

Castle climbed the steps to the second floor and searched the bathroom and Margaret's bedroom, finding nothing of interest. When he entered the boy's room however, he felt himself drawn to the dresser. He remembered Larry building the dresser, creating it. He patterned it after the old Victorian Eastlake style dressers, with handkerchief drawers and carved handles.

Castle had helped a little, but Larry really did everything on it. Cut the board, sanded it, used the jigsaw to cut the scrollwork in the top. He was such a perfectionist about everything with the dresser. The dovetail joints in the drawers had to be just right, no gaps.

Larry's friend and fellow former soldier stood in front

of the dresser, running his hand over the dark, smooth wood.

It was ironic how Castle hadn't been driven to the same perfection when he was sawing through Larry's limbs. The sides of his mouth curled up slightly as he remembered that day in the woods next to Baylor Lake.

He didn't intend on killing Larry that day, of course. Charlie had decided to join Larry and Slim for fishing and got to the marina a few minutes beforehand. Larry arrived and together they walked into the woods to dig up some night crawlers.

Once in the woods, Charlie casually asked Larry about his affair with Brenda and if he had socked enough money away to run off with her. Yes, Larry replied, he had been taking a few hundred at a time every month or so. Making his rounds as a security guard gave him easy access to the office at night and half the time the safe wasn't locked properly. It was the manager himself who frequently neglected to give the handle a final downward push to lock it into place.

He hit the jackpot when the cannery manager himself had hit the jackpot. An after-hours poker game with other company managers from around the country had been held in the conference room of the factory. The local manager brought in booze and some "entertainment" from Rochester, Larry explained. They played into the night, some of the men taking a break to wander off with the ladies into various offices.

The game finally broke up around four o'clock and the manager had scored almost ten thousand dollars from his fellow plant managers. Some had suspected him, correctly, of cheating. They weren't sure how he did it, but they definitely weren't happy about it. Larry had been on duty that night and the manager decided to put his winnings in the office safe rather than take it home with him, not wanting to be possibly waylaid on the way home.

Larry went on to say how he simply decided to take the money. There were still some of the managers milling around and suspicion would probably fall on them when the money was discovered missing the next day. The plant manager trusted Larry and he probably wouldn't go to the police as there would be a lot of company violations he would have to explain. Larry went to the office after everyone had left, pulled up on the handle of the safe and it sprang open easily. There were stacks of cash just sitting there.

Charlie's eyes grew wide when Larry revealed just how much money he had stolen. Thanks to sloppy bookkeeping, his skimming of about two thousand dollars over the last couple years went undiscovered. And in one night he added almost ten thousand to his total. With pride, he told Charlie that he had over eleven thousand dollars squirreled away.

Castle had asked if the money was safe and Larry assured him it was, without revealing where it was hidden. He had made some references to Brenda having some money as well, so Charlie wasn't sure in whose house the money was kept. Maybe it was split between the two.

Charlie had suddenly turned on Larry, demanding a third of the money to keep quiet about it. *Tell me where the money is, Larry, or I'll tell the plant manager what happened.* When Larry refused, Charlie gave him one more chance to tell him. Larry was stubborn about how he had assumed incredible risk in stealing the money and how he was going to surprise Brenda with it and they could run away together. He wasn't sure where they were going to go, but he needed all of the money.

That day in the woods beside Baylor Lake after Larry had laid out his plans to his friend, Charlie demanded part of the cash and when Larry refused, he killed him. In a flash, Charlie punched Larry in the carotid artery. The blinding speed of Charlie's strike gave Larry no time to react, and its accuracy stopped the blood flow to Larry's brain. He crumpled to the ground, unconscious.

Based on what Larry had said when he first arrived at the lake, Slim was going to be about forty-five minutes late. *That gives me about a half hour to finish the job.* Breaking Larry's neck and leaving his body in the woods wouldn't do, even if he dragged it further in. It was quiet at the marina that day, so nobody noticed Charlie trotting over to his car and opening the trunk. He rummaged around a bit and pulled out a few blankets.

On a nearby dock, he spotted a small tool shed. Once inside the dimly lit structure, he quickly grabbed a hacksaw hanging on a pegboard and darted back out.

Back in the woods, Larry's breathing was shallow. He was still unconscious as Charlie hoisted his victim's leg up and began sawing just above the knee. Larry squirmed as blood spurted out from his thigh. Then he popped his head up wild eyed and screamed. Charlie left the saw in his leg and turned toward Larry. A quick punch brought Larry back to darkness. Charlie rather enjoyed the thought of dismembering Larry while still alive, but screams coming from the woods would draw undue attention.

Castle moved to Larry's head and hoisted him up to a sitting position. He wrapped one arm around his neck, pressing his hand against the shoulder. With his other hand he jerked Larry's head to the left. There was some resistance, but after two more twists, the vertebrae finally broke, and Larry's darkness was permanent.

No more screams came as Charlie sawed off his late friend's legs. Charlie's plan came together as he began to work on Larry's arms. He took off Larry's shirt and tossed it aside, then used the saw to shred through the flesh just below the shoulder. Each of the limbs was then cut in half. *Larry should have kept himself in better shape. So much fat.*

He put on Larry's red flannel shirt over his own to cover up the blood that had spurted out. It was a tighter fit, but manageable. He wrapped the limbs in the blanket and carried them to the nearest boat tied up at the dock. Norwood was asleep or passed out in the marina office, as Charlie knew he would be, so he didn't see him ferrying bundled body parts to the small motorboat.

Castle picked up a few good sized rocks along the way and placed the rolled blanket into the boat. He jogged back to the woods and wrapped the torso and head in the remaining blanket. He added some rocks to the bundle as he returned to the boat. He quickly tied the ends of each blanket up and placed the rocks inside for weight.

He jogged back to his car and moved it out of the marina's parking lot, across the street to the back of a shuttered warehouse where it wouldn't easily be seen. He also gathered a few empty beer cans he found at the warehouse and placed them outside Larry's car.

A few minutes later and Charlie gave the starting rope on the small motor a quick pull. It coughed to life and he was soon steering the boat out of sight of the marina. He gunned the outboard and sped across the narrow lake to a rocky cove twenty yards off shore. It was near the densest part of the woods and nearly inaccessible.

Castle looked around and quietly slipped the two bundles into the water where they immediately sank to the bottom. He knew Grady and his men would dredge the lake, but only in the area where "Larry" would be seen apparently drowning.

He turned the boat toward the middle of the lake and arrived just as Slim's car was approaching the marina from the lake road.

He watched as Slim parked and approached the shore, waving his arms and calling to him. As Charlie anticipated, given the distance and that he was now wearing Larry's ever-present red flannel shirt, Slim mistook him for Larry.

Charlie watched as Slim continued to holler at him, his voice not quite carrying across the water. At that point, Charlie stood and picked up the anchor. He had shortened the rope considerably on it, ensuring that the boat would capsize as soon as he tossed it overboard. Knowing that Slim was still watching and waving, Charlie heaved the anchor over the side.

Charlie dove free of the gunwale as it pivoted upward and toward him. All Slim could see from the shore was the bottom of the boat turning skyward. He could not see the body parts of his friend spilling out of the boat, nor could he see Charlie swimming powerfully under the surface toward the opposite shore.

When Charlie was sufficiently far away from the boat, he broke the surface of the cold water just enough to gulp in some air. Slipping back under, he continued his strokes to the shoreline. He repeated this several times. When his strength finally started giving out, he felt the sandy bottom underneath him. He had swum over half a mile and now pulled himself onto the gravelly shore. Drawing on a deep down reserve of strength, he crawled through the rocks until he was inside the safety of the thick woods surrounding the lake. He would rest and then make his way around the southern, unpopulated end of the lake, and back northward until he came to his car.

Charlie's memories of that day faded and he re-focused on the task at hand. Over eleven thousand dollars was hidden in this house somewhere. He actually would have been disappointed had Larry agreed to his demands of a third. *Why would I want three or four thousand when I could have all of it?*

He pulled open one of the handkerchief drawers on the top of the dresser and noticed a small, black stone. He recognized it immediately from his time in the Philippines. He felt like it represented something far darker in spirit than he had ever seen. Castle was surprised by its presence here, but awed by it at the same time, and he welcomed it.

He picked up the stone from the drawer and grasped it in his hand. He felt the vibrations in it, the icy coldness coursing up his arm. His eyes rolled back in their sockets and Charlie collapsed to the floor, his grip on the stone loosening.

The black stone jerked out of his hand and rolled to the floor. Its quivering grew more pronounced. Charlie watched out of half-closed eyes as the stone cracked in front of him. Pieces of the stone fell away. A small shape, all black, emerged from a void in the stone. The shape grew and fluttered to get free of the pieces of stone. With a little effort, the black bird, a chick, shook off the remaining bits of stone.

The chick, completely black, stood among the remains of its thousand-year home and cocked its head to one side, spying Charlie lying on the floor.

Charlie blinked out of awe and a little fear. Time slowed down as he recalled the dying Filipino soldier he and Larry had come across during the war. He found the stone in the guerrilla's pocket and had given it to Larry before their raid on the POW camp. Think of it as a good luck charm, he had told Larry.

Now Charlie thought of the word the soldier had said with a cracking voice as he lay still in the tall grass. He had pulled the stone out of his pocket and the man had reached toward it, trying to take it back from Charlie.

Charlie remembered now what he said as the chick with the black body and wings and eyes hopped over to his face. His mind was swirling, it was like he was in a trance of sorts. Charlie opened his mouth and whispered, "*Aswang*." He opened his mouth wide and the chick climbed in, over his lips and past his teeth. Charlie closed his eyes.

Barely conscious, he felt the chick fluttering on his tongue. Charlie was hungry for the power the chick was sacrificing to him. What the bird was about to become also needed Charlie. With all the strength his weakening body could muster, he closed his mouth around the black bird. He bit down, his jaws crunching through the tiny bones of the bird.

After a moment he swallowed.

The transformation began.

## Chapter Twelve

MARGARET HELPED DAVEY out of the car as George grabbed the bag they had taken to the park. They waved to Dick and Fran as they walked into the kitchen through the side door. Davey ran to the living room to play with the pinwheel all the children at the concert received.

"What a fun afternoon!" Margaret said. "How about some lemonade? I know I'm thirsty."

"I'd love some," George replied. "Here, let me get the pitcher down for you."

"Oh, I've got it, but thank you." Margaret nodded toward the living room. "I don't hear Davey though. That usually means trouble. Could you check on him?"

George smiled and headed into the other room. He saw Davey at the window and noticed the pinwheel in Davey's hand spinning in the breeze. Frowning, he looked again and saw that the window was completely open. Davey had just stuck his head above the sill and was on tip-toes trying to see out when George ran to him.

"No, Davey," George chuckled. "It's only a few feet down but you're not wearing a parachute." He lifted Davey up and sat him down on the floor. "Margaret," he called. "Did you leave the window open when we left for the concert?"

Margaret ducked her head into the living room. "Pardon? Leave the window open?"

George smiled. "Davey was very curious about the open window."

Margaret shook her head. "I've been meaning to get a screen for that window and just haven't gotten around to it. I always keep it closed." She walked to the window and closed it, then turned to George. "You don't think somebody broke in, do you?" She brought her hand to her mouth and looked around the room.

Both Margaret and George jumped when the doorbell rang. Margaret walked briskly down the hall and to the front door. George watched from behind as she opened it and saw Sheriff Grady and Inspector Perkins on the front stoop.

The sheriff spoke first, taking off his hat. "Mrs. McConnell, it's been a while. How are you?" He motioned toward Ted. "I think you know Investigator Perkins with the State Police."

"Of course. Won't you come in?" Margaret stepped back and the two lawmen entered. She escorted them to the living room and introduced George to Sheriff Grady.

"Mrs. McConnell," Grady said, holding up a paper bag. "We don't want to take up too much of your time but—"

"Actually, we were about ready to call you, Sheriff," Margaret said, looking at George.

George pointed to the open window. "We think the house may have been broken into. We just came home from the concert in the park and found the window open. Margaret said she hasn't opened it since last summer."

"How long have you been home?" Grady asked.

George shrugged. "Just a few minutes, I guess."

"Have you been upstairs?"

"Um, no. We came in through the side door," Geoge said. "We just noticed the window open when you rang the bell."

"Ted, stay here with them. I'll check upstairs." George and Margaret both noticed that Grady had placed his right hand on the butt of his revolver as he walked swiftly to the bottom of the stairs. Pausing to listen but hearing nothing, he crept up the stairs. After a few minutes of exploring the upper levels of the house, he returned to the first floor.

"Everything appears normal. Except for what I assume is your son's room," Grady said, looking at Margaret.

"What is it?"

Grady held out his hand toward her and opened it. His palm was filled with broken pieces of a small, black rock. "I found this in front of your little boy's dresser. And his window was broken out."

Margaret gasped. "That looks to be the stone that was in the top dresser drawer. Something Larry had brought back from the Philippines." She looked from Grady to Perkins. "The window is broken?"

"Yes. Only a couple small fragments inside, but some pretty good sized pieces outside on the ground. Whoever broke the window was going out, not coming in. Unless they had a ladder propped up against the window, I'm not sure how they got down from the second floor. That would have been a hard landing." Grady paused and reached in his pocket for a toothpick. "Darndest thing though. The window was unlocked. No reason to break the window, which could have brought attention. Just slide it open to get out."

The sheriff twirled the toothpick between his teeth. "Oh, something else. That dresser in your son's room.

Looks like someone took a chisel to it."

George interjected. "Yes, it's a woman's name. L-I-L-Y. We're actually not sure how the letters got there. It's a bit of a mystery." He chuckled. "We've even enlisted the help of a palm reader, and Lily happens to be her name, making it even more of a puzzle."

Grady looked at George and squinted slightly. "No... I'm not sure exactly what those letters say, but it's definitely not Lily." He pulled out a small notebook from his back pocket and flipped it open. "I drew the markings as best I could. No L's or I's or Y's in there. I don't understand what it means, it just a bunch of odd curves and lines. Doesn't look like any letters I'm familiar with. Maybe Egyptian." He looked to Ted. "What are those things called, hiero, something or other?"

"Hieroglyphics?" Ted replied.

"Yeah, that's it. That's kind of what they look like. Definitely not 'Lily,' though." Grady picked up the paper bag he had come in with. "Mrs. McConnell, I did want to show you something and don't want to forget." He reached into the bag and pulled out the red flannel shirt. Holding it out toward Margaret, he asked if it was Larry's.

Margaret stood a little straighter and took it from the sheriff, turning it over in her hands, finally holding it in front of her by the shoulders. "Yes, it's definitely his. It was his favorite. I remember he wore it the last day I saw him. He was going fishing with Slim and, and he never came back."

George placed his hand gently on her shoulder and she continued. "The bottom button is missing. I noticed it shortly before he left and told him I could sew another one on in no time, but he seemed to be in a hurry. Then we started arguing and..." Her voice trailed off.

Grady pulled a slip of paper out of the bag and handed it to Margaret. "Is this your handwriting? I know it's pretty faded, but do you recognize this?"

Margaret took it and examined it from a couple different angles. "Yes, it must be a grocery list I had given Larry. I always signed my little notes to him with just my first initial. Where did you find this? And the shirt?"

Perkins spoke up. "We were searching Charlie Castle's apartment and I found it in the back of his closet. The note was inside the shirt pocket. You say this is what Larry was wearing the last day you saw him?"

"That's right."

Perkins and Grady looked at each other. Grady looked at Davey before he spoke. "Mrs. McConnell, perhaps we could speak somewhere...out of earshot of your son."

George led Davey by the hand to the kitchen. "I'll fix him up with some lemonade, Margaret. Go ahead."

"Thank you, George," Margaret said with a faraway look in her eyes. She had tried to forget all about that final day. As much as it was a relief to not have Larry and his temper around any longer, she really didn't like to dwell on that last day.

"Maybe we should sit down," Grady said.

"Oh yes, I'm sorry. Please make yourselves comfortable."

"Mrs. McConnell," Perkins said after they had taken their seats. "We believe that your husband was murdered two years ago. We're not sure of the motive, but we have a strong suspect in the case."

"Is it Charlie Castle?"

"That's who we think it is, yes."

Margaret turned to Grady. "Isn't he one of your deputies?"

Grady sighed. "Former deputy. He's gone off the deep

end." He looked at Perkins. "We've been searching for him for a few days now." He turned back to Margaret. "I'm not sure how to put this, Mrs. McConnell, but were you aware of a relationship between your husband and a Brenda Singer? She's a barmaid—"

"Yes, I know who she is, Sheriff." Margaret paused and looked down slightly at her hands folded in her lap. "I had heard the rumors about Larry and her, and I had my suspicions."

"Well, I'm sorry to confirm those rumors, but we've talked to Miss Singer and she has admitted to having an affair with your husband. In addition, I'm afraid that Mr. McConnell had stolen a sizable amount of money from his workplace over the years and had socked it away so that he and Brenda could run away at some point."

"Mr. Perkins mentioned something about that when he was here the other night. I honestly didn't know anything about that, Sheriff."

"Oh, you're not under any suspicion at all, Mrs. McConnell, believe me."

She smiled warmly and said, "Please, call me Margaret."

"Thank you."

"I take it you have not found any large sums of money stashed anywhere around the house?"

Margaret chuckled and shook her head. "No, just some money I had found in Larry's boot when he was still alive. I had told Mr. Perkins about that, but I've never come across anything like that since. If I do find anything, I'll certainly let you know."

"I appreciate that," Grady said. He took a full breath and continued, pointing to the window in the living room. "Now this is sheer speculation and something I haven't even discussed with Ted obviously, but I'm betting that that open window and the broken one upstairs has something to do with Charlie Castle. Brenda —er, Miss Singer—indicated that Castle was searching for the money that Larry had squirreled away for the two of them. I can't see a connection to the vandalism to your son's dresser, but I have a feeling that Castle has been here recently looking for that money."

"Sheriff, would you mind if I took a look at the dresser?" Margaret gestured to George. "Like Mr. Carmichael said, it definitely had a woman's name carved into it. In fact, I was the first to see it, along with the palm reader we had over."

George brought Davey in at that moment and Perkins volunteered to stay with him while the other three went upstairs to inspect the dresser.

Margaret was first in the room and noticed the broken window first. As she went to it, George called to her, "Don't worry about the window, Margaret. I can get a board in there today and get the glass replaced tomorrow."

Margaret turned and looked at the surface of the dresser and the odd markings carved into the wood. As the sheriff had explained, *LILY* was gone and in its place was a strange set of symbols:

ꙮꕚ꒰ꙮ ꙮ꒰ꙮ꒱ꙮ

"Sheriff Grady," George began after staring himself at the carvings, "I was certain that seeing *LILY* gouged into the wood was explainable. But the fact that *LILY* is gone and these 'words,' if you can call them that, are here..." His voice trailed off. He rubbed his hands over his arms and shook his head. "I know what I saw earlier and much as I hate to admit it, maybe there is something to the notion that this house is haunted. At the very least, I can't explain it."

Margaret looked at him, her eyes wide. She suddenly felt very afraid. As long as George was reassuring her that there was an explanation to everything that was going on, she had felt safe.

Grady pointed to the floor where some remnants of the black stone still remained. "What do you make of that?" he said to both of them.

"You say it was a black rock that Larry had brought back from the war," George asked Margaret.

"Yes, I kept it in that drawer," she said, indicating the right-hand handkerchief drawer. "I don't really know what it was, just a stone that he had with him when he came back from the Philippines. He didn't say anything about it other than it was a good luck charm. I put it in the drawer and haven't looked at it since."

"Looks like somebody smashed it with a hammer," Grady said, holding out the pieces in his hand. "Any idea why?"

Margaret shook her head and George shrugged. "I haven't the foggiest idea."

George looked at Margaret. "This is going to sound crazy, but I think we should have our new friend Irene Adler take a look at this."

"Who's she?" Grady asked.

"She's the palm reader who came over last night," Margaret replied. "Her real name is Lily, but that's a long story. Anyway, she had asked about that stone yesterday. She was very upset about seeing her name carved into the dresser but I bet she would be very interested in this."

"I have an idea," George said. "Let's get a piece of paper and pencil and make a rubbing of these symbols. We could mail it to her to see if she has any ideas. It would save her a trip from Rochester."

Margaret smiled slightly. "For someone who was so skeptical just a day ago, you're certainly an enthusiastic believer."

"Well, I'm still reserving judgment, but I'm definitely open to any explanations, 'cause I'm stumped now."

## Chapter Thirteen
## Thursday, June 17

THE DOORBELL RANG and Margaret walked briskly to the front door. She opened it up and a late afternoon shaft of sunlight lit up some dust particles in the foyer. "Irene, I'm so glad you could come for dinner! Please, come in."

Irene smiled and entered the house with Winston in her arms. She set him down on the hardwood floors and he rubbed between Margaret's legs, purring softly. "We shouldn't have any problems with him today, as long as I don't force him to go upstairs," Irene said with an uneasy laugh.

Margaret led the way to the kitchen where George was sitting cleaning his pipe. Davey was in the living room playing and while he didn't take much notice of Irene, his face lit up when he saw Winston. He held is hands out and the cat trotted over, walked around him a couple times and sat down.

"Winston is an excellent judge of character," said Irene as she and Margaret sat down at the kitchen table. "I think he and Davey will become good friends."

George reached for his pipe and began filling it with

tobacco. "So what did you find out, Miss Adler? These last few days have been filled with anticipation." George smiled and continued. "I must say, I was deeply skeptical during your first visit, but now I truly don't know how to explain these recent events."

"Has anything happened since the break-in and the symbols appearing on the dresser?"

"No, it's been quiet. Thankfully." George tamped down the tobacco and struck a match.

"Do you mind if I take a look at the carvings in the dresser?" Irene asked. "Your rubbings proved most valuable, but I'd like to have a firsthand look."

"Of course," said Margaret. "I'm just finishing up dinner. I think you know the way." She gestured toward the living room and Irene got up from her chair.

George lit his pipe and the gentle sweet aroma of Royal Yacht tobacco filled the room. "Well, do you think we'll get to the bottom of this now, Margaret?" he asked after Irene had made it to the second floor.

"I don't know. I hope so. At the very least I'd like to get Davey back to his own bed. He squirms around a lot and keeps me up half the night." She turned to the pressure cooker and took it off the burner. "The meat should be ready in about twenty minutes. Hope it's okay."

George grinned. "Well, if your pork roast is like everything else you've whipped up, I can't wait to try it."

After a few minutes Irene returned to the kitchen. As she walked through the living room she patted Davey on the head. "Lovely boy you have, Mrs. McConnell. He does so well with Winston. Now then, is there anything I can help with?"

"No, dinner is almost ready. You can just relax."

After supper, George offered to clean the dishes while Margaret and Irene sat in the living room with Davey.

Margaret's son began to yawn while he was petting Winston and finally he lay down on his side on the floor. Margaret took a pillow from the sofa and placed it gently under his head. Winston turned in a circle and curled up next to the boy.

George joined the women and lit his pipe again. He didn't want to admit it, but he was quite eager to hear what Irene had to say about the carvings.

Satisfied that Davey was asleep, Margaret said, "I'll take him up in a little while, but could you make out what those strange symbols are on his dresser?"

Irene took a deep breath and looked toward the ceiling and back at Margaret. "When you sent me the rubbings, it was certainly nothing I recognized. I checked several books in my library, from encyclopedias of ancient alphabets to *The Discoverie of Witchcraft*, but could find nothing."

"Witchcraft?" Margaret exclaimed. "Is that what we're dealing with?"

"No, I don't think so. That book was actually written in the late 1500's and was more of a treatise on magic, explaining that witchcraft wasn't real and so-called witches were really sleight of hand experts. Similar to today's modern magicians, who accomplish their tricks through legerdemain or gimmicks of some sort. The book was practically heretical at the time but, like I said, I don't think what you're experiencing is the stuff of witches and spells."

"Are the symbols a type of hieroglyphics or cuneiform?" George asked.

"Not in the traditional sense. That is, it doesn't match the writing systems of the Sumerians, Hittites, Assyrians, or others I checked. Nor does it match any of the ancient Egyptian dynastic systems." Irene folded her hands and placed them in her lap. "I finally consulted with a professor who teaches at the University of Rochester. As it happens, their Anthropology Department specializes in east and southeast Asia. Most fortunate."

"Why is that...?" George asked.

"It turns out that, according to Doctor Hughes, what has been gouged into your son's dresser is a writing system called Baybayin. Its root is the Brahmic family of languages from India, but Baybayin actually comes from the Philippines. It's their pre-Colonial writing system. The first recorded use dates back to the early sixteenth century."

There was silence in the room as George slowly removed the pipe from his mouth and cradled it in his hand. Margaret's mouth hung open as she looked from Irene to George.

"I don't understand." Margaret shook her head and her brow furrowed. "The Philippines?"

"That's right." Irene started to speak but George interrupted.

"But your true name—Lily—was in English, or to be correct I suppose, the Latin alphabet. And," he puffed quickly on his pipe, "what happened to your name and how did that mumbo jumbo appear in its place?"

"We are dealing with something very powerful. Manipulation of matter is not difficult for—"

Before Irene could continue Margaret spoke up. "Wait! If you know what the language is, does that mean you know what the symbols mean?"

Irene nodded, pulled a small notebook from her bag and unfolded it. "Doctor Hughes was able to translate it." She paused for a moment. "This may prove to be unsettling," she said, looking at Davey sleeping quietly on the floor.

Margaret looked at George for a second then turned back to Irene. "Go on."

Irene spoke deliberately. "The first set of symbols says simply, 'Aswang.'"

"'Aswang', what is that?" George asked.

"The *aswang* is a vampire-like creature prevalent in pre-Spanish Filipino culture. Stories of it abound throughout the various—"

George couldn't stifle his laughter. "A vampire? Like Dracula? You can't be serious, Miss Adler."

"George, please," Margaret said, giving him a stern look. "Let's keep an open mind. Please continue, Irene."

"Mr. Carmichael, I shared your surprise when I had my follow up visit with Doctor Hughes, although I don't recall being as churlish with him."

George regained his composure and apologized. "It's just that this information is more, surprising, than what I thought you'd find."

Irene nodded and went on. "According to Doctor Hughes, the *aswang* is more than a vampire. It also has characteristics of a werewolf or were-dog, depending on the region. Ultimately, they are ghouls, demons if you will, and quite powerful. In the Visayan region of the Philippines, they take the form of the *manananggal*, which is usually female, although not always. It has the power to separate at its waist and its upper half can take flight thanks to large bat-like wings. It preys on fetuses but, failing to find an expecting mother, will feast on a small child."

Margaret's eyes darted toward Davey and she covered her mouth with her hand. "How horrible."

George smirked as he brought his pipe to his lips but didn't say anything.

"*Aswangs* and *manananggals* can reproduce with

themselves, they're hermaphrodites, although—and Doctor Hughes offered this himself with no prompting from me—they sometimes use eggs. Those eggs have the appearance of small, black stones. Out of them hatch black chicks which then are ingested by their victim. The person becomes the next *aswang*."

George's smug smile turned to a frown. "Are you saying that that black rock in Davey's dresser was an egg?"

"That is my belief, yes. An egg, or a seed, if you will. In my first visit here, I touched the rock and felt distinct vibrations from it. It was like nothing I've ever felt before. It represented an otherworldly and evil presence." She paused and looked at Margaret, whose eyes were open wide. "You wrote in your letter that the stone had been smashed, correct?"

Margaret nodded as George spoke up. "Yes..." he said, suspecting now where Irene was going with this.

"May I see the fragments of the stone?" Irene asked.

George got them down from an upper shelf of the hutch and handed them to Irene. She turned over the larger pieces in her hands and rubbed them between her fingers.

"I get no such vibrations or tremors now. They are... inert."

"Well, let's get back to this *aswang*, or whatever you call it," said George, puffing a large cloud of smoke upward from his pipe. "We should be on the lookout for a big bat-winged woman and call it in to the sheriff when we see her?"

"According to Professor Hughes' research, *aswangs* are shapeshifters. In the villages of the Philippines, they can assume the shape of the townspeople and go unrecognized. They can appear as dogs or other animals.

Typically, they maintain their humanlike appearance during the day and transform during the night to their demonic form. They then go on the hunt."

Irene referred to her notes again. "Their nighttime appearance is quite frightening. Their hair becomes long and wiry, nails grow to become long claws, the skin darkens, and the eyes turn red. The tongue grows into a long proboscis, able to suck the fetus from an expectant mother.

"The creature also makes a peculiar clicking sound, kind of a *tik-tik* sound which, paradoxically, is louder when the *aswang* is farther away."

"This is all just so fantastic, Miss Adler," said George. "These are stories similar to ancient Greek and Roman mythology. They had monstrous creatures like the minotaur and Medusa. How is this any different?"

Margaret had been silent for some time, but spoke up in little more than a whisper. "Irene, do you believe it?"

"I do. Doctor Hughes has an encyclopedic knowledge of the Filipino culture and filled me in on most of what I'm telling you now. He did some post-graduate work in the Philippines before the war and was surprised that much of the population still regards the *aswangs* as real."

"Oh, that's ridiculous—" George started to say.

"No, no." Irene held up her hand. "You spoke of ancient Greek mythology. Being from the U.K., I'm sure you're familiar with ancient Celtic myths and stories of Welsh creatures from long ago like the *gwyllion*, and so forth. The Japanese have ancient folklore and evil creatures as do the Chinese, Mexicans, Brazilians, and most other cultures. My point is that around the world these ancient mythologies have come and gone throughout the centuries. But for the most part the Filipinos still believe."

George considered this for a moment and gestured with his pipe toward Irene. "The believers are probably those who live in the rural areas, folks who haven't had any formal education. They've relied on oral traditions to create a plausible story as to why a woman miscarried, for instance."

"That's actually what I thought at first, too. But Doctor Hughes assured me that it isn't just people in the far flung provinces that believe. Professionals and educated people in the largest cities take the whole belief system quite seriously. Engineers, doctors, businessmen in Manila, Davao, and Cebu, many are fervent believers. And they fear the *aswang*.

"The Philippines are, for the most part, Roman Catholic. But Catholicism was imposed on them by the Spanish in the mid-1500's, and the ancient beliefs never died out. Based on what Hughes told me, and my own... impressions...these beliefs aren't just myth. The professor did indicate that there have been numerous sightings but only recently have a couple incidents been verified by academics like Dr. Hughes. He believes that the creature is nearly extinct. But it is still highly feared.

"Irene," Margaret began. George and Irene both looked to her. "You said that these creatures can look like other people?"

"That's right. During the day they can adopt the appearance of anyone. Apparently though, if you look in their eyes closely enough, the images reflected in their pupils are inverted. Also, they don't have a...hold on. Let me find the term Doctor Hughes used." She flipped through her notebook and stopped on a page. "Philtrum. In their human form they won't have a philtrum." Before the other two could ask, she pointed between her nose and upper lip. "This thing, this indentation. Everyone has one. Doctor Hughes explained that it's some sort of evolutionary throwback but, in any case, *aswangs* don't have one."

Irene paused and looked at Margaret. "There's more, if you're willing to hear it."

Margaret took a deep breath and nodded her head. "Go on, please."

"Very well. Some type of *aswangs* prey on children or the unborn. That's the kind that Doctor Hughes believes we're dealing with here. In one instance that Doctor Hughes reported, an *aswang* kidnapped a child and replaced it with a double of sorts, made from plant material. The 'child' became sick and died after a couple days, while the creature, um, feasted, on its victim. The child's parents did not suspect anything until their daughter became sick. The village doctor could not identify the nature of the disease but suspected the involvement of an *aswang*.

"Doctor Hughes was in the province at the time and investigated shortly after the child's death. He took tissue samples from the body and brought them to a biologist in Manila. Without telling him what they were, he had the biologist look at them under a microscope. The scientist identified them immediately as plant cells. They were rectangular in shape and had other characteristics that were completely different than animal cells but consistent with cells found in plants."

"But if this is true, why hasn't this been made public?" Margaret exclaimed. "I would think just from a scientific standpoint your Doctor Hughes would want to publish this. And wouldn't the government in the Philippines want to warn parents about this danger?"

"Actually, Doctor Hughes did publish his findings. It almost cost him his job. Nobody believed him. His academic peers laughed at him. He was completely discredited and now teaches basic freshman-level courses at the university. He tries to maintain some standing in the anthropology community but has lost most of his friends. He works mostly with some people in the Philippines who admire his work and host his visits to the islands every year so he can continue his studies."

George's pipe had gone out as he was listening intently to Irene. "Can they be stopped? You know, killed?"

"They can. The person possessed by the *aswang* can be, well, 'cured' I suppose is the right term." She referred to her notes again. "The person must be hung upside down and a fire lit under them to drive the chick out. The chick will try to make it back into the person's mouth, but it must be hacked to death with a knife or hatchet."

Margaret shivered while Irene described this gruesome ritual. Irene continued. "To actually kill the *aswang* one must be very precise. It must be stabbed in the exact middle of the back with a bolo or a sharpened bamboo spear. That way it will not be able to reach the wound. Striking it in any other place will allow the *aswang* to smear its saliva on the cut and close the wound. The *aswang* is not only incredibly strong but can heal itself. It is a most dangerous creature."

"Is there any way to protect yourself against it?" Margaret asked, her voice a little shaky.

"Salt. You can sprinkle salt around the outside of the house and that will prevent the *aswang* from entering. There are other oils and plants that can deter it, but most are only found in tropical areas so not readily obtained here in western New York. Salt, however, is plentiful."

"Irene, you said that the first set of symbols said *aswang*. What about the other symbols?" Margaret asked.

"Margaret, you will find this especially disturbing.

Please prepare yourself."

"I'm ready."

"Doctor Hughes translated the last set of symbols as 'this child is mine.'"

## Chapter Fourteen
### Friday, June 18

"FRAN," MARGARET SAID. "I didn't get a bit of sleep last night. Every noise I heard I thought it was that horrible creature coming for Davey." She poured another cup of coffee for her neighbor who had stopped over after breakfast, anxious to hear about Miss Adler's visit.

"That's quite a tale she spun. Do you believe her?"

Margaret looked sharply at Fran. "You were the one who convinced me to invite her in. Now you're suggesting that she's not being truthful?"

"Not at all." Fran patted her on the arm. "I'm sure she's being honest with you, but perhaps she's simply mistaken. Or that she misunderstood this professor." She picked up a sugar cube from the bowl and dropped it in her coffee. "What does George think about the whole thing?" She looked around the kitchen, leaning her head out into the living room. "Where is he, anyway?"

"He went to the hardware store to get some things for the new window in Davey's room. He's going to finish installing it today." Margaret sighed. "George is very skeptical of Miss Adler's story, but even he admitted that he doesn't have an explanation for the carvings on the dresser."

Margaret finished her coffee and stood up. She placed the cup in the sink and turned to Fran. "I think after George gets back I'm going to visit Mother. I was going to take Davey, but she doesn't want me to bring him 'cause she's convinced she has a summer flu. The doctor thinks it's just a cold, but you know how she is. Anyway, I'll probably wait 'til he goes down for his nap. George is so good about watching him."

"Are you going to tell her about what's been going on?"

Margaret laughed. "I don't think so. I don't want to worry her for nothing. That's probably all it is." She was trying hard to convince herself that she was suffering from an overactive imagination. Miss Adler was surely mistaken. The house wasn't haunted or possessed by some Filipino monster. As George had said, just because there wasn't an easy explanation didn't mean that there was a supernatural explanation.

Fran stood and handed her empty cup to Margaret who placed it in the sink with the other. "Well, it does sound pretty crazy after all. I'll tell Dick to keep an eye out for giant bat-creatures," she said with a smile.

Fran gave Margaret a quick wave as she left through the side entrance and headed back to her house next door. She glanced to the street as a black Hudson coupe pulled up to the curb, but thought nothing of it.

\* \* \* \*

Later that afternoon, Margaret was gathering things to take to her mother. She had finished making chicken noodle soup and ladled some into a container. "George," she called, turning toward the living room. "You're sure you don't mind watching Davey? I won't be gone too long."

Davey was playing quietly on the floor with a coloring book and barely heard his mother. "I'm happy to," George replied. "He's never any trouble." George nodded toward Davey and chuckled as he yawned. "I think he's headed toward that nap pretty soon."

"I think you're right," Margaret said. She picked a few of his books up from the end table and placed them in the easy chair. "Davey, why don't you sit up here and look at your books?" Margaret winked at George. "I know you won't fall asleep, but just in case you do, you'll be more comfortable in the chair."

Once her son was settled, she knelt down and gave him a kiss. "I'm going to visit Grandma, but I won't be gone long. I'm stopping by the drug store to get some cold tablets for her and maybe you'd like a new book?"

Davey looked up and grinned. "Oh yes, Mommy. New book! Farm book!"

"A book about farms and animals?" Margaret laughed. "Okay, I'll try to find one for you. Be good for Mr. George. I'll see you soon." Davey turned back to *The Poky Little Puppy* and was eagerly turning pages by the time Margaret had left.

George was taking a break from his reports and was turning pages in a book of his own, at a much slower pace. He was puffing gently on his pipe and after a time he glanced over at Davey. The boy was slouched over in the chair and the book slipping from his grasp. His eyes were almost closed and George smiled, thinking back to his own son and the books he enjoyed.

The light coming in from the window dimmed slightly as if a shadow passed in front of it. George looked up from his book, frowning slightly. He looked back to the book but after a moment set it on the sofa and walked to the window. He looked out to the back yard but nothing seemed amiss. George checked the lock on the window and returned to his book.

A few minutes later, Davey had slumped over completely in the chair and the book had fallen to the floor. A sad smile returned to George's face as he thought about his own family. He considered himself very lucky however, for finding himself in the midst of this small and welcoming family. Margaret was different than Maureen. Maybe it was the "English" in his late wife. She was a little more reserved than Margaret. He was enjoying getting to know Margaret and the rest of the decidedly American townspeople in Kingsbridge. Even Dick and Fran. They were a little brash, but still fun.

Perhaps Margaret would agree to a dinner in the next week or so, he thought. Nothing overtly romantic, of course, just a simple night out. He had heard good things about the Avon Inn, with its Ionic columns and beautiful gardens. The menu was one of the best in the area and he couldn't think of a better person with which to share the dinner.

George found himself having to read the same paragraph several times, and he finally simply put the book down and puffed away on his pipe. As he reached for his tamper, there was a knock at the kitchen door. He glanced at Davey who hadn't stirred and quickly walked to the door. Looking through the curtains, he saw Fran's toothy smile staring at him.

He opened the door and invited her in, but she held her hand up. "Sorry, George, can't come in. But I need your help again with the pilot light."

"Fran!" George said with a smirk. "You always need my help when Margaret's away. Davey's sleeping, but I don't like leaving him alone. Can't it wait? Margaret will be home in an hour or two."

"Now George. You know how quick you were in getting that stove lit the other day. You'll have it done in a jiffy."

George sighed and looked back into the living room. Davey was sound asleep as George slipped through the kitchen door and over to Fran's house. Once inside, George made sure all the stove knobs were in the off position, then lifted the top up. He fished around in his pocket for his box of matches and struck one, holding it near the left side gas jet. Nothing happened. He held the lit match near the right side jet, but it didn't light either.

Not concealing his sigh, he pulled the broiler out and laid on his back on the floor. Peering into the darkness, he could see a small blue flame. "Oven's okay, Fran," he said as he started to get up.

"Well, of course, silly. I just can't seem to get the burners going. I thought I told you that."

George got up and pushed the broiler drawer back in with a chuckle. "No, you failed to—did you hear that?" George swiveled his head toward Margaret's house.

"Hear what?" Fran said. "I didn't hear anything."

George shook his head. "I don't know. Sounded like a pop or something." He stood and looked out the kitchen window toward's Margaret's house but saw nothing out of the ordinary. He turned his attention back to the stove. He bent over, peering closely at the gas jets. "When's the last time you or Dick cleaned these?"

Fran looked down. "I don't think we ever have. You know, neither one of us have any business owning a house. We don't know how to do anything. That's why we have you now!"

"Hmm-mm. Well, that's probably the reason they're not staying lit. Do you have a screwdriver?"

Fran rummaged in a kitchen drawer and handed

George a screwdriver. He tapped each of the jets a few times. "This might dislodge some dirt and dust and get it working again."

Fran clapped a minute later when both pilot lights glowed with a soft, blue light. "You're my hero, George!"

"Happy to be of service. I'll stop over later with some sandpaper and give the jets a more thorough—" He was interrupted by the squeal of tires from the street. Without a word, he rushed out of the door and turned toward the street. A black car was racing away.

George's heart was racing as he ran to Margaret's house, ignoring Fran's confused calls. From the kitchen, he noticed that Davey's chair was empty. Worse, he saw that the window leading to the back yard was broken. George ran into the room and to the window. He ducked his head out but saw nothing. He bounded up the stairs yelling Davey's name, his voice cracking. He checked the second floor rooms and sprinted to the third story. The house was silent except for his own wretched cries.

Back on the main floor, George kept calling Davey's name as he ran down the hall and burst out the front door. "Davey! Davey—it's Mr. George. Davey, where are you?!" The rain-drenched street was quiet. Nothing out of the ordinary except for a pair of fresh tire marks where the car had peeled out. "*Davey!*"

\* \* \* \*

Margaret was humming the melody from the last song she had heard on the radio while visiting her mother as she rounded the town circle. It was probably a good thing she didn't stay too long. Just long enough to fix her some tea and honey and get her settled in. Her mother always felt like she had to entertain everyone, even family. All this rain and humidity wasn't good for Mother's breathing.

Margaret wasn't sure if she was getting a summer flu or not, or if it was maybe allergies. She'd check on her tomorrow, maybe bring her some—a black coupe burst out of a side street careening in Margaret's direction. She had to jerk the wheel to the right to avoid getting hit as the car flashed by, its engine roaring.

She pulled back onto the street from the grass and looked over her shoulder at the crazy driver who...had come out of *her* street. Margaret knew everyone on the street and although the car looked vaguely familiar, she couldn't place who owned it. And she was positive none of her neighbors would drive as insanely as that.

Margaret turned left onto her street and as she approached her house she saw a man running toward her in the middle of the road. Not just a man. It was George! What in the world was he doing in the street in the rain, she thought. When George spotted Margaret's car, he started waving his arms and running faster.

Margaret pulled up next to him and rolled her window down. "George! What on earth—"

George yanked open the door. "There's no time to explain. Slide over!"

"What's going on? Are you all right?" Margaret sputtered as she slid over. George wrestled himself into the car, pushing her to the passenger side.

George spun the wheel to the left and mashed the gas pedal to the floor. The motor screamed and the car fishtailed around to face the other direction. George whirled the wheel to the right to correct the spin and once the car was straightened out he rocketed down the street.

"George! You're scaring me! What's going on?" Margaret clenched the dashboard with both hands as they sped toward the main road.

"Did a car pass you just as you made the turn?" George asked, panic gripping his voice.

"Um, yes. Yes. He almost drove me off the road."

"What kind of car was it? What color?"

"I don't know. It was dark, probably black. What's happening? You're scaring me to death."

"Did you get a look at the driver? Think, Margaret. This is critical!"

"No, I'm sorry, I didn't." Tears filled her eyes. "What's going on?"

"Whoever's in that car has Davey."

*"What?!"* Margaret shrieked. Her hand flung to her mouth, her eyes wide in terror.

The road was wet from the light rain and faint tracks from the car George was pursuing were visible as they approached the intersection. The fading tracks revealed a sharp right turn and swerves as the driver fought to keep his car under control.

George glanced left and turned the wheel to the right, gunning the engine again. As they approached the circle, more and more cars filled the streets, obliterating the already faint trail.

They entered the wide circle and George slowed at each of the incoming streets, desperately seeking... anything.

Margaret was sobbing, searching George's face for an explanation. George made six laps around the circle, peering intently down each street. He explained what happened to Margaret, whose sobbing turned to hysteria.

"Davey...!" she wailed. She could barely breathe. Her words came out in short chops. "Who would take him? Why? Where is he?"

George could offer no explanation. He could only drive in circles.

* * * *

Sheriff Grady and Inspector Perkins were staring at the file on Charlie Castle when they heard a car skid to a halt outside their office. George and Margaret spilled through the doorway. Margaret ran to the sheriff in a barely controlled frenzy.

"Sheriff. Sheriff! Someone took Davey! They're in a car, a black one, I think. We tried to follow them, but—"

"Mrs. McConnell. Please, calm down. What's happened?" He looked to George, who was only slightly calmer than Margaret.

George quickly explained and the sheriff looked to Perkins. "That's got to be Castle."

Margaret gasped. "What would he want with my son?" She tried to wipe the tears from her eyes. "Why?!" She broke down again, sobbing harder. "Please find him!"

Perkins jotted down notes from George and Margaret while the sheriff called his part-time secretary and dispatcher at home to come to the office. He also called Sheriff Rauber and the offices in the surrounding counties to be on the lookout for Castle and the boy.

"Listen." Grady addressed both Margaret and George. "I need you to be calm. You'll be no help to us if you're hysterical." He stood squarely in front of Margaret and grasped her shoulders. "I will find your son. Count on it."

He stepped back and motioned toward a couple chairs. "My dispatcher will be here soon. Jean will communicate with us and monitor the search efforts from here."

"Sheriff, we have to come with you," George said.

"Out of the question, Sir. The best way to help us is to remain here. If you think of anything else, anything at all, let Jean know and she'll radio the information to us."

Grady fastened his belt, checked his revolver and grabbed a fistful of rounds from the box in his desk drawer, inserting them into the holders on his belt. The sheriff retrieved two of the shotguns from the back room and as he and Perkins were leaving, looked over his shoulder at Margaret.

"I *will* get him back. I promise."

## Chapter Fifteen

CHARLIE CASTLE WHIPPED the black coupe through the streets of Kingsbridge, sliding around rain-soaked turns as he made his way to the edge of town and toward The Grotto. Davey was screaming but his cries were muffled from the trunk, barely audible above the engine noise and the squeal of the tires.

Castle lurched to a stop in the gravel parking lot of the tavern. It was early afternoon and there were only a few other cars present. He flung open the door and sprinted inside. He spotted Brenda and in five strides was across the floor. Brenda was serving a customer a beer at a table next to the pool cue rack and didn't see Castle until he grabbed her by the arm. He spun her around and she dropped the beer on the floor with a shout.

"Hey! Charlie?! What are you doing?"

"Shut up! You're coming with me."

The commotion drew Brenda's uncle out of the back room. He started out from behind the bar but stopped when Castle drew his revolver and aimed it at his head. "Stop right there, old man." The man froze. "Brenda's coming with me. And you're not going to call the sheriff or anyone else, understand?" Brenda's uncle nodded his head slowly, not taking his eyes off Castle's face. There was something odd about it, but he couldn't place it.

Castle jerked Brenda's arm toward him, forcing her to step beside him as they walked out the entrance into the rain. Now pointing his gun at Brenda, he motioned toward the passenger side. "Get in. You're gonna play babysitter for awhile." he growled.

Castle slammed the door shut and Brenda sat still, too shocked to move. In a flash she realized the motor was still running. Charlie was running around the back of the car. She started to slide across the seat but it was too late.

Charlie whipped open the driver side door and forced her back, his gun aimed at her. "Don't even think about it," he growled. He threw the car in gear and popped the clutch violently. The car pitched forward and onto the road, spewing gravel in its wake.

"Charlie! What the hell are you doing? Where are you taking me?" Brenda yelled.

"What did I tell you inside the bar? Just be quiet. I have to think."

Brenda started to say something but Charlie raised his right hand, ready to strike. Brenda remained silent. A minute later they were still headed out of town when Davey started to cry again from the trunk. His screams could be heard faintly and Brenda twisted her head toward the back in horror.

"What have you done?!"

Charlie stared at her as he sped over the concrete. "Do not say another word," he said slowly.

"Charlie!" Brenda shrieked and grabbed the steering wheel pulling it to the right. "Stop right now!"

Charlie wrenched the car back onto the road and slapped Brenda across the face with the back of his hand. "Shut your mouth, I said!"

Brenda fell back into the seat and felt her lip, instantly swollen. She probed her teeth with her tongue and felt one of them give a little. Her eyes filled with tears and she wiped them away, staring straight ahead as the trees rushed by.

As Brenda cried softly, Castle sped west on 408 through Mt. Morris. An idea was forming and he made another sharp right onto the road leading to the dam construction site. He knew that with all the rain in the past days and weeks, construction on the massive dam had been suspended. Nobody would be at the site until it stopped raining and the steep cliffs dried somewhat.

Castle sped up when he saw the locked chain link gate stretched across the road. The padlock and chain yielded instantly to the mass and speed of the Hudson, and Castle drove on until he reached a small parking area at the top of the cliffs.

Both Davey and Brenda were quiet as Castle opened his door and got out. He ducked back in and looked at his frightened passenger. "Don't move," he snarled.

Castle walked to the edge of the parking lot and peered over the fence. Almost three hundred feet below, the engorged river was spilling past the cofferdam. The giant corrugated steel cylinders were waiting for more concrete to be poured, but the rain had delayed construction. The water churned in front of the cofferdam as it raced northward.

He traced the switchback roadway carved into the side of the cliff with his eyes and spotted a small construction shed at the bottom.

He ran back to the car and got in. Brenda was shaking, afraid of what Castle would do next. *Why was there a child in the trunk? Who was it? Will I survive the day?*

Castle eased the car down the roadway, carefully

negotiating the muddy hairpin turns. Brenda's hands clenched the door handle until they finally made it to the bottom. Castle drove to the shed and stopped. "Get out and get that kid out of there."

Castle found the construction shed's door locked but quickly kicked it in. Brenda had Davey in her arms as he motioned her toward him. She was horrified to recognize who Charlie had kidnapped. *Oh my God. What is he doing with Larry's son?*

He waved her up the steps with his gun and followed her in. Inside was a desk and chair, shelving with rolled up blueprints, a drafting table and stool, and a dirty couch. There was an overhead light and lamps on the desks.

"Put him on the couch," Castle said. "Make sure he stays quiet. And no lights." Brenda obeyed and he went to the desk, pulling open the center drawer. He drew a piece of paper out and took a pencil from the coffee mug under the lamp. He began to write, then scratched it out, finally crumpling the paper and shoving it aside. He took another sheet of paper out and scrawled several lines on it.

He folded the paper several times and stuffed it in an envelope, folding over the flap and sealing it. He looked to Brenda who had laid Davey down on the couch. The boy's eyes were wide, but he remained still. "Come here," Castle said.

She got up slowly and walked across the small structure. Davey whimpered and she paused. She turned to him and put her finger to her mouth. "Shh…"

When she reached Castle, he thrust the envelope at her. "Take this to Larry's widow. Don't open it. Just deliver it and come back. Grab some food and beer from your house first, but don't make any other stops. If you're not back in two hours, I will hunt you down and kill you. Remember how Slim screamed as I stuck my knife in him? That will be you. But before that, I'll do to that kid what I did to his old man."

Brenda took the envelope with quivering hands. She looked back at Davey who was still quiet on the dingy brown sofa. She turned back to Castle as he spoke again with an even tone that chilled her soul.

"That's right. I'll cut his arms and legs off. I'll carve him up into little pieces." He looked past Brenda at Davey and chuckled. "His pudgy little thighs will make good bait for catching bass."

Brenda stared at Castle, unable to look away from such evil. Something didn't look right. Something on his upper lip, through the stubble. It didn't look natural.

"What are you waiting for? Get going. Remember what I said. Deliver the letter, find out if she's playing ball and get back here right away." Brenda turned toward the door and glanced at Davey as Castle spoke again. "And for his sake, he better stay quiet."

\* \* \* \*

George and Margaret were pacing in the sheriff's office when his secretary Jean entered. She greeted them and immediately went to her desk to monitor the radio.

"It's been quiet," George said, motioning to the radio set.

Jean looked up at them. "Why don't I make us some coffee."

"Um, yeah, that would be fine," George said absently. He watched Margaret walking aimlessly around the small office and finally went to her. He touched her arm lightly and she jumped.

"Margaret, this is all my fault. I am so sorry. I never should have left Davey. He was sleeping so soundly..."

George's voice trailed off and he slumped into a chair, covering his eyes with his hand.

Margaret knelt beside him. "Just tell me they'll find him," she said softly.

Before George could answer, Jean interjected. "Sheriff Grady and the others are the best. He'll find your little boy. Don't you worry." She smiled warmly. "Now give me just a few minutes and I'll have some coffee brewing."

Margaret stood and touched George's shoulder, squeezing gently. George looked up, unable to say anything. Although he never felt responsible for his wife's and son's death, he experienced tremendous guilt over it. *But I'm directly responsible for Davey's disappearance. If he isn't found, or worse—.*

"George," Margaret said. "I'm going to call Fran. I want her here."

George nodded. "Of course," he whispered.

"May I use the telephone?" Margaret asked, walking slowly towards Paula's desk. "I want to call my next door neighbor."

"Of course, hon. Call whoever you need to. Use the phone on the right side of the sheriff's desk."

Margaret dialed Fran's number and after a few seconds, the call connected. Margaret tried to tell her what had happened, but couldn't choke the words out. Jean came over and took the phone from her and explained. "Why don't you come down to the sheriff's office? I think your friend could use you about now." She turned to Margaret as she hung up. "She'll be here right away."

The radio squawked and Jean hurried to her desk, picking up the microphone. Sheriff Grady's voice came through the speaker. "Jean, Grady here, come in please."

"Go ahead, Sheriff."

"Nothing yet. Perkins and I are headed over to Mrs. McConnell's house to see if we can find any evidence."

"Okay, Sheriff—I mean, 10-4."

She put the mic down and smiled at George and Margaret. "We just started using these new ten-codes and I'm just not in the habit yet." She got up and reached for the coffee pot and some mugs. "Now then, how do you take your coffee?"

\* \* \* \*

"I don't know how much more I can take," Margaret said, her voice breaking. She looked at George as he set his coffee cup down. "Why haven't they found him yet?"

"They're doing everything they can. You heard Jean calling the FBI's field office in Buffalo, right? Between Sheriff Grady and that Perkins fellow, plus the other deputies and the surrounding county sheriffs, and now the FBI, they'll find him. I'm confident." George lowered his voice. "Again, Margaret, I can't even begin to tell you —"

The front door to the sheriff's office burst open and Fran ran in, making a beeline to her friend. "Oh Margaret, I'm so sorry." Fran wrapped her arms around Margaret, pulling her close. After a moment, she smoothed Margaret's hair and stood back slightly, looking at her face. She wiped the tears from Margaret's cheeks and from her own eyes as well. "I'm here. Everything's going to be all right."

"I'll die if anything happens to him," Margaret said, trying to blink back a new wave of tears.

"Now c'mon. Don't talk like that, dear. They'll find him. You must stay strong." Fran hugged her again and stepped back. "Now I went ahead and called Irene. I talked with her secretary and she was actually conducting a reading or something in Geneseo. She's dropping everything and is racing here as we speak. I know you've grown quite fond of her and she may be of some help too."

"Help? What could she..."

"Well, she seems to know a lot about this whatchamacallit that's been haunting your house. Don't you worry, she'll be here soon."

"Oh my god," Margaret gasped. "I'd forgotten all about that hideous creature." Her voice started to rise, the hysteria returning. "George! Didn't Irene say something about it transforming at night into that monster?"

George sputtered a bit before he spoke. "I think so, but let's not get carried away. I think what we're dealing with is just a human being. Evil, I will admit, but still completely human."

"You were there!" Margaret exclaimed. "You saw the carvings on the dresser, you saw the shell of that black egg. That's not normal. That's not human!"

George took a step toward Margaret. "I'm just trying to be rational about all this. Irene can spin a tale and, I must say, it sounds somewhat plausible, but I'm still not convinced that we're dealing with some supernatural demon."

Margaret sighed and looked at George and Fran. "I just don't know what to think anymore," she said in a voice barely above a whisper.

Fran gave Margaret a quick hug. "It will be okay. They'll find—"

The phone rang at Jean's desk, startling Margaret. Jean answered and took notes for a minute, thanked the caller and hung up. She turned around and reached for the radio set.

"Was that the sheriff? Did they find Davey?" Margaret asked quickly.

"No," Jean said. "I do have to call the sheriff though. He'll want to know this." She turned back to the microphone and called for Grady. "Sheriff Grady, Sheriff Grady, this is Jean. Come in please."

After a moment of static, Grady's voice came through the radio. "Go ahead."

"Sheriff, I just a got a call from Roy Singer at the Grotto. He said that Charlie Castle just came in and practically dragged his niece Brenda out of there by her hair. Roy tried to stop him, but Castle drew a gun on him."

"I don't suppose he had the McConnell boy with him?"

"Not that Roy could see."

"Did he notice where he went?"

"Roy said he was headed toward Mt. Morris in a dark Hudson."

"Got it. Thanks. Listen, I'll be stopping in soon. Ted wants to make some calls to Albany, get some more help here. I'm less than five minutes away."

"Ten-four." Jean put the microphone down and looked at Margaret. "We're doing everything we can, Mrs. McConnell. I hope you know that."

\* \* \* \*

Only as Brenda drove north from Mt. Morris towards Kingsbridge did her adrenaline rush finally level out. At first she was going to do exactly as Castle had instructed. She was terrified of what he would do to her if she disobeyed. Of what he would do to Larry's son.

She had always been jealous of Margaret, especially when she gave birth to Davey. Brenda deserved to be the mother of Larry's child. Margaret was so...weak. She couldn't make Larry happy like Brenda thought she could, and eventually did.

Brenda entered the town of Kingsbridge and drove past the sheriff's substation. She continued on in the direction of Margaret's house, ready to deliver the note. The closer she got, however, the more she realized how easily manipulated Larry had really been. How easily he been seduced by her once she set her sights on him. He had actually been a good husband to Margaret until he had started coming by The Grotto once in awhile after work and Brenda began flirting with him.

Brenda pulled to a stop in front of Margaret's house and looked at the note on the seat beside her. How much of this whole thing was actually her fault, she wondered. She had convinced Larry to sleep with her, to steal the money from the cannery, and to leave Margaret for her.

After a moment, Brenda pulled into Margaret's driveway and put the car into reverse. She backed out and drove back the way she came. For once, she would do the right thing. She would try to put right every evil that she had caused.

Brenda came to a stop in front of the sheriff's office behind a dark green Packard and took a deep breath. She grabbed Castle's note and walked inside. As she shut the door beside her, everyone in the room turned and looked at her.

Sheriff Grady was at his desk with another man, talking with his secretary. She recognized Margaret, of course, and her neighbor, Fran. Margaret was standing next to a handsome fellow and they had been talking with an older woman who was holding a cat, of all things.

The sheriff stood from his desk and walked toward her. "Brenda! Are you all right? Jean just received a call from your uncle that you were practically kidnapped by

Charlie Castle."

"I'm fine," she answered. "He didn't hurt me. Too badly." Brenda looked tentatively toward Margaret, then back to the sheriff. She held the note out, her hands trembling. "I'm supposed to give this to Mrs. McConnell."

At that, Margaret rushed toward Brenda, snatching the envelope from her hand. She tore out the note and read it quickly, then looked to Brenda. "What is he talking about? What money? How am I supposed to get eleven thousand dollars to him in just a few hours? I don't have that kind of money!"

Sheriff Grady took the note gently from Margaret and read it. "Perkins, take a look. I think it's a good thing we've called Hoover's boys in for this."

## Chapter Sixteen

CHARLIE PACED IN THE foreman's shed while the rain pelted the metal roof and streaked down the windows. It was getting later in the afternoon and although it couldn't be seen through the thick clouds, the sun was drifting in its arc to the horizon. Davey had squawked a little after Brenda left but was quiet for now.

Charlie was so focused on the ransom money he would soon collect that the sharp pain in his belly startled him. He came to a stop and frowned. Something had happened in that little brat's bedroom but he couldn't remember what. It was the damnedest thing. He had opened a drawer and found...what? That's right, he vaguely recalled spotting a smooth black stone, polished like a river rock. And then...nothing. His next memory was waking up in his apartment, his clothes soaked with sweat.

There was a foul taste in his mouth then and he tasted it again just now as his stomach fluttered. What was happening to him? There it was again. It felt like he had swallowed charcoal or something. He had a strange, gritty feel in his mouth. He also sensed a new strength and awareness that he had never experienced before.

He looked at the clock on the foreman's desk. It was approaching 3:30 and Brenda should be back soon. Then the short wait begins and soon he would be well over ten thousand bucks richer and on his way to Las Vegas. The city was building casino after casino and he wanted some of the action. He had no reason to keep Brenda or the kid alive, of course, and he smirked a little at the thought of killing them both.

*How will I do it? Something different. I could tie them up in here and set the trailer on fire. I've never burned someone alive. That would be new.* He peered out the window and saw tanks of diesel fuel in the distance. Perfect, he thought.

As soon as that traitorous bitch returned and confirmed that the note was delivered and the grieving widow was going to cooperate, he would tie her and precious Davey up, splash some fuel around and strike the match. Ooh, not so fast, he thought. Maybe one last roll in the hay with her. Or Margaret. She needed to be with a real man, he thought.

His pants tightened as he imagined ripping her blouse off and—there it was again. His stomach turning summersaults. Now his shoulders ached. What was going on?

Charlie shook his head and re-focused on the real prize. The money. Ten thousand dollars that he would parlay into fifty thousand, and fifty into a hundred. There was no stopping him now, he thought. He looked outside again, this time towards the foot of the dam that had just gotten underway. Burning Davey and Brenda alive certainly had its merits, but drowning them in the raging river would be fun, too.

He had heard that during construction of the Boulder Dam, or Hoover Dam, or whatever the hell they were calling it now, some workers had fallen to their deaths from the scaffolding. And their bodies were just left there, cemented over. It was too difficult to retrieve their bodies, so construction just carried on. Castle wondered if he could do something like that with them. No, as much as that excited him, he simply wouldn't have the time. Grady and his boys would be after him and he would have to get out of the area as quickly as possible.

Charlie pictured himself counting all that money. He would take a train to Las Vegas, but he would first drive to Cleveland or even Chicago. He couldn't take the risk of going to a train station in Rochester or Buffalo. Too much heat. He could grab a New York Central or Pennsylvania train in Cleveland and take it to Chicago or St. Louis, and head west from there. Just be patient another couple days, he thought, and you'll be richer than you ever dreamed, and away from all this scrutiny.

Davey rolled over on the dusty couch and looked up. "Where's Mommy?" he said in a thin voice.

"Shut up," Charlie growled. Was there any reason not to kill the kid right now? The last thing he wanted was Davey crying or screaming. Nothing worse than a hollering kid, he thought, as he moved closer to the boy.

Charlie stopped in front of the sofa and realized that he had to keep him alive at least until Brenda came back. Find out if Larry'w widow was bringing the dough and then have some fun with Brenda. *Once I have the money, I'll kill 'em all.*

\* \* \* \*

The sounds of ringing phones and squawking radios ricocheted through Sheriff Grady's office while Margaret and George sat numbly in their chairs, being comforted by Fran and Irene. Brenda had told the sheriff that Charlie was hiding out with Davey at the site of the new dam in Mt. Morris. Jean was coordinating with the other deputies and sheriffs from the surrounding counties on the radio while Perkins called the State Police barracks in Geneseo and Warsaw for reinforcements. They had a short window of time before Brenda was expected back at the construction shed and needed as many men as possible to converge on the site.

The ransom note demanded that Margaret bring the eleven thousand dollars that Larry had squirreled away in her house by nightfall to the dam, just a couple hours from now. Failing to show up, or coming without the money, or going to the police, would end Davey's life immediately.

The sheriff and Ted Perkins were gathering up all the weaponry from the office when Irene approached them. "Gentlemen, please give me a few minutes to tell you exactly what you're dealing with."

"Ma'am, I appreciate you supporting Mrs. McConnell, but this is a police matter now," Grady said. He wasn't short with her, but made it clear that he was in charge and didn't need civilian interference.

"Sheriff and Investigator Perkins," Irene said only slightly perturbed. "Give me your undivided attention for just one minute and you will have a good chance of returning with Margaret's son, and your lives."

Grady sighed and nodded to Perkins. "Fine, go ahead."

Irene took a breath and began. "You are no longer dealing with your deputy." She looked at the clock. "For the next two hours, he will maintain the appearance of Deputy Castle as you knew him. If you capture him before sunset, you can perform a ritual to rid him of the evil, an exorcism of sorts. But when darkness comes, he will transform. He is an *aswang* and I do not have the time to fully detail what that means. In brief, it is a monstrous creature originating in the Philippines. Come nightfall, your deputy will be taken over by the evil residing in him. He will mutate into a demon of unimaginable power and evil."

"Okay, Miss Adler," the sheriff said, interrupting her. "We don't have time for fairy tales. Come on, Ted, let's get going."

"Sheriff Grady," said George, rising from his seat. "I didn't believe at first either, but based on what has been happening at Mrs. McConnell's house over the last several days, I think you should at least hear her out."

Grady looked at his watch. "Make it quick." He nodded at Margaret. "Her son's life is at stake."

Irene looked between Grady and Perkins. "I can't tell you exactly what he will change into, but most likely its skin will darken and its hair will become long and wiry. It will grow long, sharp claws and wings. It has the power of flight once fully transformed."

Grady started to interject but Perkins touched him lightly on the arm and indicated for Irene to continue.

"Know that once the mutation is complete, you are not dealing with your deputy at all. This creature cannot be reasoned with or threatened. You can only attempt to exorcise it or kill it."

"How do we kill it?" Perkins asked.

"One way—a knife thrust into the exact center of its back. Your guns will slow it, but as long as it can reach its wounds, either with its fingers or tongue, it will use its saliva to heal. A knife wound in the middle of its back is unreachable, and only then will the *aswang* die.

"If you are successful, there are specific protocols to follow to dispose of its body. If you do not stop it and do not follow the directions fully in getting rid of it, it will continue to breed. Its species is near extinction but it has a very strong survival instinct."

Grady rolled his eyes. "Thank you very much, Miss Adler. I'll keep everything you said in mind when capturing my former deputy." He turned quickly to Perkins. "Let's go."

\* \* \* \*

Sheriff Grady and Investigator Perkins loaded their weapons and ammunition in the sheriff's patrol car and pulled out of the small parking lot onto the wet asphalt. After they left the city limits, Grady mashed the accelerator down and the heavy cruiser built up speed.

"You don't put much stock in what that Adler woman had to say, do you?" Perkins asked.

Grady glanced at him and smirked. "Do you?" He shook his head. "Ted, you're a smart guy. College educated, even. I'm surprised she was able to take you in like that." He paused. "When this is all over are you going to have her read your palm or see what the tea leaves say about you?"

"Don't be so quick to dismiss her. Especially when you consider what Mr. Carmichael said. He struck me as a pretty level-headed guy. And earlier I heard her mention something about a professor she'd been working with."

"I'm just surprised at you," Grady said with a laugh.

"Hey, I bet there's all sorts of creatures that science hasn't discovered yet. Take mountain gorillas in Africa. They weren't known until the turn of the century. Less than fifty years ago. And even our own Lake Champlain has its monster."

"Champ? Oh, please. The best explanation for that supposed sea monster is a hoax or simply someone mis-identifying a known creature. An eel, or a large sturgeon, something like that."

"Well, there have been dozens of sightings over the years, as far back as the Iroquois Indians."

Grady eased up on the gas as he approached a curve in the road. "I can't believe we're even discussing this seriously, Ted. Do you know how many motels and diners use that sea serpent as their mascot? I've been fishing up there dozens of times. I take 'Champ's Ferry' from Plattsburgh to Burlington. They have a big green sea monster painted on the boat. It's all a money-making scheme. The tourists flock to the lake every summer trying to get a glimpse of the thing and every time a log floats by everyone goes nuts." He straightened the wheel and sped up. "The biggest thing I've ever seen in that lake? The seventeen pound pike I took out of there last year!"

The rain pounded harder and the wipers were fighting to keep the windshield clear. Ted took a cigar from his pocket and used his knife to clip the end off. "How much farther?" he asked between puffs as he lit up.

"Ten minutes. I'd get us there quicker if it wasn't raining so hard."

"Who's meeting us?"

"I've got four of my deputies who are probably there already and three more on the way. Sheriff Rauber's bringing his dogs and three men from Wyoming County. Sheriff Gill is sending two from Allegany County but they might be a little late to the party. It's kind of far for them. What were you able to line up?"

"I rang up Sergeant Michaels in Warsaw. Good man. He's on his way with three troopers. I also called the superintendent and he's authorized additional manpower from other barracks if we need them."

"You called Gaffney himself?" Grady whistled. "Don't you rank?"

Ted chuckled and took another puff on his cigar, blowing a thin stream of smoke out between his lips.

"Don't forget the FBI. Your girl Friday got on the horn to them, right?"

"Yeah, Jean's really the one in charge around here. She called their Buffalo office, I think. Heck, maybe she called Hoover! In any case, she's calling them back with directions to the dam site."

Grady slowed as he saw a group of police cars at the turn off to the construction site. He looked at Perkins who had his knife out again and was trimming a stray piece of tobacco from the head of the cigar. "Hope that thing's sharp enough to kill the beast."

"Go ahead and laugh, Jim. If I see your deputy start to fly, forget the gun. I'm flinging this at him. I'm a pretty good knife thrower."

"I'll remember that the next time we play mumblety-peg."

\* \* \* \*

"Margaret," George said quietly so Jean couldn't hear him. Fran and Irene were sitting several feet away and were engaged in their own conversation. "Can you give me directions to this dam they're talking about?"

Margaret's eyes widened. "What are you going to do?" she whispered. "You heard the sheriff. He didn't sound like he wanted any of our help, although I hate just sitting here. I feel so useless"

"This is all my fault," George replied. "I have to do something. I'll never forgive myself if I don't. Now I don't know exactly where he is, but say Davey is wandering around that construction site. He may hide and not come out if strangers are calling him. Hey may come out if he hears my voice."

Margaret nodded, tears forming again in her eyes. She took George's hands in hers. "When you first told me about your wife and Ian being killed in the war, I couldn't imagine how it would be to lose a child. Now I can and I don't think I'm strong enough to survive it. Please get my son."

George withdrew his hands and wiped his own tears away. He reached out to her and squeezed her shoulder. He nodded and slowly, hesitantly, drew her in. Margaret pressed her cheek against his chest and quietly sobbed. He held her close and after a minute they stepped back. She spoke just above a whisper, giving George directions to the construction site.

Without saying a word, George left the sheriff's station and got in Margaret's car. Heading south toward Mt. Morris, he fought to keep the car on the road. The driving rain made it almost impossible to see the shoulder and twice he slipped off the asphalt. He slowed when he saw dozens of blinking lights in the distance through the rain.

George pulled onto the shoulder of the road and turned the car off. As he started to get out of the car a state trooper appeared at the driver's window. George lowered the window a crack so he could hear the trooper. "Sir, you have to either keep going or turn around. There's no stopping here, I'm afraid. We have a situation at the dam."

George looked at the unflagging expression on the trooper's face and the rain dripping off his campaign hat. He decided to stretch the truth a little and opened the window wider, speaking up so the trooper could hear him.

"I'm working with Investigator Perkins. He's expecting me."

The uniformed trooper stepped back and turned his head toward a large group of men standing outside their cars. "Oh, I see. Go ahead then. You'll find him over there."

George rolled the window up and jogged to the men conferring at the entrance to the dam site. Most ignored him, but Sheriff Grady stepped forward to meet him with an angry face. "Mr. Carmichael, I thought I made it clear at the office that this is a police matter. That crystal ball gazer seemed to get the message. You need to go back. Now."

"Sheriff, I'm responsible for this mess. I promise I won't get in your way. Whatever you're planning, I'll stay well behind. But I may be of some help. Davey knows me. He might come to me if he's hidden away somewhere or wandering around lost."

Grady started to interrupt but considered the last part of what George said. "Okay, but I don't want to see you. In a few minutes, we're going to head down the road toward the dam on foot. No sense in Castle seeing a parade of cop cars swarming in. When we get about halfway down, we get off the road and into the woods. You stay well back of us, understand?"

George nodded in agreement.

"When I need you, I'll call for you or wave you up. Got it?"

"Yes sir. Thank you, Sheriff."

Grady moved back to the growing crowd of fellow lawmen. He and Perkins gave orders as to how they would proceed down the steeply inclined road and then through the trees. Two of Sheriff Rauber's men stayed behind with the dogs, to be called up if needed. They all checked their weapons and quieted their radios, then moved out silently.

Ten minutes later they came to a bend in the road and Grady held his hand up. Everyone stopped as he turned to face them. He motioned for half of them to take to the left side of the road and the other half the right. They crept into the woods. George was about thirty yards behind the rest of them and he took to the right side, following the sheriff.

Once in the woods the rain didn't come as hard but it was much darker. Mosquitoes and gnats swarmed in front of George's face and he tried unsuccessfully to wave them away. Footfalls were virtually silent on the wet ground as the assorted group of twenty state police and deputies advanced on the construction shed.

George tried to be careful and walk slowly, but he tripped over a root and landed on all fours, slapping the wet ground with his hands. The ten or so lawmen ahead of him froze and whirled around, staring at him as he crept to his feet. They continued on down the steep hill, making their way between the trees and muddy hollows.

The trees began to thin as they approached the construction clearing and all the men instinctively knelt closer to the ground as they moved ahead. The white shed was now in site through the trees and Grady raised his hand to halt his men. He motioned to Perkins who was a few yards to his right. He moved quickly and quietly to Grady's position.

They both studied the corrugated metal shed. It was elevated and a set of wooden steps led to the door. The shed was located about twenty feet from the edge of the drop off that led to the river. Normally it was a thirty foot drop to the water, but the swollen river was now only ten feet down.

Four large cofferdams were in place and stretched almost halfway to the west side of the river. Concrete had been poured in the nearest two and the rough shape of the dam's base was soon to be apparent. The brown water boiled violently around the cofferdams as it tried to race its way past the constriction.

Grady motioned to Sheriff Rauber who had advanced to a parallel position on the left side of the roadway. He would lead his men to the rear of the shed while Grady and Perkins and the others would make their way as quickly as possible across an open area in front of the shed to some construction equipment. If they made it unseen, they would be closer and still behind cover.

Before the sheriff gave the signal, Perkins showed his watch to Grady. "It's almost sunset, we better hope this gets wrapped up quickly."

"Oh c'mon, Ted," he said. "Not this monster crap again."

"No, it's not that. Well, not completely. But these cliffs are going to block out whatever light we have very quickly."

"Agreed." He turned to the shed and then looked across the road to Rauber. He was about to motion Rauber forward when Perkins grabbed his arm.

"Look!" Ted said, pointing to the shed.

Castle had just emerged from the door and was standing on the small landing at the top of the steps smoking a cigarette.

Ted hoisted his rifle up and waved the barrel toward Castle. "I can hit him easily from here," he whispered.

"No. There's no sign of the boy. If we kill Castle and he's got Davey squirreled away somewhere we may never find him."

"Who said anything about killing him?" Perkins said with a wry smile.

"It's too risky," Grady responded. "The boy could be just inside behind the wall. A miss could send that round through the metal."

They watched as Castle drew on his cigarette. The waves and turbulence in the river were loud, but not loud enough to drown out the sudden blast of static from a police radio across the road. Everyone looked to one of Rauber's men who was fumbling with the controls of his two-way radio. In one movement, Castle's eyes darted into the woods and he ran back inside the shed.

"Shit! Let's move!" Grady cried, a surprise advance now spoiled. Grady and Perkins were closest to the clearing, but still had twenty feet of trees to navigate through and another sixty feet before they would be at the shed. Everyone rushed as best they could toward the construction site.

An instant later Castle reappeared at the door of the shed, but he was not alone. He had a squirming and crying Davey McConnell wrapped up in his left arm. He had the boy positioned to block the possibility of a body shot from one of the lawmen. In his right hand he held his revolver, which he slowly brought up to Davey's head as he moved down the steps.

Grady and his men ran out of the woods but stopped when they saw Castle with Davey. George ran through a few seconds later but noticed that it wasn't much lighter in the clearing than it was in the woods. The diffused, overcast light was dimming. And he picked up a faint *tik-tik* noise coming from Castle. Was it Davey making that sound? Maybe it was something on Davey's or Castle's clothes that was rattling as the little boy squirmed. No, he was quite sure it was coming from Castle's partly open mouth.

Sheriff Grady and the others were formed in a loose semi-circle around Castle as they took one step at a time toward him. Most had their guns drawn. Perkins had his rifle at the ready.

Castle had reached the bottom of the steps and was moving away from the men. Walking backward toward the river.

Grady was about to call to him to surrender when they witnessed the unexpected. Castle lowered his weapon and opened his hand slowly. After a moment, the gun dropped to the ground.

## Chapter Seventeen

IN SHERIFF GRADY'S office, Margaret paced while Jean brewed another pot of coffee and monitored the radio. Fran and Irene talked quietly and encouraged Margaret to sit with them. She was too nervous to sit. Whenever the phone rang or the radio barked, she jumped. Jean handed her a cup of coffee which she took in her hands, cupping them around the mug. Margaret felt cold and shivered slightly, either from fright or the cold rain falling outside, or both.

"Irene," Margaret asked, stopping in front of them. "This creature, the *aswang*, what is it exactly? You mentioned that it can be driven out of a person through a ritual…a what did you call it?"

Irene gestured to the open chair beside Fran, and Margaret sat down after a moment. "It's a kind of exorcism," she said. "People often attribute exorcism to Roman Catholicism, but most all major religions have a form of it within their doctrines."

"Exorcism?" Margaret said.

"I asked Father Peterson about it once, but he said he wasn't trained in it," Fran interjected.

"In Catholicism," Irene continued, "exorcism is a

formal rite performed by a specially qualified priest who invokes the word of God, specifically Jesus Christ. Judaism has its own form of exorcism, as does Hinduism and Islam. In all cases it is a formalized series of steps that, if successful, drives out the demon that has taken possession of the person.

"In the case of the *aswang*, this is a spirit that does not fit neatly into the major religions with which people are familiar. Filipino folklore is varied and goes back well before the introduction of Christianity to the islands in the 1500's. The *aswang* is actually a group of creatures ranging from ghouls and vampires, werewolves and demons. The particular *aswang* we are dealing with is more along the lines of a vampire. Remember, however, that each area and province of the Philippines has its own take on these mythological creatures."

Margaret spoke up. "Mythological? Wait, I'm confused. Is this thing real or not? "

"For hundreds of years stories of these creatures were part of the Filipino folklore, carried on mostly as part of an oral tradition and often used as a way to simply get children to behave. Similar to the 'boogie man' here in the United States. Only in the last few decades have anthropologists such as Dr. Hughes begun to study the mythologies of the Philippines.

"In their studies, they have discovered that, yes, the vast majority of sightings and stories throughout the islands are just that. Stories. Nothing more. They are the continuation of the myths. But a handful of the cases have turned out to be, well, true. It's as if one or two of the gods of ancient Greek myth actually existed."

Margaret sipped her coffee and shuddered. "I just can't imagine what my boy is going through." Her voice caught and she bent forward in the chair, almost dropping her cup. Fran grabbed it and Margaret brought her hands to her face, quiet sobs wracking her body.

Fran touched her gently on the shoulder. "It'll be okay, dear," she said. "The sheriff has two dozen men with him and George is there too, remember."

Margaret swept her red hair back behind her ears. She placed her palms firmly on her legs and smoothed out her dress. She was determined to get through this madness.

\* \* \* \*

Rain continued to pour down in sheets from the dark sky, forming large, muddy puddles in the clearing at the dam site. Charlie Castle held Davey close to him and continued to back up toward the raging water. His eyes darted from deputy to deputy, trooper to trooper. He was initially scared, not sure if he could escape, but the flips he felt in his belly turned to fire. He wasn't sure what was happening, but he could feel raw power coursing through his body.

The skin around his shoulder blades drew tight and he lifted his free hand up to his face. It was getting darker but he found that he had excellent vision. His nails had grown. How is this possible, he thought. *They looked like claws, talons almost. Interesting.*

He knew the deputies wouldn't attempt a shot at him but he was growing tired of Davey's incessant crying and squirming. He felt a hunger and looked at the boy. Castle wondered what human flesh tasted like for he was suddenly aware that besides escape, he wanted nothing more than to feast on this wriggling twenty-five pound mass of fat and muscle.

Castle stuck his tongue out briefly for it felt different, longer, sharper. At the same time, he felt a sharp pain in his upper back and heard his shirt ripping. His short hair grew longer and fell into his face. He tossed it back and looked with amusement at the lawmen arrayed before him.

Castle sensed a weight on his shoulders, drawing him back slightly. "What the hell?" he heard one of the deputies say. He saw a man with a rifle taking aim at him but he adjusted the boy's body slightly to block the shot. Castle uncoiled his tongue again, this time brushing it against Davey's face. Oh yes, he thought, I must devour this, gorge on it. *I'll have to fly away to do it though.* Wait, he wondered, why did I think that? He realized at that moment that he had the power of flight. He sensed a great number of powers that he now possessed. But they all had to be fed with human flesh, young human flesh.

\* \* \* \*

Perkins' eyes grew wide as the transformation of Charlie Castle began. When the wings began to unfold, he brought his rifle to his shoulder. But Castle turned slightly, obscuring most of his body with Davey's. Castle's tongue flicked out and touched Davey's face. His tongue penetrated Davey's cheek, drawing blood. The boy screamed. Perkins looked around and saw that most of the men were transfixed on what was happening to Castle, unsure of what to do.

He looked to Grady who had his revolver aimed at Castle as he stepped slowly toward him. Perkins and the others followed suit, steadily advancing on him. It was just too dark and Davey was moving around too much to risk a shot. Castle held Davey with one hand that seemed to have grown sharp claws, which were now clenched around his small body.

"Castle!" Grady shouted, startling everyone. "Drop the boy."

As the men drew closer, most of them could hear a

faint *tik-tik* sound coming from Castle, or whatever Castle was morphing into. Strangely, as they moved forward the sound faded. A vicious smile spread across Castle's face and his tongue scraped across Davey's face again. As Davey shrieked, Castle spread his wings and slowly beat them back and forth.

With a little jump and some rapid flapping of his wings, Castle was a foot or two off the ground, landing with a start. He continued to retreat toward the embankment leading to the water. His wings were a dark yellow color, with veins that channeled the rainwater downward.

Perkins realized that, bizarrely, Castle was learning to fly. And that very shortly their chances of rescuing Davey would vanish with this creature once he figured it out. He kept his rifle aimed at Castle, hoping that Davey would wriggle out of his grasp and he could get a clean shot.

Perkins glanced around him again and saw that Mr. Carmichael had come up behind him. "What do you make of it?" he asked.

George looked at him and the creature. "I haven't the foggiest idea. I'm just trying to remember everything Miss Adler told Margaret and me about it." He paused to swat at a mosquito. "Would probably be a whole lot easier if it wasn't holding Davey."

"Yeah, I just don't have a shot that doesn't risk hitting the boy."

They watched as the creature's hair continued to spill out of its head and its wings beat slowly against the rain. The creature turned its head from side to side and took a quick look behind it. Only a few feet separated it from the drop off to the river.

In a flash, the creature jumped up, its wings beating

furiously. It started to gain altitude and turn away from the men.

Perkins took aim and fired, hitting the creature in one of its dangling legs. The demon screeched and loosened its grip on Davey. The lawmen saw the boy drop to the embankment and they rushed to the edge. Perkins aimed again and pulled the trigger, this time hitting one of the creature's wings. It looped in the air, wings flapping violently.

Perkins saw George run past him toward the water's edge. He made a quick decision to try and bring down the demon. There were enough other deputies and troopers tending to Davey. He fired again at the monstrous creature but missed. It was difficult to see his target against the darkening sky but he fired one more time anyway. He caught a glimpse of it flying upriver through the gorge, heading south.

\* \* \* \*

When George arrived at the edge of the bank he was horrified by what he saw. Or rather, by what he didn't see. There was no sign of Davey. A dozen or more men in uniforms were scrambling down the muddy slope searching for the boy. Light was fading fast and he heard Sheriff Grady calling to the other sheriff to get his men down here with the dogs as quick as possible and to bring as many flashlights as they could gather.

George rushed to the edge of the roiling water and yelled over the roar to one of the deputies. "What happened? Where is he?"

The deputy turned to him and pointed downriver. "He fell onto the bank when that, that thing, let him go. Must have rolled down and got swept away by the current." He turned back and clambered along the edge of the river.

George was frantic as he followed in the deputy's footsteps. He slipped numerous times as he made his way downriver and toward the cofferdams. He heard Grady shouting into his radio for some men to get to the bridge in Mt. Morris. It was a long shot and there probably wasn't enough time anyway as the dam site was only a couple miles to the downtown area of the small village.

It was almost completely dark now and the men were now searching mostly by feel along the bank. George watched as one of the state troopers slipped and got caught up in the current. A deputy reached out and grabbed him, holding him fast against the water until two more men could help him out.

The rain was lessening, but still coming down steadily. George took a few steps along the muck and stopped to call Davey's name, positive that the thundering of the water was drowning out his voice.

From behind, George saw lights bobbing up and down, casting long shadows into the river. Two German Shepherds raced past him and along the water's edge. One of the deputies had positioned his car at the edge and turned on the spotlight, illuminating the embankment. Another deputy ran past him calling to his dogs and passing out flashlights.

George heard shouts from downriver. He hurried as best he could but kept slipping in the mud. He finally arrived at the cofferdams and saw several men aiming their flashlights at the base of one of the corrugated steel structures. Thirty feet from the bank was Davey's body, tumbling in the waves against the dam.

* * * *

Margaret jumped when Sheriff Grady's voice crackled through the radio. She ran to Jean's desk as the call was answered.

"Jean, find out how quickly we can get a State Police SCUBA team here. Perkins said they can do water rescues, but he didn't know how close a team was. Then call for an ambulance. Make it two—we may need 'em."

"Ten-four, Sheriff. Stand by."

Margaret spoke up. "What's going on? Have they found Davey?" She was near hysterics as Jean reached for the phone.

Fran and Irene rose and brought her back to her chair. "She'll tell us, Margaret. But let her do her job first," Fran said. "Come on, sit down."

* * * *

"Find a rope or chain!" Grady shouted. "Check the foreman's shed. There's got to be one around here!" He pointed to one of his deputies. "I know I've got one in my car. Get up there as fast as you can."

Three men started up the embankment, fanning out to search the site while another headed up the long drive toward the road. A trooper shined his flashlight through the window of a maintenance shed and spotted a length of rope hanging on the wall. He smashed the glass and crawled through the small opening. He emerged a second later with the rope, cutting his hand and arm on the glass.

"Rope!" he shouted as he ran to Sheriff Grady and the others.

"Give me some light over here!" Grady called, pointing to a steel piling halfway up the embankment. He ran up with the rope and ran it through one of the piling's holes. He cinched the knot tight and slid back down toward the water.

"We don't have time for the rescue team." Grady pointed to several men. "Follow me in, wrap your arm around the rope, form a chain. Let's go!"

The sheriff waded into the rushing water and immediately fell as the waves smashed him against the cofferdam. He came back out and took a few steps away from the dam, upriver. "There's too much turbulence against it," he shouted. "I'll have to angle in."

Grady tried again, several feet away from the cofferdam. The water was fierce but he was able to maintain his balance. Other deputies followed him into the rushing river. Precious seconds ticked by as he made his way to Davey's bruised, limp form.

Waist-high in the water, Grady finally reached the boy. He wrapped his arm around Davey's cold body and hoisted him out of the water. He turned and passed him to the man behind him. Each of the six men in the water did the same until Davey reached the bank. Eager hands grasped him and set him gently on his stomach on a rain jacket one of the troopers had laid on the ground.

The trooper knelt down at Davey's head and tilted the boy's face sideways. He brought up Davey's arms, bending them at the elbows, then placed his own hands on the boy's back. He rocked back and forth several times but with no effect.

George had rushed over and watched in horror as Davey remained lifeless. He looked up at Grady. "Sheriff! This isn't working. When I was in the RAF, I was taught a technique by one of your pilots. Let me try—please!"

Grady tapped the trooper on the shoulder and gestured him to the side. George knelt down and rolled Davey on his back. He directed the trooper to lift the boy's legs slightly. George bent down and covered Davey's mouth with his own, blowing air in while pinching his nose shut. Davey's chest rose but nothing else happened.

George raised up slightly and took another breath, blowing it again into Davey's mouth. Once again, Davey's chest rose. George repeated this three more times with no change.

He moved to the boy's chest and placed three fingers just below the center, pressing down several times. He swiveled back to Davey's mouth and blew rapidly in again.

Finally Davey coughed and spit. His body spasmed. George blew twice more into his mouth and Davey coughed up a spray of water. George turned him on his side as the boy vomited. Davey fought to catch his breath and George sat back, keeping his hand on the little boy's head.

George was surprised to hear applause break out from the crowd around him. Several deputies and troopers patted him on the back.

"Nice job, Carmichael," Perkins said, squeezing his shoulder.

Several more minutes of hard coughing and Davey began to cry. Large tears rolled down his cheeks and George helped him sit up. A deputy had found a blanket in the foreman's shed and handed it to George.

"Let's get you out of those wet clothes, Davey," George said. "There's someone I know who's worried sick about you."

George wrapped Davey tightly in the blanket and they made their way to the patrol car. Grady opened the door as George and Davey got in. "Well done, Limey," Grady said to George with a wink.

* * * *

Twenty minutes later, Sheriff Grady and his men arrived at his office in Kingsbridge. Margaret heard the cars pull up and ran to the door. In the lead car she could make out George in the passenger side opening the door and getting out, a wrapped bundle in his arms.

She gasped when George hurried to her and uncovered Davey's head. New tears welled in her eyes as she reached for her boy, who was still coughing a bit. "Davey!" she cried. "You're alive! You're okay!"

When he saw his mother, Davey cried and flung his arms around her neck. "Mommy!" He buried his head in her shoulder and she looked at George, who was covered in mud and shivering. He touched her gently on the shoulder and simply smiled.

A soaking wet Sheriff Grady came up behind George and greeted Margaret. "Your tenant here is the man of the hour. Without him, we would have—" his voice caught for a moment. He quickly composed himself and continued, "We would have lost your little boy if it wasn't for Mr. Carmichael."

"Don't be so modest, Sheriff. You pulled him out of the river."

Grady's face turned serious. "Mrs. McConnell, your son was dead when I pulled him from the water. I'm as sure of that as I am my own name. Perkins' man was just going through the motions. George breathed life into him." He looked through the door to the warm office. "Now if you'll excuse me, I need to change into some dry clothes."

\* \* \* \*

The sheriff's office was busy with activity as deputies and troopers came and went, calling their respective offices and giving reports. Jean canceled the SCUBA team and the FBI, but Grady wanted the outlying deputies who were en route to meet at his office. Davey was safe but they still had to find Castle, or whoever or whatever he had changed into.

Margaret wouldn't let Davey out of her arms and she and George found a somewhat quiet corner in the office. They were joined by Fran and Irene while George explained what had happened. Someone had handed him a winter coat that he wrapped around himself. When he was done with the story, Fran looked at Margaret who had fresh, happy tears trickling down her face. She made no attempt at wiping them away, but just squeezed Davey harder.

Fran gripped George by the arm. "You're our hero!" she exclaimed.

"Oh, Fran, don't embarrass him," Margaret said with a smirk.

"Honestly, I still feel terrible for allowing this to happen in the first place. I'm just grateful I remembered what one of you Yanks taught me in the war."

Fran and Irene talked and Davey settled down in his mother's lap, the memories of all he had endured already fading. Margaret looked at George and smiled. George shrugged off the coat, no longer feeling cold.

## Chapter Eighteen
## Saturday, June 19

FOR THE FIRST time in days, the sun was shining brightly. Davey was happily playing in the living room while George worked on the broken window. It took a couple trips to the hardware store but he was almost finished with it. Margaret found herself not wanting to leave Davey alone, even as she cleaned up from breakfast. She brought Davey into the kitchen to play while she washed the dishes.

George and Margaret had talked again this morning about having Davey checked out by the doctor, but he seemed fine. Even last night, once he was home and in dry clothes and away from the ruckus at the sheriff's office, he was back to his normal self. After a full night's sleep, it was as if yesterday never happened.

George came into the kitchen to wash his hands, stepping over Davey's toy cars on the floor. Margaret was drying and stacking the dishes. "Window's all fixed," he declared.

"Thank you. That didn't take long."

"It was pretty easy. That carpet by the window is still pretty damp though. Maybe put a fan on it for the day to help dry it out." George paused and Margaret turned to face him. "Margaret, again, I am so sorry for leaving Davey alone. That was an unforgivable lapse of judgment on my part."

Margaret held up her hand. "George, I don't blame you at all. And I don't blame Fran either. Charlie Castle did this. He's the one responsible. You, on the other hand, saved my son's life." She leaned over, placed her hand against his cheek and lightly kissed the other. She stepped past and draped the towel over the sink. George felt his face reddening as she walked out of the room.

\* \* \* \*

Sheriff Grady arrived at his office followed by Perkins. Grady plugged in the percolator and started brewing some coffee. Neither man had gotten much sleep last night and today promised to be just as exhausting as they continued the search for Castle.

They had witnessed firsthand his transformation into the creature, or *aswang*, as Miss Adler had described it. Once George and Margaret had left for home with Davey, Grady gathered more information about the creature from Irene. Several deputies and troopers had returned to the dam site to look for it, but found nothing. The sheriff conceded that searching for it in the dark was probably futile, so he dismissed everyone and returned home to try and get some sleep. They would regroup in the morning.

"Here you go, Ted." Grady handed the investigator a steaming mug. "I probably don't make as good a cup of coffee as Jean, but it'll do."

"Thanks. So if that Adler woman is correct, now that it's daylight, we're back to looking for Charlie Castle, not a flying demon, right?"

"That's what I understand," Grady said.

"Unfortunately, she didn't have any idea how far he, or it, could have flown last night. But she's under the impression that it would stay in this general area. You said you shot it once or twice?"

Perkins nodded. "At least once, I'm sure of it." He took a sip of coffee. "But remember what Miss Adler said about it being able to heal itself, unless it's stabbed dead center in the back. Plus this area has a lot of ground to cover. I guess we should start at the dam site and work outward from there. Good thing most of the boys from last night are able to help out."

Grady started to reply but the phone rang. He picked up the receiver. "Sheriff Grady here." He listened for a moment while Ted took a cigar out of his pocket. "You're sure she's—I understand." He paused. "Of course. I'm very sorry, Mr. Singer. I'll have one of my deputies come out there. Please accept my condolences." He hung up the phone and sighed deeply.

Perkins had struck a match but was waiting to light it, wanting to hear what this latest call was about.

"That was Brenda Singer's uncle. She hanged herself in her garage. Left a note about how she couldn't take the guilt over the McConnell boy's death."

Perkins blew the match out. "But we found him. He's okay, right?"

Grady looked down. "Yeah, but she didn't know that. I had asked Jean last night where Brenda was and she said that she had slipped out of the office sometime during all the commotion. She probably heard some of the radio traffic and figured that Castle had killed the boy."

Perkins thought for a second. "Is there any chance that Castle had something to do with her death? I mean, made it look like a suicide?"

"That's a possibility, but I think Brenda had left the

office sometime after dark. Castle had already turned into that, that thing. I don't think Castle, as the creature, flew to Brenda's house and forced her into a noose. Miss Adler said that once the creature takes over, it lies dormant inside the body during the day and only transforms at night. It's almost like a Jekyll and Hyde type thing. The one version doesn't know what the other is doing."

"So you're saying that the creature would have no reason to seek out Brenda and do any harm to her?"

Grady reached for a toothpick from a shot glass on his desk. "According to Miss Adler, the creature is operating on pure instinct. It needs to eat and reproduce. It feeds on young children or expecting mothers. And apparently if it doesn't find one of its own kind to mate with, it can reproduce on its own with these black egg-like stones." He wedged the toothpick between his teeth and continued. "She called it something. A 'herma' something or other."

"Hermaphrodite?" Perkins suggested.

Grady snapped his fingers. "That's it! How'd you know what it was called?"

"I'm a smart guy, Jim. College educated, remember," he said with a laugh. "And smart enough not to say 'I told you so' too!"

"All right, all right. But I still don't believe there's a sea monster swimming around Lake Champlain."

Perkins struck another match and lit his cigar. They heard other patrol cars arriving in the small parking lot. "Let's hope we can find Castle in the daylight and not have to face that thing again. 'Cause I shot it twice and didn't stop it."

"I'm with you. The good news is that it's stopped raining. Newspaper says we've got three or four days of fair weather ahead."

Perkins nodded as he puffed on his cigar and the two men gathered their weapons and headed out to meet the others.

\* \* \* \*

Charlie Castle woke to the shrill sound of a train whistle. He then heard rushing water. He was lying on the ground below a canopy of thick trees, wet and shivering. He started to sit but felt a sharp pain in his stomach and laid back down. The late morning sun was shining through the leaves and felt warm against his face.

*Where am I? Where's the water coming from?* Dozens of confused thoughts jumbled through his head. He managed to get to a sitting position among the leaves and mud on the forest floor. *The last thing I remember was Grady and his boys closing in. I had the kid in my arms and he was squirming around. I felt hungry, hungry for something I've never eaten before.*

Castle whirled his head around. *Where's the boy? Where's Brenda? Where the hell am I? Nooo! Without the kid, Margaret's not going to give me the money. Damn!*

He stood but his knees buckled and he collapsed. Taking his time, he gathered his strength and slowly rose, grabbing a tree for support. He took a few steps toward the sound of the water. It was loud, a waterfall. He made his way through the trees, finally stopping at the edge of a high cliff. He looked down to see the Upper Falls of the Genesee River raging underneath the Portage Bridge. He squinted into the sky and saw a line of boxcars rolling across the towering steel trestle.

*How in the hell did I get here? I was at the dam in Mt. Morris. That's over fifteen miles upriver from here. Did I get drunk last night?* Confusion held sway in Castle's brain as he struggled to understand and remember what had happened the night before. He felt cold wetness on his shoulders and twisted his shirt around, feeling holes in the back of it. *What the —?*

Suddenly thirst was all he could focus on. His mouth was painfully dry. He thought about trying to make it down to the river to drink, but the cliff was far too steep.

Looking at the bridge and the high falls he got his bearings. Castle realized he was on the east side of the gorge, in a little-used area of the park. If he walked southeast for a mile or two he should come to the main road that leads to Portageville. From there, he could find water, and probably a car to steal.

Another realization hit him as he watched the red Erie Railroad caboose rumble across the bridge above him. His original plan involved getting to Cleveland or Detroit by car, then buying a ticket for a train to Las Vegas. He was sure Grady and his men were still looking for him and stealing yet another car could be risky. Hopping aboard a freight train might help him get out of the area quicker and with far less chance of being seen.

Castle wasn't sure where an eastbound train like the one he just saw was headed, but if he saw a westbound one, it would surely end up in Buffalo or beyond. Perfect, he thought, as he stepped away from the cliff and began the walk toward town. In Portageville he could find water and maybe some food and come up with another plan for getting that money.

Before long, however, his mind was consumed with thoughts of nothing but water. He was so thirsty. Whatever happened last night really sapped his strength. He was deep in the woods, the sounds of the water had faded, and he leaned against an oak tree to catch his breath.

*I'm thirsty, but not dehydrated. More tired than anything. Exhausted actually. So very tired.* Castle slid down the tree, his knees barely able to hold him up. He stretched out his legs with his back against the trunk and quickly fell back asleep.

\* \* \* \*

Grady and Perkins led a convoy of patrol cars to the dam site. Once there, they searched the banks of the river, which was still running high and fast. They found no sign of Castle or the creature. Grady ordered a group of men to drive through the town of Mt. Morris across the river and enter the west side of the park. It would be a tedious search through the forest but at least the morning sun was bright.

One of Sheriff Rauber's deputies and his dog accompanied the west side party while another stayed behind to search the east side of the park. Everyone agreed that heading south through the trees and avoiding the town to the north was the best course of action. Castle would probably be holed up under cover of the forest and the two parties walking south on either side of the deep gorge would have the best chance of finding him.

Sheriff Grady, Perkins, and a handful of deputies and troopers spread out through the woods, maintaining visual contact with each other as they trudged through the still damp forest floor. Perkins was nearest to the edge of the gorge and he could make out park visitors walking along the trail on the west side of the park, almost a mile across the canyon. What would they think when the other deputies arrived on the scene, he thought. *Would they tell the visitors they were searching for a mythical Filipino monster? Probably not.*

Perkins walked to the edge of the tall cliff, noting that the visitors across the gorge were protected from the three hundred foot drop by a low stone wall that his side lacked. He paused and brought his camera to his eye, adjusting the lens focus. The shutter quietly clicked as Grady approached from behind.

"See something, Ted?"

"Uh, no, just snapping a quick picture. Don't know when I'll make it back here. Sorry."

"It is spectacular scenery, I'll give you that." Grady pointed his toothpick at Ted. "But do your sightseeing on your own time." Grady winked to let him know he wasn't too upset with him.

"Ten-four, boss," Perkins said with a smile.

The two men plodded through the dense trees, keeping the others in sight. Perkins turned to the sheriff. "What do you think our chances of finding Castle are?"

"Frankly, I'm not optimistic. There's so much ground to cover and, like we all witnessed last night, the man flies."

"That thing could be anywhere."

"Yeah, the Adler woman didn't have any information as to how far or long these creatures could travel in the air."

Ted drew a cigar from his pocket and sliced the end off. Puffing it to life from a match, he turned to Grady. "How long is this gorge?"

"The gorge is roughly seventeen miles long, extending from Mt. Morris in the north to Portageville at the south end. Letchworth State Park is on both sides of the river that whole distance. The dam is being built here while upriver are the three main waterfalls," he said, pointing south. "They're named, appropriately, the Lower, Middle, and Upper Falls. Above the Upper Falls is an old train bridge that's still in use."

"If the terrain is all like this, we'll never cover that much distance before nightfall."

The sheriff grunted his agreement. "That's even

assuming that Castle, the creature, whatever you want to call it, is still in the park."

"It's the most logical assumption," Ted said, blowing a stream of smoke skyward. "But each day that we come up empty is more area we have to cover as he tries to put more distance between himself and us."

"I know. Good thing everyone is equipped with lots of food and water. I think we're going to be out here all day."

Before Ted could say anything, one of Sheriff Rauber's dogs sounded three loud barks from fifty feet away. A flash of movement erupted from the underbrush and sprinted away from the dog and the men. Deputies and troopers whirled as one, training their guns on the sudden commotion.

"Hold your fire! Hold your fire, everyone!" Rauber's deputy raised his hand and held the dog's leash firm. "Scamp just flushed out a deer is all. Good lookin' one too."

The men resumed their slow walk south. Grady looked at Perkins. "Where's your cigar? What'd you do, eat it?"

"Oh damn. I dropped it when that dog barked."

"Mm-mmm," Grady laughed. "I think you got scared thinking it was the *aswang*."

Ted chuckled as he looked around the ground for his fallen cigar. "Maybe, but that was a good one. Joyce gave me a box of 'em for my birthday last month." He spotted the cigar and picked it up. "Didn't get too dirty," he said, wiping it off with his handkerchief. "And still lit."

Grady shook his head as they continued walking.

\* \* \* \*

The sun was low in the sky and an assortment of mosquitoes and other flying insects were swarming around the various deputies and troopers. Each lawman had exhausted his water supply but continued the trek through the woods until Grady finally called the search over for the day.

"We still need to take some time to hike outward from the gorge and to the road and I don't want to do that in the dark," he told his assembled men. "You've all put in a good, hard day's work, and I appreciate everybody's effort. I've radioed in our approximate position where we'll exit the park onto River Road, and Sheriff Rauber will have a couple cars waiting to take everyone back."

Looking at his compass in the dimming light, he pointed eastward. "We've got about a half mile or so 'til we're out of these woods. It's getting dark, so stay close to one another." He looked around one last time, disappointed they were unable to find Castle. "Let's go."

\* \* \* \*

Jean poured Grady and Perkins a last cup of coffee and said goodbye to the troopers and deputies as they left the small office. "Have a good night," she called. "Drive safe."

She turned to the two men. "Decided not to be heroes and go find that thing now that it's nighttime?"

The sheriff stood a little straighter. "Now wait a minute, we've been—"

"I know, I know. I'm just teasing you. Drink your coffee. I don't want you out at night chasing after that demon thing." She turned to Ted. "You either."

"Yes ma'am," both men said in unison.

Grady looked at his watch. "It's past eight-thirty, why don't we call it a night. I told the others to meet here at seven tomorrow morning, but if you want to come a little early we can work out our alternate strategy for finding Castle. Or at least figure out what areas we want to search. We barely made it through half the park today.

That'll still give you a decent night's sleep."

Perkins yawned. "Sounds good to me." He sipped his coffee and was putting it down when the phone rang.

Jean picked it up on the second ring. "Sheriff's Department, this is Jean." After a moment, she looked up at Grady and Perkins and waved them over. "Wait, say that again." Another pause, and she spoke again. "Your boys are all right, though?" She nodded her head. "Okay, thank you. Yes, I believe you. I'll send Sheriff Grady to check it out."

Jean hung up the phone. "You boys aren't clocking out yet."

"What is it?" Grady asked.

"Two teenagers—brothers—were on the approach to the Portage Bridge, daring each other to cross it, when a train started across from the other side."

"Stupid kids! The trains run slow across the bridge, but someone's going to get killed one of these days," Grady interrupted.

"No, they didn't get hurt from the train. Or hurt at all. But the headlight of the train lit up something on the tracks, in the middle of the bridge. They said it looked like the devil, big wings and everything. As the train moved closer, it flew up and came back down after the train passed. They live in Portageville. That was their mother that called. Said the boys ran all the way home and were scared to death. They think the sound of the train drowned out their running through the woods. But she said that the boys are good kids, and wouldn't lie about something like that, as unbelievable as it sounds."

Grady took a last gulp of his coffee and sighed. "Call Rauber, have him drive to the bridge on his side of the river. We'll drive to it from our side. He'll probably get there before we do, but have him sit tight until we arrive.

Unless he's forced to do something. But that's a long bridge and I don't want him going after this thing alone."

Grady and Perkins were almost out the door when the sheriff turned back to Jean. "Oh, and try and get a hold of the Erie Railroad. I don't want to be two hundred and fifty feet up when one of their freights comes through. See if you can't get them to divert or hold any trains."

They reached the car and got in, pulling out onto the road and heading south. "How did you say your knife-throwing skills were, Ted?"

"Pretty good, I'd say," Perkins replied with a confident smile.

"How many knives do you have?"

Ted's smile faded. "Just the one."

Grady rolled his eyes. "Swell."

**Chapter Nineteen**

GEORGE FROWNED AS he realized that his supply of his favorite English blend of tobacco was almost gone as he was filling his pipe. The after-dinner pipe was his most anticipated of the day and there wasn't much left. He had tried a couple tins of Prince Albert but, although it was popular with the Yanks, he hadn't gotten used to it. He was afraid it might appear too decadent if he had some of his tobacco shipped from England, but perhaps...

"Everything okay, George?" Margaret asked, glancing up from her needlework to adjust the lamp.

"Um, yes. Well, not really. It seems I'm about out of my good tobacco."

"Oh dear. I enjoy that one. I hope you can get some more."

"Yes," George replied with a smile. "I was just thinking how I should splurge and send a wire to my tobacconist in London. See if he can send some via air mail." He lowered his pipe into the pouch a final time to fill it.

George sensed he was being watched as he lit his pipe. He puffed on it quickly, producing great volumes of blue smoke. Finally, he leaned back and blew out a doughnut-shaped smoke ring. Margaret clapped her hands and George nodded his head in appreciation.

"So George," Margaret said, her eyebrows arched. "Did you, by chance, ever apologize to Irene for doubting her about that, that *aswang* creature?"

"I don't think you should be teasing me so," George said with a laugh. "Haven't you heard about the delicate male ego?"

But Margaret persisted playfully. "I mean Irene never once said 'I told you so'. The least you could do is apologize for not believing her."

George pointed the stem of his pipe at her with mock exasperation. "Now see here. We're having a nice evening, we are. Our nice little family—" He stopped himself, not sure what to say. Before he could feel too awkward, Margaret filled the silence.

"It's all right. You've only been here a few weeks, but I feel it, too. It's like you've been a part of our lives forever. And I wish it would last...forever."

George felt his face redden as he smiled. "You know just what to say or do to make me blush, don't you?" He sat up straighter on the sofa, cleared his throat and drew from his pipe. He glanced to the steps leading to the second floor. "It's remarkable how quickly Davey recovered from everything, don't you think?"

"I know you're changing the subject, Mr. Carmichael, and that's okay." Margaret followed his gaze up the stairs where her son was quietly sleeping in her room. "And yes, it's like nothing happened. I feel better with him sleeping in my room, at least for a time. What I'm most surprised about is how there's not a mark on him, especially from when that thing pierced his face with its tongue." She shuddered and closed her eyes.

"Agreed. If I didn't see it myself, I wouldn't have

believed it. Castle, or the demon, or whatever, definitely drew blood. But now there's not even a scab or a scar. But, I've given up trying to explain anything. Maybe when I call Miss Adler to apologize, I'll ask her about it." He winked at Margaret and tamped down the ashes in his pipe.

She smiled but wrapped her arms around her shoulders. "I'm still afraid, George. The sheriff said he would call when they captured Castle, or killed the creature, but he hasn't. I know it's only been a day but that means it's still out there. What if it comes back for Davey?"

George put his pipe down and looked at Margaret, his voice unwavering when he spoke. "I will not let anything happen to Davey, or you. Your family is safe."

Margaret relaxed and her eyes softened. "Our family," she whispered.

\* \* \* \*

Sheriff Grady looked at his watch as they turned onto the dirt road that would lead to the tracks. "It's just after nine o'clock. The road ends next to the rail line and from there it's only a few hundred feet to the trestle. Rauber should be in place." He looked at Perkins and within a few minutes they reached the tracks.

They checked their weapons but before they left the car, Ted asked, "How high up is this bridge again?"

"Roughly two hundred and fifty feet, directly above the Upper Falls. Why? Don't tell me you're afraid of heights?"

"No, no, not at all. How long is it?"

Grady paused and thought. "About eight hundred feet."

Perkins whistled as he stepped out onto the gravel. "Just a thought...what if Jean wasn't able to get the railroad to stop their trains and one comes while we're on the bridge? That's a long way down. Is there enough room for a person and a train on the bridge at the same time?"

Grady smiled. "Only just."

"Swell," Ted replied.

A few minutes of walking on the railroad ties through the woods and they could see in the moonlight the opening ahead where the trestle began.

Grady held his hand up, motioning them to a stop. They peered across the bridge but didn't see anything. He whispered to Perkins. "I hope Rauber doesn't get jumpy and start shooting. We're in his crossfire."

Perkins nodded. "I think he knows that shots might slow it down, but aren't going to stop it. I'm afraid we're going to have to flush it out and take care of it at close range. Good thing I brought the shotgun." He squinted in the dim light down the long bridge. "If it's even here. All I see is the bridge. I can barely make out the other side."

"Nothing to do but start walking."

Both men tensed when they stepped off solid ground and onto the trestle. In the ghostly light of the nearly full moon they could see the terrain fall away below them through the bridge deck with each step. The criss-cross of iron and steel supports cast muted shadows on the ground. The sound of the Upper Falls grew louder as they approached, its water tumbling seventy feet to the rocks below.

"Is that Rauber?" Perkins said in a low voice, pointing to the other side of the bridge.

"I think so. He must have seen us and started across. I don't see wings, so I'm assuming it's not that damned creature."

"This is a lot tougher than it should be without

flashlights, but they'd give us away in a heartbeat."

Grady nodded. "We're probably pretty easy to spot anyway against the sky."

Before long they were almost above the river. Rauber was getting closer from his end. They could see each other more clearly now in the moonlight. It was apparent that Castle or the *aswang* was not on the bridge. Another minute and the three met directly above the river. The rushing water was loud even from this height.

"See anything?" Sheriff Rauber asked.

"Nothing," Grady said, shaking his head.

Perkins leaned against the slender railing and watched the water pour through the cataract and surge north toward the Middle Falls. "Wish I had my camera. It's quite the view, even in the dark."

"Probably a little dark to be shooting pictures, Ted." Grady shook his head. As he did, something caught his eye against the western cliff. The vague shape he noticed suddenly leaped off the rocks toward the river. "There!" he cried, pointing to the gorge wall. The man-shape fell a few feet but its wings beat powerfully to overcome gravity and it gained altitude.

The men watched as the *aswang* flew out over the water. With each beat of its large wings, it climbed in the air until it was above the height of the bridge. It ducked and swooped, and changed direction, heading toward Grady and the others in a fast dive.

The demon was flying straight up the river toward them. The men froze for a moment. But only for a moment. Then almost simultaneously, Grady and Rauber drew their revolvers and Perkins raised his shotgun. All at once the bridge lit up with muzzle flashes and the gorge erupted with the roar of shots being fired.

The aswang was hit, at least by a few rounds. It jerked

in the air and flew straight down toward the river. Just above the falls it beat its wings furiously and straightened out its course, flying upriver underneath the bridge. Grady and the others ran to the other side of the bridge and looked down, straining against the rusty railing.

Peering upriver, they couldn't see anything except the fast moving water and the surrounding trees. Sheriff Rauber spotted it. "Look," he shouted, pointing almost straight down. "It's flying back the other way."

Grady leaned over the railing as far as he dared, aiming his pistol downward. He felt the railing flex as he got off a shot, then stood back. "I don't think I came close. That was stupid, wasting a shot like that."

Grady and Rauber stayed, looking upriver. Perkins stepped to the opposite side, almost tripping over the rails. None of the men saw anything. Grady joined his friend and the two of them looked downriver, into the dark sky and at the rocky cliffs. They searched for any movement, any sign of the demon.

"Anything?" Grady called to Rauber, who was still peering upriver.

"Nothing," he answered.

Perkins pointed to something far off against the rocks at the water's edge. "Is that it?"

Grady turned and looked, following Perkins' finger. "No, I saw that earlier. I think it's a log or something."

"I just think I would have seen it fly downriver," Perkins said, frustrated. He looked over his shoulder to Rauber. "Sheriff, you're sure it flew back under the bridge?"

"Yeah, positive!"

The thought hit Grady and Perkins at the same time. "It's directly under us!" Ted cried. "It's probably climbing or flying up the supports."

Perkins and Grady backed away from the railing and off the solid steel deck onto the ties of the tracks. Now with a view of the water rushing below them, they looked but didn't see anything.

Ted turned back to look over the railing just as the *aswang* appeared, flapping its huge wings and landing on the thin steel beam in front of him. The creature lunged at Perkins before he had a chance to raise his shotgun.

Ted yelled as he was knocked backward and Grady and Rauber turned. The monster spread its leathery wings and hissed, thick saliva dripping from its teeth.

Grady and Rauber emptied their revolvers into it. It staggered back. In moments though, the creature had wiped its spit on the wounds and it rose again, seemingly taller than before.

Perkins tried to rise, tried to reach the shotgun, but the *aswang* swiped its clawed hand across his chest, knocking him to the side. Ted looked down quickly to see blood seeping through his shirt through three ragged lines.

Rauber and Grady rushed the monster but it fended them off easily, sending both sprawling onto the deck. Rauber struck his head hard against the rail and didn't get back up.

Grady got to his knees and charged again just as Perkins came at it from the side. With no effort, the *aswang* flapped its wings and rose a few feet in the air. Ted tried to reach for it and ran into the railing instead.

His body bent at the waist as he scrambled to grab the railing. The creature was hissing and screaming as Ted felt himself going over the railing. His momentum was carrying him too far. He could feel it and was powerless to fight it. His legs were scrambling above the bridge deck but his feet found nothing but air.

Grady dove at Ted and was able to grab his pant leg above the ankle. He reached up with his other hand and pulled, letting his weight bring Ted back from the edge. Ted drew a breath just as the creature descended onto the deck in front of him.

The demon swiped again at Perkins, tearing flesh from his face. Ted screamed in pain and fell to one knee, reaching for the railing for support.

He looked for the shotgun on the bridge deck and found it resting across the ties in the middle of the bridge. He tried to crawl for it as Grady launched another attack.

Grady came in low but the creature wrapped its powerful arms around him and drew him off the deck. Waves of unbearable pain ripped through the sheriff as the demon sank its long, serrated teeth into his shoulder.

The creature threw Grady onto the tracks in the middle of the bridge, knocking the shotgun through the ties and into the river over two hundred feet below. With two flaps of its wings, the devil sprang onto the sheriff's back and began tearing at the muscle and sinew of his shoulder.

Grady was writhing and trying to escape, but the creature's strength was too great. He felt his own strength ebbing. Searing pain wracked his body. He heard the monster's jaws snapping through his collarbone and he arched his body in fresh shards of agony.

Its head shaking back and forth like a dog, the *aswang* continued its vicious attack, pulling meat and flesh from the sheriff's weakening body.

Sheriff Grady was on the edge of consciousness when he felt the creature stiffen violently. In an instant, an unholy shriek pierced his ears. The weight of the creature was off him and he was able to work himself free. The onslaught had stopped, and the surge of adrenaline kept him moving, but he knew he was quickly weakening, and might not survive the night on the bridge.

\* \* \* \*

Perkins watched in desperation first as the shotgun slipped through the ties, then in horror as the *aswang* knelt over Grady, ripping flesh from his shoulder. Ted struggled to his feet, weakened by the blood loss in his chest and face. He touched his hand to his face and felt flaps of skin hanging below his eye.

He staggered forward, eyeing the back of the demon. He drew his knife from the sheath strapped to his leg. It was an M3 Trench Knife, given to him by his brother, designed for combat only, not a utility knife. Perkins adjusted it in his hand, aiming the point downward.

Ted took another step forward, now just two steps from the ongoing grisly assault. With both hands, he gripped the knife's leather handle. He raised it skyward and closed the distance to the creature.

Perkins thrust the knife solidly into the center of the monster's back. His own feet lifted slightly off the deck as he drove the blade its full seven inches into the demon.

The *aswang* instantly arched upward, releasing Grady. It screamed in defiance, the demonic screeching echoing off the walls of the gorge.

The creature desperately tried to reach the knife with hands covered in blood and saliva. It thrashed and twisted, but couldn't reach the knife or the stab wound.

Perkins fell to the bridge deck, exhausted. He crawled to Grady's position as the creature continued to flail and scream. He watched it warily as he took his shirt off and wrapped it around the sheriff's shoulder, tying it tightly.

Perkins watched as the creature reared up, panting and shrieking, its long tongue uncoiling and wrapping around its neck, trying to reach the knife wound. Its tongue wasn't long enough and it couldn't reach with its clawed hands.

Grady had faded into unconsciousness but Perkins kept holding pressure on his friend's shoulder, blood seeping through the shirt in no time.

Still thrashing, the monster flapped its massive wings, rising a few feet from the bridge. As its feet dangled against the railing, Ted screamed in rage at the creature and leaped up from Grady. He charged and pushed the *aswang* back. Its wings were flapping chaotically now and it lost its balance. Ted watched it fall from the bridge to the water below. He caught a glimpse of it going over the falls and lost sight of it in the darkness as it made its way to the Middle Falls. He was sure its wings weren't beating and that it did not survive the fall.

Perkins turned back to Grady and resumed the pressure, trying to stop the bleeding. "Come on Jim, stay with me," he pleaded. The sheriff's breathing was shallow but steady. If he could get help soon, the sheriff might make it.

Sheriff Rauber stirred, lifting his head from the rail. He made a low, muffled sound as he struggled to sit up. Ted noticed him moving, relieved that he was still alive. "Sheriff, don't get up. You took a nasty hit to the head. Just lay back down."

Rauber groaned and touched the back of his head, but stayed still. "What about the…" he mumbled.

"It's dead. I stabbed it and pushed it into the river. But it took some bites out of Jim and he's bleeding badly."

Rauber started to roll over as his head cleared, eager to help his fellow sheriff.

"Sheriff, please, you're hurt too," Perkins said. "I've got this."

Rauber waved him off, crawling on all fours to his

position.

"Sheriff Rauber, I work for the state. You work for the county. I'm in charge. Stay where you are."

Rauber snorted. "I was elected by the people. You weren't. I'm helping."

"Fine," Ted sighed as the sheriff reached for the bloody shirt. "There's a large area that was torn away. Put your hand here."

Perkins looked up to see a white light approaching from the east side of the bridge. For a moment, he panicked. *Train!* Then he realized it was the beam from a flashlight. He could then see several flashlights and, for the first time in what seemed like an eternity, took a deep breath and relaxed slightly.

"Sheriff?" a man called from a third of the way across the bridge.

"Over here," Perkins said. "Hurry!" He was relieved to see several men with stretchers approaching. "How did you...?"

"Sheriff Grady's dispatcher called us when she hadn't heard from you. Said you were responding to trouble on the bridge."

The medics took over, hoisting Grady onto a stretcher and making their way back over the bridge to the waiting ambulance. Two more stretchers carried Perkins and Rauber to their own transports and before long they were being wheeled into the Dansville hospital.

## Chapter Twenty
## Sunday, June 20

THE SHARP SMELL of bacon filled the kitchen as Margaret walked in. "What's all this?" she said, seeing the two eggs boiling in a saucepan. The toaster popped and George almost succeeded in grabbing the slices in mid-air. He placed them on a plate with a flourish.

"That would have been a nice trick," he exclaimed. "It'll take me a loaf or two to practice, though."

Margaret stepped beside him to butter the toast but George put his hand up.

"Uh-uh! You've been doing enough cooking around here. This morning it's my treat."

"But your rent includes room and board," Margaret protested. "Really, I don't mind."

"Just have a seat and enjoy some eggs and soldiers, a true English breakfast."

"Eggs and what?" she asked, moving to the table.

"Eggs and soldiers. You'll see. A little butter on the toast, slice them up into soldiers, and we're almost ready." His actions followed his words and a moment later there were eight long strips of buttered toast divided between their plates.

The egg timer ran out and George removed the eggs, placing them in the egg cups. With a sharp whack of the butter knife, he neatly removed the top of each soft boiled egg.

"And there we have it, eggs and soldiers." He picked up a strip of toast and plunged it into the liquid yolk, then popped it in his mouth. "Mmm-mm!" He smiled and wiped his mouth with a napkin. "If only we had some English Breakfast Tea. The tea from Kenya is the best."

He watched as Margaret dipped her toast in the egg. "Oh, that *is* good," she said. "Hey, wait a minute. You're always drinking coffee. I didn't think you liked tea. I've offered to buy it a couple times and you've always said no."

George looked down at his egg and toast, his lips pursed in embarrassment. "I, um, only like Twinings. I doubt you can find it here."

"Why, George Carmichael! You know what you are?" Margaret said, laughing. "A snob. A British snob!"

"I am not!" he cried, his eyes wide with mock indignation. His voice softened. "Well, maybe when it comes to tea." He paused, then said in a lower voice. "And tobacco. Oh, and sport, too. Your baseball is a dreadful imitation of cricket."

Margaret smirked playfully and took another bite. They finished their breakfast with more banter and laughter and began clearing the dishes.

"George, do you feel it?" Margaret said, washing the silverware.

"Feel what?" he asked, wiping a plate dry.

"I don't know, I can't quite explain it. I tossed and turned for hours last night trying to fall asleep. I was so scared that that creature would come back."

"But I told you that I would—"

"I know, George, you're very sweet." She smiled warmly and continued. "When I woke up this morning, I felt different somehow. I'm not afraid anymore. It's almost a sense of lightness. Like the creature is gone. I don't know if Sheriff Grady killed it or it flew away, but I'm not afraid now."

George put his towel down and embraced her. "I'd like to think it's because of me that you're not afraid anymore," he said with a chuckle. "But I'm glad you're feeling better." He stepped back and reached for the towel.

Margaret extended her hands, her fingers touching his. She looked up slightly at his face. She took a half step toward him. George hesitated briefly, then bent down. He had often wondered if this moment would happen. He had noticed a simmering inside, a gentle bubbling. Something he hadn't felt in many years. A feeling only Maureen had stirred...

George stopped. He closed his eyes. Margaret was only inches away. She was so beautiful, but it was more than that. She had a sweetness about her, a kindness. He hadn't even thought of being with another woman since that terrible day, let alone falling in love. Could he be in love, he thought. *I've known her less than a month.* How long had he known Maureen, he asked himself. *About the same time.* The corners of George's mouth turned up slightly. Had they been able to meet, Maureen would have liked Margaret, he decided.

He sensed that Margaret was being patient, knowing what was going through his mind. Not wanting to rush him. Giving him time to fold away the old feelings without guilt or regret. He felt like she would stand there for hours if need be, watching and waiting.

George wasn't sure how much time passed but, almost imperceptibly, he bent down further and their lips touched. Softly. George felt her arms reaching up and around him, drawing him closer.

They pressed their lips together more firmly. George's arms slid around her waist. Her lips soft and smooth, supple. He wasn't surprised to find himself aroused accompanied by a fleeting instant of shame. The shame wasn't because of his wife, he realized. It was a reaction to a base desire that he hadn't felt in years. But more than the desire was a tremendous liberation, his heart reaching out to hers.

He felt her heart respond in kind as he reached up and stroked her hair with his hand. George breathed in her fragrance, her essence. They parted slowly, wordlessly. He watched as she brought her finger to his cheek and wiped away a tear he didn't know was there.

\* \* \* \*

Perkins said goodbye to Sheriff Rauber in the lobby of the hospital. Rauber's diagnosis was a mild concussion and, after a night's observation, he was released. Perkins was sporting some stitches and bandages on his face and chest but was also released. He had seen Rauber off but wanted to stick around and visit Sheriff Grady.

Grady's wounds were serious, but not life-threatening. The doctors were confident they could patch him up, but he'd be in the hospital at least a week. They told Ted he could see him at lunchtime. He spent the morning on the phone to Jean, filling her in, and also made a call to Mrs. McConnell, assuring her that the *aswang* was dead. He himself had killed it and watched it plunge into the Genesee River. She thanked him and asked him to send her regards and thanks to Sheriff Grady.

He also called his supervisor in Albany who didn't

believe any part of his story. He was disappointed, but not surprised. His boss's reaction confirmed in his mind that he wouldn't be calling the FBI with a follow up report.

Ted did decide to call Irene Adler and let her know what had happened. Miss Adler asked if she could give Professor Hughes his contact information as she was sure he would want to talk to Ted. He agreed, and said that he would be in the area for the next couple days. The professor could reach him at his motel or at the Sheriff's office.

Shortly before noon, Perkins was allowed to see Grady. "Hey buddy," he said as he entered the room. "How are you feeling?"

"Like I got run over by a train on that bridge."

"Understandable. Doc says you're going to be okay, but you're stuck in here for a while."

"How's Rauber?"

"He's fine. He just got released. Bump on the head, but he'll be all right. Said to get well and get back to work."

Grady sat up a little in his bed, wincing in pain. "Please tell me that thing is dead."

"It cost me a fine knife, but it's dead. Right in the center of its back, flung itself over the railing trying to get it out. With a little help from me."

"Did you see where it ended up?" Grady asked.

"Definitely hit the river and went over the falls. From there I couldn't see it. It was too dark. And I had to get back to playing nursemaid to you. A little thanks would be nice," Ted said with a wry smile.

"Of course. Sorry, Ted. Thank you. I thought I was a goner when that thing started snacking on me."

"Glad to do it. Oh, I made some calls this morning getting Jean and others up to speed. Talked to your senior deputy, Bill Malden, too."

Grady's face lit up. "Bill? How's he doing? Is he still in here?"

"He's doing fine. He got out a few days ago and has been at home. He's getting around pretty well. Says his wife is waiting on him hand and foot and threatens to leave him if he goes back to work for you."

The sheriff smiled. Malden was a good man but he would understand if he didn't return to police work. He had a feeling his wife would come around though.

"Investigator Perkins?" A nurse had ducked her head into the room. "There's a call for you. You can take it at the nurse's station."

"Be right back," he said to Grady.

\* \* \* \*

When Ted returned a few minutes later, he shook the sheriff gently to wake him.

"Everything okay?" he said as his eyes fluttered open.

"Yeah, but we may have a bit of a public relations problem."

"What do you mean?"

"That was the park superintendent at Letchworth. Seems a group of hikers have spotted our friend's body wedged against a stone bridge, near the Lower Falls."

"Oh no."

"He's blocked off the bridge and the trails leading to it, but we've got to get that thing out of there. I guess when I saw it go over the railing, I figured it would end up in Lake Ontario, especially with all the rain we've had."

Grady thought for a moment. "Wait. Is it that *aswang*, or did it change back to Castle since it's daytime?"

Perkins shook his head. "Apparently once it's dead it stays in whatever state it was in. So those hikers got a good look at a large bat-like creature with lots of hair."

"Well, maybe this is how legends like Champ start. I'm not too worried about word getting out about it. Nobody'll believe it and the rumors will just die down." Grady leaned back in his bed in thought. "Get ahold of Rauber. Make sure he's feeling all right first. If he can help, get a few men down to the bridge and get it out of there. Wrap it in a tarp or something. It's a long climb down and back up from the rim of the gorge and you're gonna have a devil of a time hauling that thing up. Fortunately, there's stone steps but be careful. It's pretty steep in places."

"So, once we get it out...what do we do with it?" Ted asked.

"Good question. You're sure you stabbed it in the center of its back?"

"Positive. I mean, I didn't take the time to measure it." Ted pointed to Grady's arm. "It was making hamburger out of your shoulder, you know."

Grady laughed, then grimaced at the sharp pain. "Maybe call that Adler woman and see what she suggests. Bury it, burn it, throw it in the lake, I don't care. Find out from her what we're supposed to do and get rid of it as soon as possible."

A nurse brought in a tray of food for the sheriff. He gritted his teeth as he struggled to sit up in bed, Ted helping him. The nurse placed the tray on the table and wheeled it in front of her patient. She smiled and lifted the cover off the plate with a flourish. "Hamburger and French fries today. It's actually pretty good."

Ted turned toward the door and looked back. "Hamburger, huh? Enjoy!" He smiled and touched his own shoulder. "Eat your lunch. I'll call Miss Adler and see what she says."

\* \* \* \*

A half hour later Ted rejoined Grady in his room. "Hey, you only ate half your shoulder—I mean your hamburger!"

"All right. Leave the comedy to Bob Hope. Stick to your knife throwing act." Grady shook his head in mock dismay. "What'd you find out?"

"Miss Adler said that once we haul it out of the gorge, the best thing to do with it is to throw it in the ocean. The creature is native to the Philippines which is, of course, surrounded by the sea. I asked her if dumping it in Lake Ontario was good enough and she said no, because it's fresh water. It needs to be essentially soaked, or buried, in salt. I guess we'll have to drive it overland to the coast. Don't suppose we can get a ticket for it on the $20^{th}$ Century Limited."

Sheriff Grady looked at Perkins and cocked his head slightly. "She said it could be buried in salt?"

"Yeah, dumping it in the ocean is best but it could also be buried in the mineral itself. How much table salt do you have at home?" he said, grinning.

"Even better. There are dozens of salt mines in this area. They've been mining salt here for over a hundred years. In fact, I know the plant manager at the Retsof mine. See if you can call him and patch the call in to me."

"Retsof? That's a funny name."

"It's 'Foster' spelled backward. Foster's the guy who founded the town. Long story." Grady looked at his watch. "Anyway, the plant manager is Thomas Bush. He's probably home from church by now. Lives in Leicester. Operator will know him."

Perkins went to the nurse's station and returned to the room a short time later, just as the phone was ringing.

Grady tried to reach over to the nightstand to pick up

the receiver, but was stopped by what felt like a thousand needles in his shoulder. He rolled back over gently and let Ted hand the phone to him.

"Tom? Sheriff Grady here." He paused for a moment. "Well, I've had better days. Listen, I'll fill you in later, but I have kind of a strange favor to ask."

## Chapter Twenty-One

IT WAS LATE afternoon when Perkins, Sheriff Rauber, and a couple deputies arrived at the gate of the Retsof salt mine. Waiting just inside was an older, barrel-chested man who looked imposing but strolled over to Perkins' car with a friendly smile. He took Ted's hand in his and shook it vigorously. "Tom Bush. Nice to meet you." He bent down and peered in to the car. "Gentlemen. Welcome to the Retsof operation of the International Salt Company."

Bush straightened up and pointed about fifty yards away. "See that building with the big tower on top of it? That's the head of the mine shaft. Drive over and I'll meet you there."

A few minutes later they were all out of their cars. Perkins and the others were at the base of the tower, craning their necks to see the top. Bush played the proud tour guide. "The Fuller Number One mine shaft stands just over one hundred feet above ground but, like an iceberg, its most impressive part is underground. It stretches to a depth of one thousand feet below ground. Below you, stretching out for three thousand acres, is the largest salt mine in the western hemisphere. This is the production shaft, where the salt is brought up by large scoops."

Perkins and the others waited patiently while Bush explained the layout of the mine. He finally stopped and gave them a quizzical look. "Now then, Sheriff Grady said you had a package you wanted to, er, bury in my salt mine?"

Perkins nodded and replied, "Yes, we do. It's kind of hard to explain and I think he said he'd give you the full story over a beer when he got out of the hospital, but—"

"Now let me interrupt you if I can, son." Bush wasn't rude about it, but he wanted to get his point across. "I'm good friends with Jim Grady, but there's been talk about burying radioactive materials in salt mines. You know, stuff contaminated from the A-bomb tests. And, I'm not so sure I'm ready for something like that. Plus, I haven't heard anything official about it from my headquarters in Scranton."

"No, no." Perkins held up his hand. "Nothing like that. Nothing dangerous." Ted looked around. "Well, let's put it this way. It was dangerous at one time, but it's dead now. But to be safe, we need to bury it in a salt mine. And yours was the closest."

Bush shook his head. "I don't know what Grady and you boys got cooking, and I kinda thought Jim was pulling my leg. But you seem serious enough. And the sheriff isn't the type to pull practical jokes." Bush clapped his hands. "So, what do you need me to do?"

Perkins looked at the large steel paneled building in front of him. "Is that how you get down to the mine?"

"No," Bush replied. "There's another, smaller shaft in there." He turned around and pointed to a four story office building. "How big is this thing we're burying?"

Ted stuck his lower lip out and thought for a moment.

About six feet long, three feet wide, a foot thick. Weighs about two hundred pounds."

"Sounds like a coffin," Bush said.

"You're not far off."

Bush looked at Perkins, furrowing his brow slightly, then got in his car. Perkins and the others got in their own car and drove to the office. They got out and went to the trunk. Perkins unlocked it and the lid swung open.

The plant manager joined them at the back of the car. When the trunk opened, the putrid smell was more overwhelming than it had been when they first stuffed the *aswang* into the car. Everyone stood back, holding their hand over their mouth.

"What the hell is that?" Bush cried. The rope securing the black tarp had come loose and about a foot of the creature's dark, leathery wing was visible.

"You don't want to know," Sheriff Rauber said flatly.

"Friends or not with Grady, I'll be damned if I'm putting that in my mine until I know what it is."

Investigator Perkins stiffened. "The sheriff said he would tell you about it later. He was calling you from his hospital bed." He pointed to the open trunk. "This is the thing that put him there, but I assure you, it's dead now. Burying it in salt is...well, it's part of the killing ritual."

"Ritual? I don't understand."

"Ask the Filipinos. This is their monster anyway," Ted said. "Can we just get it into the mine? Grady said you had some unused areas that nobody messes with and that would be perfect. We don't want one of your miners stumbling across it."

"Son, if it wasn't for my twenty year friendship with Sheriff Grady, I'd tell you and your Filipino monster to get the hell out of my mine." Bush unlocked the main office door and held it open.

Perkins and the others struggled to hoist the *aswang* out of the trunk. The stench was overpowering but they continued on with the lifeless creature.

Bush led the way through the hallways of the building until they were finally at the door to the skip. He flipped some light switches but no lights came on. He met Perkins' curious look with a curt reply. "Turns the lights on along the mineshaft and at the bottom." He pulled on the metal door and it scraped along the tracks, disappearing into the wall. It revealed a cage constructed of thick metal with its own accordion-like door. Bush yanked it open.

Dim lightbulbs illuminated the elevator car as the men and their cargo piled in. Bush was the last one in and he pulled the door shut. He pressed the green button and they felt the car jerkily begin its descent.

There was enough room in the car to put the creature down, which the men gladly did to rest their arms. "How long does it take to get to the bottom?" Perkins asked.

"It's just over a thousand feet down and it takes about five minutes," Bush said.

Ted asked questions about the mine itself and that seemed to put Bush in a better mood. He was obviously proud of the vast enterprise he was in charge of and enjoyed talking about it.

They reached the bottom and stepped out of the skip. Bush walked to a large electrical panel and flipped six levers to the up position. Circuits and relays sounded and sodium vapor lights came to life, illuminating an expansive room measuring fifty feet in all directions, and upward to the ceiling.

Perkins whistled. "Wow! This is much bigger than I was expecting."

"Salt mines aren't like coal mines," Bush said patiently.

Coal mines have to follow thin seams of coal, so the ceilings are sometimes barely high enough to stand in. The salt bed we're mining is sixty to a hundred feet thick. It spreads underneath most of the Great Lakes, including Lake Ontario."

Perkins was listening attentively but when the smell of the creature reached him, he looked back to the skip and remembered what they were here for. "We should probably get to work on that thing," he said.

"Yes, whatever that is, it's stunk up my mineshaft pretty bad, I'm sure."

The lawmen dragged the creature's body out of the skip while Bush fetched a foreman's pickup truck from the livery. When he arrived, they hauled the *aswang* into the bed of the truck and piled in. Perkins climbed into the cab with Bush, who put the vehicle smoothly into gear and drove off across the floor of the mine.

Bush motioned to a rolled up blueprint on the dashboard of the truck and Perkins picked it up. He smoothed it out on his lap. "It looks just like a city map," he said, looking at Bush.

"Exactly. The 'roadways' are what's been mined out. The 'blocks' are what's left. We don't touch them. They provide ceiling support."

After a few turns and more than a mile from the mineshaft, they came to a halt alongside one of the heavy curtains that directed the flow of air through the labyrinthine mine. "If I can get you to pull back the corner of the curtain, I'll drive slowly through. These things can rip the aerials off trucks if we're not careful."

After the truck drove slowly to the other side of the curtain and stopped, Ted quickly ducked through the small gap between the curtain and the wall of salt and rejoined Bush in the truck. They drove for another twenty minutes and came to an area that was obviously no longer being maintained. The roadway was rougher and there were no more air curtains. Very little of the fresh air supply made it this far into the mine and Perkins could tell by the stale smell that lingered.

They stopped in front of a dead end in the mine. A room, of sorts, that was piled high with chunks of salt. Each one was about fist sized and the pile stood almost to the ceiling, fifty feet high.

Bush hopped out of the cab. "Let's go gentlemen. The air's no good here so we need to work quick. Grab that Filipino thing and some shovels and get to work."

They worked in the light of the truck's headlamps, all of them taking turns digging a spot for the creature. The temperature was barely above seventy degrees and there was little humidity, but it was still hard work. Before long, everyone's shirt was spotted through with sweat.

They dug out a cavity between the sloping pile of salt and the wall. It was difficult holding back the crumbling rocks of salt, but the men managed to hold the hole open long enough to drag the body into it. Perkins and the rest began to cover the creature with salt.

The *aswang's* body was lying face down and Perkins could see the outline of the end of his knife's handle in its back, under the tarp. It was like the center pole of a tent, sticking straight up. That was his favorite knife, he thought. *Once we leave here, I'll never see it again. No man will ever see it again.* There was a connection between a man and his knife, and this one was very special. Not only did it save the life of a friend, but his brother had given it to him when he returned from Germany. It had saved his brother's life on more than one occasion. He couldn't leave it behind.

Bush and the others were finished, having shoveled the

last bits of salt on the body, satisfied that the creature was completely covered. They were throwing the shovels back in the truck, but Ted walked back to the body and with his hands, pulled some of the salt rocks away. He dug at the knots in the rope and tore the tarp open, revealing the butt of his trench knife. Dried blood had pooled around the wound, a thick maroon colored crust.

Perkins heard Bush start the truck. He heard him honk the horn for him. But he couldn't leave without the knife. He knew he should leave it right where it was. But the creature was dead anyway. And the power of the knife, and family, was too great. He quickly reached in amongst the salt rocks and grasped the hard leather handle.

Ted wasted no time, but for a moment he felt something, a faint tingle, like electricity, in his hand. He pulled firmly and the knife came free. *Did that thing move? No, it must have been from me pulling the knife out.*

He quickly jogged back to the truck and got in. He wiped the blade clean on his handkerchief and held the knife on his lap as they drove back through the dark mine.

Nobody said anything as they ascended to the surface. The warm rays of the sun and the blue sky was a sharp contrast to the environment they had just left. Perkins thanked the plant manager and shook his hand.

Investigator Perkins drove out of the gate, not listening to Sheriff Rauber and his men talking quietly. Ted glanced down briefly at his trench knife laying on the bench seat between him and Rauber. He touched the knife, lightly placing his fingers on the flat of the blade. The faint tingling he felt was obviously in his mind, his adrenaline still pumping, or something.

## Epilogue
### Sunday, September 13, 1964

"DAVE!" MARGARET CALLED from the base of the stairs. "Brian's here. Do you have everything?"

"Yeah, Mom," her son responded from upstairs. "I'm surprised you haven't tripped over it in the hallway yet. I'm bringing the last of it down now."

Margaret watched as Dave's best friend backed his battered pickup truck into the driveway. She met him at the side door and opened it for him. "Is that thing going to make it to Oswego?"

"Of course!" Brian stood a full foot taller than Margaret. He had an eager face and reddish-brown hair. "Nothing's fallen off it yet today!"

They both turned at the sound of Dave bounding down the stairs. "Hey buddy," he called to Brian. He pointed to the hallway at his pile of belongings. "I'm surprised you haven't loaded everything in for me."

"Hah!" Brian laughed. "I'm chauffeuring you to college and you want me to be your porter too?"

Dave smiled and added a final duffel bag to the boxes and suitcases by the front door. "Actually, would you mind getting started? I want to make sure Mom knows

I'm going to be okay." He turned to Margaret. "No tears, right Mom?"

She smiled but her lip quivered a bit in protest. "No tears. I hope."

Dave watched as Brian picked up a couple bags and headed out the door with them. He led his mother to the kitchen. "Mom, it's cool. Really. I'm going to be fine. Heck, I'm going to be living with Aunt Sarah. How much trouble can I get in?"

Margaret looked at her son. She was so very proud of him. He received excellent grades, was editor of the school newspaper, was on the debate team, and tutored other kids. She had nothing to worry about. "It's not that. It's just that, well, the house is going to seem so empty once you're gone."

"Empty? What are you talking about? Did you forget George?" he said with emphasis. "Your husband?"

Margaret laughed, the lines around her eyes deepening for a second. "Of course not, silly. You just have such an energy about you. You always have, from the moment you were born. That's what I'll miss."

"Speaking of George," Dave said. "I hope he makes it in time to see me off. Brian wants to get back before dark. I don't think either of the headlights on his truck work."

"Oh, don't tell me things like that. Now I'll be worried sick. And don't worry about George, he'll be here any minute. He wouldn't miss it for the world."

"Good!" Dave trotted down the hall to help Brian with the last of his boxes.

When they came inside, Dave could see his mother dabbing at her eyes with her fingers. "Come on," he said to Brian. "The only thing left is the dresser."

As the young men started up the stairs, they heard a car screech to a halt out front. "Sounds like George's car!"

Dave exclaimed, taking the steps two at a time with Brian close behind.

They reached Dave's bedroom and he looked around, many of his pictures already taken off the walls and packed away. The top of the dresser was bare and all the clothes gone from the drawers. He ran his hand over the smooth wood surface, then put his hands on his hips and frowned.

"Hey, don't get all sentimental on me Dave," Brian said, lightly punching him on the shoulder. You'll be back at Christmas."

"I know, it just already looks bare. The only furniture I'm taking with me is the dresser. Aunt Sarah has everything else I need in her spare room. But it's so... empty. I guess I know a little of what Mom's feeling."

George and Margaret came up the stairs and entered the bedroom. "Darned if that train wasn't running late from Cleveland," he said. "That never happens. I probably drove a little faster than I should have from the station, but didn't want to miss you."

"I'm glad you made it," Dave said.

"Me too, Mr. Carmichael," Brian said with a grin. "Now I can supervise the moving of the dresser instead of doing the grunt work."

George laughed heartily. "Not on your life, son. And just for that, I nominate you for walking backward down the stairs."

"Oh, man!" Brian turned to Dave and the two of them lifted the dresser a few inches off the floor.

"This thing is solid," Dave cried. "We'll never get it out of here."

Brian stood up. "Hey Einstein. Let's take the drawers out and take 'em down separately. You did empty them first, right?"

Dave smirked. "Of course I did. But yeah, I guess taking the drawers out will help." He pulled out the small handkerchief drawers and turned around, placing them on the bed. He reached for the top drawer and pulled it out, putting it next to the smaller drawers. He repeated his movements for the middle drawer and then came to the bottom one.

He knelt down and pulled on the handles. The drawer came out easily and he stood up, turning to place it on the bed.

"Wait, what's that?" George said, pointing to something on the back of the drawer.

Dave tilted the back so it was facing upward and they saw a manila envelope taped to the wooden slat. The corners had a brownish tinge from age and the tape was dry. He reached his fingers underneath the envelope and pulled gently. The tape yielded easily and he turned the envelope over in his hands. It had a good sized bulge in the middle.

"Nothing written on it. Any ideas, Mom?"

Margaret shook her head. "I don't have any earthly idea. I sure didn't put it there. Are you sure you didn't? Remember a couple years ago you were almost obsessed when Kingsbridge deposited that 'time capsule' in the foundation of the new city hall. You said you wanted to do something similar."

"Well, I wouldn't say I was obsessed with it. And I pretty much forgot about after a day or two."

George spoke up. "I have a novel idea. We could open it."

Everyone laughed. Margaret gestured to Dave. "You found it, son. Go ahead and open it. Finders-keepers."

Dave took a breath and bent the metal prongs upward on the clasp of the envelope. He slid the flap open and reached inside. He frowned a bit and pulled out the contents.

Margaret gasped and George's eyes widened.

"Holy cow!" Brian exclaimed.

Dave was holding a bundle of money, wrapped tightly with a thick rubber band. His mouth hung open as he flipped through the stack of bills. The brittle rubber band snapped and flew across the room.

"Oh my God," Margaret whispered.

Dave spread the bills between his hands—twenties, fifties, hundreds. Lots of hundreds.

Brian broke the silence. "You've been holding out on me, man. All those burgers I bought for you this summer at Tom Wahl's. You coulda been treating the whole gang!"

Dave protested. "I had no idea this was—"

His mother interrupted. "You know what this is?" She looked to Dave and George. "This is Larry's money. The money he…" Her voice trailed off.

"Obviously we can't keep this," George said. "Sorry to break the finders-keepers rule, Dave."

Dave stuffed the money back in the envelope and handed it to George. "I know where it came from. I don't want it."

"I'll run it down to the sheriff's office in the morning." He looked at Dave and Brian. "Now then," he said cheerfully. "Let's get this dresser loaded onto the truck."

\* \* \* \*

Brian was waiting in the truck while Dave returned to the house to say his final goodbyes. He walked in and met George and his mother in the kitchen. Margaret had tears in her eyes and Dave frowned. "Now Mom. I thought you weren't going to cry."

"You knew I would. I knew I would." She smiled. "I'll

be okay."

Dave started to lean in for a hug, then stopped. "Oh, don't forget to call that ad from the *Penny Saver* for me, the one that had the '54 Chevy for sale. I circled it for you." He handed over the newspaper. "I wasn't able to get a hold of him yesterday and I really want a set of wheels at school."

Margaret pursed her lips. "Mmm...we'll see. I haven't decided if that's a good idea or not yet." She stood up straight. "Okay, now get going before I completely fall to pieces."

She reached out her arms and held him for a long time, her tears spotting his shirt. When she released him, Dave turned away. She pretended not to notice as he wiped at his eyes.

He turned back around and shook George's hand. George pulled him in for a quick hug and then stood back.

"We're very proud of you, son. Really proud."

Margaret wiped the last of her tears away with both hands. "Tell Brian to drive carefully, and here's some money for him for gas. And call when you get to Aunt Sarah's. Tell her you're calling collect." She reached in her dress pocket and gave him a slip of paper folded in half. "This is a check for Sarah. I know she said she didn't want any money, but you make sure she takes it." She handed him another check. "And this is for you."

"Thank you, Mom. And George. I'll be fine. And I promise to call when we get there. I'll write you in a couple days, too."

Dave McConnell kissed his mother on the cheek and opened the kitchen door. He turned and waved and jogged out to his friend's truck.

George took his wife's hand as they followed Dave out

the door. The truck rumbled to life and headed down the street. "He's going to be just fine, you know. Your sister will see to that, plus he's a good kid. You've done a great job raising him."

"*We've* done a great job raising him," Margaret said as she squeezed George's hand. They stood in the driveway long after the truck had disappeared from view.

**Author's Note**

The heroic World War II raid on the Japanese POW camp at Cabanatuan featured in the prologue was an actual event and was responsible for liberating hundreds of Allied prisoners of war. The characters and actions depicted in this book are, of course, fictionalized and the timeline has been condensed for brevity and pacing.

Interested readers wanting more information on this operation are directed to *Ghost Soldiers: The Epic Account of World War II's Greatest Rescue Mission* by Hampton Sides (Anchor Books, 2002) and *The Great Raid on Cabanatuan: Rescuing the Doomed Ghosts of Bataan and Corregidor* by William Breuer (Wiley, 1994).

The mythological creature depicted in the book, the *aswang*, is deeply rooted in Filipino mythology, dating back to at least the 1500's. I have not strayed too far from the commonly accepted descriptions of it, nor its behavior. Not surprisingly, the *aswang* features highly in Filipino popular culture, both in books and cinema, and articles and films are readily available for those who want to draw their own conclusions about whether the creature is real or if it belongs safely in the folklore of the Philippines.

## Acknowledgments

No author works in a vacuum, and I had the help and encouragement of many people in writing *The Onyx Seed*, my first novel. Early readers of partial manuscripts include Alan, Bridget, Bryan, Kevin, Desiree, and Arleen. They confirmed that I had a story worth telling so I kept at it.

When I couldn't dream up a suitable name for Irene Adler's cat, I crowdsourced the task to my followers on Facebook. Thanks to Mary Jane Weeks who suggested Winston, the perfect name.

Thanks also to Michelle and Lally who helped with the Baybayin translation, the written language of the Philippines. Throughout the book, I have strived for accuracy and would have stumbled horribly without their help.

It's been far too long since I've had a two- or three-year-old toddler running around the house and I'd forgotten how extensive or limited their vocabulary is. Thanks to Ashley who assisted greatly in getting Davey's speech just right, so he didn't sound too old or too young.

The front cover is so striking because of my friend

Mike Legg's hard work. He is a supremely talented photographer and illustrator. From borrowing a dresser and selecting the perfect props, to hand-crafting some of the effects, he captured the essence of the book with a single image and I am highly indebted to him.

The job of editing the book fell to two people, Sara Gill Kuntz and Ryan T. Harrison. Both provided invaluable assistance in developmental editing, line editing, and copy editing. As a talented fiction writer herself, Sara helped immensely with pacing and continuity. She convinced me to jettison parts of the story that dragged to keep the momentum up, resulting in a much more readable book. Sara's husband Ron was also helpful with the prologue and I am incredibly grateful to both of them.

In reading about the writing process, I learned that one shouldn't ask the opinion of family and friends because they will provide nothing but platitudes and how great the manuscript is. So I hesitated in sending it to my son, Ryan. I needn't have worried. He was my ultimate fact-checker, keeping me honest at every turn. He was also quite adept at catching inconsistencies in the story. But he edited with a carrot and stick, always supportive of my efforts. I am most appreciative of his work on this book.

All of the above mentioned people were instrumental in getting this book written, edited, and polished, but if it weren't for my wife, Paula, it would never have been written at all. Not only did she help with the title, she provided excellent feedback on the various characters and story arcs. But more than that, she sacrificed many evenings and weekends while I clattered away at the keyboard. Her belief in me, and this journey, was what kept me going after I would write myself into a corner or staring at a blank computer screen. Thank you, Paula.

## About the Author

R.W. Harrison is a marketing professional residing in the Tampa Bay area with his wife, Paula, and their evil black cat, Tucker. They hope to move to western New York someday, where this story takes place.

*The Onyx Seed* is his first novel.

Finally, if you've read this far, I appreciate it! An honest review on Amazon, Goodreads, or other book review sites would be most welcome.

Please visit www.rwharrisonauthor.com to get the latest on upcoming books or to contact me.

Find me on Facebook at:

www.facebook.com/RWHarrisonAuthor

Thank you!
R.W. Harrison
Tampa Bay, Florida

44195189R00185

Made in the USA
Lexington, KY
08 July 2019